THE BUTCHER,
THE BANK ROBBER,
AND
THE BLONDE

ALICE WHITE INVESTIGATOR BOOK FOUR

MARC HIRSCH

Printed in the United States of America

First Printing, 2022

ISBN 9798831783629

www.marchirsch.com

TABLE OF CONTENTS

CHAPTER 1

MONKEY BARS

In the late 1800s, there were gun possession restrictions in towns like Dodge City, Kansas, Abilene, Texas, Deadwood, South Dakota, and Tombstone, Arizona. These restrictions required visitors to leave their guns at the sheriff's office when they came into town. On October 26, 1881, the gunfight at the O.K. Corral in Tombstone, Arizona, was fought over gun control. At the end of it, Tom McLaury, Frank McLaury, and Billy Clanton lay dead.

It took a little longer to bring gun control to New York state. The Sullivan Act took effect in

August of 1911. It made carrying unlicensed guns in public a felony.

Alice White needed one of those licenses before she graduated New York University's School of Law. How would it look if it got around that she'd been carrying a concealed .380 automatic, breaking the law she was swearing to uphold? On the other hand, who in New York State government could she get to permit a self-willed, irrational, impulsive woman walking around with a loaded gun? Clearly, she would have to find a way around the system.

It was a beautiful day in May in the northernmost borough of the City of New York, the Bronx, home of the world-famous New York Yankees. Alice White decided to take a break from her legal studies and walk over to the Oval, a children's playground on the far side of Mosholu Parkway. She stopped on the way to pick up a bologna hero on Italian bread, with plenty of mustard, and a bottle of Coke.

She sat in a swing chomping down on her crusty sandwich and taking an occasional pull off the

Coke. Her shoulder-length black hair shined from the shampooing she had given it earlier. Too bad there was no exam in procrastination. She chewed on the hard crust and swung gently in the breeze.

Birds chirped. Children screeched. The chatter of gossiping housewives trading stories filled the air.

After a while, Alice noticed that silence had fallen. The place was almost empty. Everyone was gone except for one young mother closely attending her little boy as he navigated the lower level of the monkey bars. Mom was masterfully resisting the urge to wrap her protective arms around her son and pull him to safety on the ground. He was doing so well too, not afraid, gripping ahead of himself, carefully making his way around a corner of the cube of metal bars.

A young, scruffy-looking man had materialized on the bench next to the mother's purse. He undid the clasp.

Alice shouted at him, "Get away from that purse, creep."

Her voice got the mother's attention. She took her son off the bars and moved to reclaim her purse.

The guy said, "Stay away, both of you."

"That's my purse," the mother said.

"It's mine now. Beat it."

Alice said, "Don't even think about stealing that purse. Whatever you need to buy is not as important as her feeding her family."

The man got up off the bench and moved toward Alice, leaving the purse unattended.

"Beat it, lady. Don't make me have to hurt you."

Alice slowly put her sandwich and the Coke down on the ground and stood to meet the challenge. A Browning .380 automatic handgun materialized in her grip.

The man moved closer to her. "Lady, you do not want to shoot me for a stupid purse."

"I don't care one way or the other. It's up to you. I haven't shot anybody in a while. I'm good with shooting you if you want."

They were within arm's length of each other. The man grabbed the barrel of the weapon, twisted it away from pointing at him, and tried to pry it from Alice's strong hand. A struggle ensued. She thumbed the safety off and fired a shot over his shoulder into a tree. The guy let go of the gun.

The young mother took the opportunity to pick up her purse.

"I can't thank you enough," she said to Alice. "The rent money is in here."

She took her boy by the wrist and exited the playground.

Alice kept her weapon trained on the man.

She gathered the remains of her lunch with her left hand and dumped it in the trash basket.

"I could've killed someone because of you. You ought to be ashamed of yourself. Lucky for you, I have somewhere to be, or I would turn you over to some people I know who don't ever want to meet. They would straighten you out. Meanwhile, you might want to consider finding another line of work."

She knew she had better get that permit soon. It was also painfully obvious she needed to learn how to control situations without a gun. She'd like to avoid killing innocent bystanders, if at all possible.

CHAPTER 2

WAR

1941

"Did you hear the news?" Thomas Laughlin asked his wife, Patsy.

"No. What happened?"

"The Japanese bombed Pearl Harbor on Oahu this morning, sunk ships, strafed barracks, killed civilians. It was a disaster."

"What does this mean, Thomas?"

"It means we are going to war. It means I will have to serve."

"I knew this was coming. You're right. We can't be selfish at a time like this. I'm proud to be your wife. Do what you have to do. Become a soldier.

I'll hold down the fort while you're gone, only, when it's over, please come home safely to me."

"I'm going to be a Marine."

Patsy said, "That sounds just like you. The toughest of the tough. First, I want us to make a baby, so you'll have a family to come home to. Off you go to the bedroom. I'll be in in a minute."

When her husband had retreated to the bedroom, Patsy closed herself into the bathroom and cried her eyes out. She was gripped by the fear that she would soon be a widow forced to raise a child on her own. She considered begging him not to go but shook it off as unpatriotic at a time like this. She washed her face, put on makeup, and sprinkled herself with Chanel No. 5, Thomas's favorite. Then she marched into the bedroom and showed her husband how deeply she cared for him. It was not such a terrible sacrifice. Everyone had to do their part for the war effort.

Even as Patsy prepared to give birth, Thomas underwent the trials of basic training and got ready to ship out wherever the Marines sent him.

1945

The gunnery sergeant said, "I know you guys are tired, but they need us now, and R and R is canceled. We're heading to an island in the Pacific the Japanese have been using to intercept our bombers. It's called Iwo Jima. It's gonna be us and the navy versus the Imperial Japanese Army. How bad can it be? Should be over before it starts. We'll be sipping beers at the bar in the Royal Hawaiian hotel on Waikiki before we know it."

"Stay down, Thomas," Hal Ferragamo yelled.

"We've been pinned down for hours," Thomas yelled back. "This was supposed to take a week, maximum. It's been over a month with no end in sight. A ton of Marines are dead and a ton of Japanese too. For what? Command probably has us on the wrong island. I don't think those guys are still out there. They've got to be as tired as we are. Probably snuck off somewhere to take a break from us."

"Stay down, man," Hal told him. "I'm telling you. These are sneaky bastards."

"I don't like just sitting here like ducks in a pond. Anyway, the odds of us ever getting off this island alive are zero. Iwo-frigging-Jima is our last stand. I don't see anyone out there. I'm just gonna stretch my legs."

Rat te te tat, te te tat, te te tat. Machine-gun fire.

"Thomas, you idiot, you're shot."

"Tell me something I don't know. Get out of here, Hal, while you still can. I'll be all right. It's just a flesh wound."

"You moron, your back is all shot up. You should be dead. If I don't get you to a medic right quick, you're gonna bleed to death."

Hal trotted miles, dodging bullets, with Thomas on his back screaming at him the whole way to let him die and to save himself. Neither man was sent home. Thomas needed his liver repaired and a nick on his heart stitched, but miraculously his kidneys were spared, and his bowels were looked at inch by inch and had no holes. He was patched up with suture and cautery, given a day of rest, and they were both sent back into battle because they were still breathing. It lasted two full weeks more. In the end, thousands of Marines died, and thousands of Japanese died. The Americans "won" the battle and took possession of Iwo Jima. A monument was erected in Washington to commemorate the victory.

CHAPTER 3

THE BUTCHER

The years since the war had not been kind to Thomas Laughlin or to his son, Benjamin.

Thomas was a broken man. He would certainly have taken his own life if it hadn't been for Benjamin. He owed it to his wife to feed and house the boy she died giving birth to. Room and board was about all he could give the child. Benjamin suffered emotionally and physically from the absence of a mother and the neglect of his dejected father.

Laughlin opened a butcher shop in Manhattan near the Financial District and lived with his growing son in a one-bedroom walk-up above the store. Benjamin slept on a couch in the living room.

The son was fifteen years old now. He spent his time when he wasn't at school hiding out from the world, lying on the couch, eating junk food, gaining weight, and reading such highbrow literature as *Mad* magazine and Perry Mason courtroom paperbacks. At night he listened to the droll, sarcastic refrain of Jean Shepherd on a cheap transistor radio, under the covers. Shepherd suited Benjamin's temperament to a tee with his sense of isolation and alienation from the human race that he reflected on in his—pretty funny—nightly monologues.

There was sawdust on the floor and the smell of fresh-cut meat in the air. THOMAS LAUGHLIN, PURVEYOR OF FINE MEATS was stenciled on the shop window. One lone older woman reached into her purse and paid the owner what she owed.

The tall, broad-shouldered butcher looked through rimless glasses at his customer and smiled.

"Thank you very much, Mrs. O'Malley."

She said, "It's a pleasure shopping here, my dear. This is the best butcher shop in all of New York

City. My family and I will eat like royalty for a week."

Laughlin said, "Thank you for the compliment. Please be careful on your way home. I'm glad daylight is lasting longer. The sky will light your path."

She said, "If you don't mind me asking, what are the butcher and his son eating for dinner tonight?"

Laughlin replied, "I don't mind you asking. I'm afraid it's going to disappoint you, though. I'm making hamburgers for young Benjamin and myself, and I'm opening a can of asparagus to go with them." He spoke with the remnant of an Irish brogue himself.

Mrs. O'Malley gasped. "Canned? Mr. Laughlin. Really? I'm going to have to bring you some fresh asparagus from the vegetable market next week when I come by. You know, Mr. Laughlin, I'm guessing it's been a while since your lovely missus passed away. You said it was before you went to war. You once told me she died in childbirth and your parents took care of the youngster while you were fighting in the Pacific. Please don't be cross with me for minding your business. If you want me to, I will stop. You won't be hurting my feelings. I know what I am, an old Irish busybody. But it's plain to see that you're a wonderful man, Mr. Laughlin, and you've been in mourning for such a long time now. It's also plain to see, the war took its toll on you, I know. It's in your eyes. You've a son to raise and it wouldn't be such a crime if you were to avail yourself of some female companionship."

Thomas Laughlin gently replied, "Mrs. O., I did not know this baby when my wife died giving birth to him. Having him killed my wife. I haven't been much of a father to him. In my darkest hours on Iwo Jima, men dying all around me, thinking these were my last minutes on earth, day after day, week after week, I thought of the promise I made to his mother to come home safely, so I fought that much harder."

Mrs. O'Malley said, "By the grace of God it was that you went off to war, and by the same grace, you came home safely. Don't you think your late wife would want you to remarry and give Benjamin a woman's presence to help raise him? Whoever the woman is, for one thing, she would keep you in fresh vegetables instead of that soupy canned asparagus, which is probably the single worst vegetable you can eat from a can, let alone feed to your son. I would love to see a smile on your face."

"That's nice of you, Mrs. O."

"My dear man, you deserve happiness more than anyone I know, and you can't seem to find it. I hate to see such a waste of a handsome eligible bachelor. Your wife must have been a wonderful person."

"She was, Mrs. O. She was full of life. There were times during the bloodiest of the fighting that I wanted them to kill me, but no matter how hard I tried, someone always came to rescue me, either that or they needed rescuing themselves, which was just as bad. Two of the most annoying of them made it out with me, here to Manhattan. We owe each other more than we can ever repay. And here's Benjamin, the son of a Marine who doesn't know how to fight. He's getting pushed around at school. It's a little late for me to start caring. I can see Patsy wagging her finger at me. We don't even have a television set. With all due respect, Mrs. O., a woman is the last thing I want in my life right now."

"I'm sorry. Please ignore the meddling of an old woman."

"Mrs. O., I appreciate your kind concern for the two of us crusty old bachelors. But, by the time I get upstairs to make dinner, it's half past eight o'clock in the evening. What woman in her right mind would have a husband with a work schedule like that? This here's a one-man operation."

"You could put a sign up, 'Out Sick,'" which would not be far from the truth. Everyone in New York City would understand."

Laughlin grinned. "Now, now, Mrs. O'Malley. My wife would be so happy to know that a respectable neighborhood woman like yourself is taking such an interest in a widower like me, and our son."

"That does it, Mr. Laughlin. I'll be removing my nose from your business and my foot from my mouth. Thank you very much for the meat and your patience. You and Benjamin have a pleasant dinner. The next time you see me, I'll be bearing fresh vegetables and keeping my mouth completely shut."

Thomas walked her to the door and held it open for her. When she was on her way down the sidewalk, he went back inside, locked the front door, and turned the CLOSED sign out toward the street. Then he began moving the meat from his display case to the refrigeration unit in the back.

"Hey, kid. Yeah, you. Come over here."

Benjamin Laughlin, the butcher's son, overweight, out of shape, once again faced a no-win situation. While he was considering his choices, he spotted the girl, Susan, who had filled his dreams ever since he first laid eyes on her. He was never able to look her in the eye before now, but after this, he would have to hide from her in shame.

Fred, the Neanderthal, finished coiffing his greased hair and returned the plastic comb to his back pocket. He smiled at Benjamin, who just stood there awaiting his fate. Benjamin reluctantly reached into his pants and handed over some of his money to the brute. "Here, take it you big jerk."

Fred punched the younger boy under his eye. That was going to swell and turn colors, Benjamin knew.

"All of it, boy," Fred told the kid.

Susan whispered to her girlfriend, Brenda, "Bren, that guy, Fred, is disgusting. One of these days he's gonna get what's coming to him, and I want to be there when he does."

"Really, Susan. That day will never come. Bullies come and bullies go, but Fred is forever. There's no one around who has the nerve to take him on, and there never will be."

The bigger, older boy reached into Ben's jeans pocket and pulled out a five-dollar bill.

"Holy mackerel," Fred said. "I hit the jackpot. You shouldn't ought'a have held out on me, boy. I would've let you keep some, but now I'm taking it all."

"Why don't you leave me alone, Fred? I'm supposed to pick up groceries with that money."

"Why don't you just run home and tell your mommy that the big bad wolf took all your cash."

"Someday," Benjamin said.

"Someday what, Laughlin? You're a loser, and it's only gonna get worse. It's sad, really. You're disgusting. Get out of my sight."

CHAPTER 4

GYPSY

Rap, rap, rap.

There was banging on the glass-paned door of Dr. Fred Brenden's Washington Heights dental office. The office was not yet open. Nurse Irene Peterson was deep into her *Journal American*. Annoyed by the intrusion, she removed the cigarette from her mouth and placed it in the ashtray on her desk.

"The office isn't open for another half hour," she said, loud enough to be heard outside.

She stood and cautiously lifted a slat of the closed venetian blinds on the door but saw no one out there. She let the slat fall back into place, sat back down, and resumed reading her paper. The banging started up again.

"Take it easy." Nurse Peterson raised her voice. "Do not break the glass."

A groaning voice came back at her, "Is the doc in? My tooth is killing me."

"I can't disturb him right now. He's setting up for the day. Come back in twenty minutes and we'll make you an appointment."

There was no more banging.

After a pause, "Lady, I'm dying out here."

She rolled her eyes and unlocked the door. When she saw who it was, she put her foot against the inside of the door and tried to push it closed with her shoulder, but to no avail. The tall, black-haired Gypsy, Christos Montes, succeeded in pushing the door open and making his way inside.

"I'm not joking," he said. "My tooth is killing me."

Dr. Brenden had fallen behind in his payments. The Gypsy had told the dentist the price was going up.

"Let's go see the doctor," Montes said, and relocked the door behind him.

The dentist had spread the word that he stopped paying Montes and nothing bad had happened. Other merchants in the area were beginning to be late with their payments.

"Stop," the nurse demanded. "After what happened last time, I'm afraid Dr. Brenden is not going to treat you. You threatened him. He gave you his answer."

"Don't get all in a twist. I heard him. I'm not deaf. This isn't about money. I need him to fix my tooth. I'll pay. It's simple. He fixes me up and I'll be on my way."

"I'll see if he's got time to take care of your problem," she said.

Before she had a chance to do anything, Montes said, "Oh, he has time. Take my word for it. We'll go see him together."

Nurse Peterson knocked on the inner office door, but Christos Montes reached around her, turned the doorknob, and pushed her inside.

She stumbled into the office to face her surprised employer.

Dr. Brenden took his feet off the desk and the lit cigarette out of his mouth and growled at his visitor, "What is the meaning of this, Mr. Montes? I will not be intimidated by your threats any longer. Can't you take no for an answer? I said no and I meant no."

The black-haired Gypsy responded, "This isn't about protection anymore. I have a bad tooth. I need you to look at it is all."

"I'm going to have to ask you to find another dentist. I'm booked all day, and your tooth won't keep. Run along now."

"Man, you must be high on your own laughing gas, talking to me like that. You must'a lost your mind. Just because I didn't burn your office to the ground doesn't mean you got home free. But I'm not here to talk business. I'm in pain, and I'm not going anywhere until you fix it. You got that?"

The dentist had alarm written across his face. It didn't take a genius to understand that he was at the mercy of his visitor. He was no hero.

"I suppose I can take a look at it, but after that, you are gonna have to get out of here and stay out of here. I don't want any trouble, but, if you bring it, I will have this place swarming with police. Show me what you're talking about."

"I got pain way in the back, doc. Right here." Montes put his dirty finger into his mouth and pulled the cheek out.

The operatory was adjacent to the office through an archway.

"Sit in the chair in there," the dentist ordered him. "And take that finger out of your mouth."

"You," Montes said to the nurse, "sit down at the desk. Just sit there and shut up."

"Don't you talk to her that way. You either behave yourself or I will have to ask you to leave."

The dentist arose and motioned to the nurse to sit in the chair behind his desk. He let the back of the dental chair down so that the unwanted patient was almost horizontal. Brenden washed his hands, and the Gypsy opened his mouth wide. The dentist lifted the man's cheek to see what the tooth and the gum looked like.

He said, "You have an abscess. Your tooth is infected. It needs to come out."

The patient replied, "Okay, do it."

Dr. Brenden said, "It's gonna hurt like hell. You're going to need Novocain and gas."

The Gypsy said, "Okay on the Novocain. Nix on the gas. You think I'm stupid? I let you gas me, I'll wake up in a jail cell."

"Okay, but you'll need penicillin after."

"You got some here?"

"Yes."

"Get it for me first."

"Nurse. Put thirty tablets in a pillbox."

Nurse Peterson got up and opened a cabinet, tapped the pills into a small prescription box, and handed it to the intruder, who put it in his pocket.

"That's three a day for ten days," Brenden said.

"Okay then, Doc. Do it."

The dentist drew Novocain into a syringe.

"Let me see the bottle, doc. Just hold it up so I can read the label."

"You don't trust me?"

"If you were me, would you? I don't want to find out too late it was Pentothal."

The dentist held the label up so Christos could read it.

"Okay, go ahead."

He opened his mouth again, and the dentist infiltrated the gum. "We have to wait for it to take effect."

"Okay, you two," the patient said, "smoke 'em if you got 'em."

The nurse opened the desk drawer and tapped out two cigarettes from an open pack. She put them in her mouth and lit them with the desktop Ronson. She got up and, her hand shaking, gave one to her employer. Her face was a mask of fear. Her boss gently gripped her wrist to steady it and gave her a reassuring smile.

It was obvious to Christos that they had shared plenty of cigarettes together, probably more than just cigarettes.

"That's right, settle down. You two can play footsie after I'm gone. Right now, I need my tooth fixed. Then I'll be out of here."

The dentist took a surgical instrument that looked like a pliers and wrestled the tooth from the gum, then put a stack of gauze squares over the bleeding socket.

"Bite down on that until it stops bleeding. It'll take a few hours."

With his jaws clamped together, the patient moved his lips. "Okay, everybody, stay calm, and I'll get outta here. I'd appreciate it if you didn't call the cops as soon as I leave."

"You don't have to worry about that," the dentist said. "You being out of this office is all I want."

Montes said, "I have to do something to save my reputation before I leave."

The dentist and the nurse looked at each other with alarm.

"What do you mean?" asked the dentist.

The Gypsy said, "My whole business depends on customer loyalty. Thanks to you spreading the news, people are beginning to think I am too weak to protect them from anything. What good is my service if I can't convince the neighborhood dentist he needs me?"

Dr. Brenden said, "I'm sorry, but you're just going to have to take my word for it that I won't tell anyone about our little arrangement."

"You think I'm stupid. I know you already have. Everybody knows. They're starting to pay me late or not at all."

"What are you saying?"

"Double. You pay me double and then you visit all the neighborhood businesses, up one side of the street and down the other side, and you tell them you were wrong, that you really do need me. Tell everyone they're lucky to have my protection, it's worth the price, that you're so satisfied with my service you pay extra."

"I can't do that."

The Gypsy said, "I understand. Believe me. I have this great idea. Why don't you call your wife and ask her if she thinks it's worth paying me whatever I say?"

"My wife? What does she have to do with this?"

"Call her and maybe she'll tell you."

The dentist's face turned red. Sweat rose from his forehead. He did not want to call his wife, but he had to. He picked up the receiver from his desk telephone and rotated the dial.

"Hello, honey. You all right?"

He listened. "No, Fred. Come home."

"What's happened? What did they do to you?"

"Fred, come home. Give them whatever they want. Just come home."

"Is our daughter okay?"

"No, she is not okay. She is terrified."

"Did they hurt her?"

"No, they didn't touch her. They hurt me while she watched. They scared the living daylights out of both of us. My face is bruised. My arm is bruised too, but I'll be all right. They told me that next time it would be worse, much worse, and I believe them. Give them what they want, Fred. Do what they say. Then come home."

Dr. Brenden said, "All right, sweetheart, I will. Try to calm down. I'll be home as soon as I can.

I have to run to the bank first. I love you, and I love our daughter. I'll be there as fast as I can."

He hung up.

Then he turned to Montes and said, "You bastard. I'll pay whatever you want. Just don't bother my family again."

The Gypsy said, "Now you are talking. I knew you were a reasonable man. Too bad about this misunderstanding. Home invasion is a serious matter. You pay me double and I will provide full-service protection for both your home and your office. Catch up on your missed payments and pay me two months in advance and this will never happen again. How much do you want for the tooth?"

"Nothing. It's on the house."

CHAPTER 5

THE BLONDE

She was five foot five, brown eyes, blonde hair, one of those rare light-haired Italian beauties. It was dawn and she was cooling down after her morning run. This was the South Bronx, her home.

She wore tan shorts, a baggy T-shirt, and running shoes.

Three strangers walked down the sidewalk toward her. She figured them for night shift workers on their way home to have a beer and get some sleep. They looked used up.

She figured on a friendly nod as they went by.

"Hiya good lookin'," the short, brown haired one said.

She took no offense, smiled, and said, "Good morning to you too."

They moved to block her way.

The handsome blond man with blue eyes, said, "Give us some company, won't you, darlin'?"

Irish.

Her smile disappeared.

The third, and biggest, said, "Didn't your mother teach you any manners?"

"More than yours taught you," she replied. "Get out of my way."

Shorty said, "Don't get smart with us."

She said, "You're not from around here, are you? Look at me. Why would a woman who looks like me walk down a street in this neighborhood without a bodyguard if she didn't know for a fact that she could tear off both your arms and beat you to death with your own fists?"

The biggest of the three guys had black hair, tattoos, was six foot tall and two hundred plus pounds. He said, "Little lady you have got to be crazy talking like that to three strapping brutes like us."

The blonde woman said, "Go home and take a shower before I put a beating on you that will embarrass you for the rest of your miserable lives. Go on, get out of my way."

Blackie said, "I got to admit you have some nerve on you talking that way to us."

She said, "Last chance. You don't get out of my way, you're gonna spend the rest of the day getting x-rays and stitches. I may not look it to you, but I am your worst nightmare." She raised her eyebrow impatiently. "Make up your mind. I got places I gotta be. On the other hand, you three could be my morning workout."

They stood their ground, crossed their arms, and grinned at her.

She said, "You win. Who's first? You." She pointed at the biggest. "A delicate flower such as myself can only take on one of you at a time. You two sit down on the ground. You'll get your turn, believe me. There's plenty of me for everybody."

The brown-haired guy and the blond man smiled and sat down as instructed.

Black-hair said, "Okay honey. It's just you and me now."

The woman said, "It's been lovely getting to know you. You start."

"What?" the man said. "I'll go easy on you so you have enough left to take on my friends. I don't want to mess up my hair."

She said, "You haven't looked at yourself in a mirror lately, have you? Your hair is the least of your problems. Your face looks like the back end of a horse. Your breath probably smells like day old manure. You and your two cretin boyfriends have no idea what you've gotten yourself into. Your two buddies are sitting on the ground. Now that is real stupid. You're making this too easy for me. That makes you both ugly and stupid."

"Why're you talkin' that way?" Blackie said. "You sayin' you can take us?"

"Take you? I will tear all three of you limb from limb if you even try to lay a hand on me. You have one last chance to get out of my way. Otherwise, you are all toast."

The two other men stood up on high alert.

"You got us real scared, lady," said Blackie. "Come closer so I can hear you better. I could swear you threatened to hurt us bad. Let's see what you got." He reached his hand out to touch her shoulder.

She gripped his wrist tightly and twisted it until he was bent forward, then delivered a front thrust kick to his stomach. His eyes opened wide, and he bent forward, but didn't go down for fear the fall would break his shoulder.

She said, "Don't make me hurt you. Walk away while you can still walk."

She let go of his wrist and he stood up straight, looking mean, getting ready to charge.

The blonde-haired woman beckoned her prey with her hands. He was feeling his strained wrist and moving his arm at the shoulder to make sure neither was broken before he moved.

Suddenly he swung his free hand at her head. She leaned back to let it pass, punched him in the ribs, then kneed him in the groin. He stood there holding his privates with both hands.

She said, "Stop now. I said I would hurt you and I meant it. It's only gonna get worse. You made a terrible mistake. There's no shame in walking away. We'll consider it a draw. Let your boys take you home. Have a beer. There's nothing but pain and hospital time for you here."

Blackie looked at his guys and said, "Don't just stand there. Get her."

Brown hair moved towards her while the chubby blond guy circled around to her other side.

She kicked Brownie with a straight kick to his solar plexus and felt his sternum crack. He went out like a light, fell to the sidewalk, slid across it, and dropped off the curb.

Black hair was on his feet and came at her, his one good hand clenched. He threw a hook, which she ducked, grabbed his extended wrist, and kicked her toe up hard under his arm, close to the armpit, dislocating his shoulder.

She told him, "That's gonna need an x-ray to make sure it's not broken before they put it back in the socket. You're gonna have to hire someone to wipe your butt after you use the toilet."

He made an animal-like growl and charged her with his head down like a bull. She side-stepped like a bullfighter. As he passed, she put her foot on his hip and pushed hard sending him sprawling on the ground.

She said, "Stay down. Don't you move or I will put you in a wheelchair for certain. I'm not playing."

He squinted up at her, defeated. He had no plans to move.

She turned in time to see the chubby guy and the now-conscious brown-haired one charging her at the same time. She side slipped and punched chubby in his ear, hard enough to put him down.

Brown hair kept coming.

Fed up, she walked up close to him, pushed her chest out, and stood still, her arms relaxed down at her sides.

He got ready to strike her but thought better of it.

"Smart," she said. "They're gonna need someone to get them to the hospital."

She reached behind her and checked under the back of her T-shirt to see that her badge and gun were still fixed in place.

Continuing her walk down the street, she said over her shoulder, "You fellas sure know how to show a girl a good time."

Thomas Laughlin came out of the frigid meat locker. The shop had been empty when he went in. The sign out front said CLOSED. Now a tall, menacing European-looking gentleman, with black hair and chiseled features, stood staring at him, too close to the locker door for comfort. The man looked to be the Gypsy he'd been warned might pay him a visit. He must've come in through the back alley. He could easily have locked the proprietor in the cooler overnight. Thomas assumed that was the message he intended to convey.

He came all the way out of the freezing compartment and thought about knocking the stranger down, but instead he shouldered him aside and closed the cold room door. The Gypsy took the physical contact without protest. Laughlin pushed a steel rod into the hasp of the meat locker handle to secure it.

"Can I help you?" the butcher asked, squaring off on the stranger.

"I was thinking it was me who could help you," the man said.

"Listen, mister," Laughlin said. "I don't want any trouble. State your business. It's closing time, and I have a boy to feed."

The stranger said, "You have a nice business here. It would be a shame if it got trashed and your customers were scared away."

Laughlin said, "Just out of curiosity, how much would it cost me for that not to happen?"

The stranger said, "Name a price and keep going up until I tell you to stop."

Laughlin said, "What makes you think you could destroy my business without me finding you and hurting you? You know, we fought a war a little while ago over this kind of thing. People were being pushed around, threatened—like you just did to me—gassed, and burned in ovens. I killed a lot of men like you and lost a lot of friends while I was at it. Almost died myself. I'm not gonna pay you to protect me from what you'll do to me if I don't pay you. That doesn't make any sense. We could save time and have it out right now. Put yourself in my place. Why don't you just start destroying my store right now and I'll signal you when to stop by breaking both your arms."

The Gypsy fumed but did not move.

The butcher said, "There's a lady in a wheelchair, sells newspapers down the street. You might want to rough her up a little and steal her money. That seems more like a fair fight for a man like you."

The Gypsy said, "I heard you were in the war, so I will cut you some slack. But, that aside, there will come a day when you will wish you just paid me off and went about your business. We all have to make a living."

Laughlin said, "If you take me on, there will come a day when you will wish you just took no for an answer and walked away."

"I don't care how many people you killed in the war. You are old and useless. Look at yourself in the mirror. You're dead on your feet, broken by the war, worn out, sick, and tired. You might as well have died fighting. I feel sorry for you. But business is business. I'll be back."

He turned and started to make his exit.

Thomas said to the stranger's back, "I'm looking forward to that."

The butcher followed the man into the alley, then watched him disappear down the street. He returned to his shop, expanded the accordion fence across the front, and locked the place up.

He didn't need this kind of trouble, but it shocked him into realizing that the Gypsy was right. He was out of shape and his mind hadn't been right for a long time. The clock was ticking. He'd better get his act together or he would become easy prey in the New York City jungle.

CHAPTER 6

MOVING IN

A cut glass ashtray slipped through the torn seam of a cardboard box, hit the hardwood floor, and broke into pieces.

There were several stacks of boxes in the foyer of the three-bedroom apartment Alice and Jim were now living in together. For years Alice had lived in a one-bedroom apartment on the other side of this building. She had a small mound of possessions. The huge pile, almost reaching the ceiling, belonged to Jim. He'd had to hire an agent to liquidate the rest of his stuff. The theoretical destinations were penciled on the sides of each carton. If this move didn't kill their relationship, nothing would.

The breaking of the ashtray signaled the end of the day's unpacking. Alice hadn't been at it for even an hour.

Jim said, "I'll tell you what, Alice. Let's take the D train all the way to the end of the line, Coney Island. Have you ever done that?"

"No, I never have. I've been riding that subway for years and it says Coney Island in big letters on it, but it never occurred to me to actually ride it to the end and visit the amusement park. You are broadening my horizons, Jim. It sounds like fun."

Jim said, "We'll go to Nathan's and have some hot dogs and sauerkraut and ride the Ferris wheel. A walk on the beach would be pretty romantic. Let's do it."

Alice carried a beach bag stuffed with all sorts of recreational paraphernalia. She and Jim approached the subway station on the Concourse and 204th Street.

"Jimmy," she said to the newsie hunched in the green wooden shed that protected him from the weather. "I got you a little present last night at the Stadium. I know you already have one, but it's old and worn out. Here."

She pulled a new, navy-blue New York Yankees baseball cap from her beach bag and handed it to him. The short, paunchy middle-aged man took the gift, smiled broadly, and put it on.

"Oh gee, Miss White. It's a perfect fit. Thank you very much."

"Jimmy, ever since I can remember, you've been standing here listening to Yankees baseball games on your transistor radio, cheering them on, Mel Allen calling the plays. You hand me my crossword puzzles and say hello. All I ever give you is pocket change. You're like my brother. I wanted to give you something more personal. My father was in the men's clothing business when I was a kid, so I can figure a man's head size. Enjoy it."

"Okay, Miss White, I will. Thanks again. Take 'er easy. You too, Mr. White . . . uh . . . sorry."

"Peters, Jimmy. My last name is Peters. And thank you for taking such good care of my friend Alice all these years. We'll see you if you're still here when we get back."

"Have fun at Coney Island, right?" Jimmy said.

Alice said, "You'd make a good detective, Jimmy. If you ever think of changing professions, let me know."

"That's not gonna happen, Miss White. I like what I do here at this little stand. I know the people and it keeps me close to my Yankees."

They read the ads on the walls of the subway car. Alice worked a crossword puzzle.

Jim commented, "Alice, you've been very quiet these last few days. Something is up with you. How bad could it be?"

"It's nothing," Alice replied.

"Alice, I can tell you think it's a whopper. It's only going to get worse."

"Oh, Jim. Really. I don't want to bother you with trivial matters."

"It's that bad, huh?"

"There was this man at the playground where I was taking a break, having a sandwich. It all turned out fine. Here I am, alive and well."

"Alice, spill it."

"Sheesh. All right, okay. I got into a little scuffle with a man over my gun. This guy was about to take a woman's purse. I told him not to do it, but he wouldn't listen. I pulled my gun. He grabbed it. We struggled, so I fired it over his shoulder. No big deal, except I could've killed someone if I missed the tree. I have to find another way to control situations like that. Let's not tell Antonio."

Jim said, "Are you trying to make me an accessory after the fact?"

"Where'd you get that 'accessory after the fact' stuff?"

Jim lowered his voice to a whisper. "Alice, you taught it to me. It's part of your pre-intimacy conversation. I think it gets you in the mood. It gets me excited too. Never give up the law. At this rate I'll be able to pass the Bar myself, in July."

Alice whispered back, "Okay, okay. I'll let you help me study. You can even tell Antonio about the thing in the park if you want."

"Alice, I'm not telling Antonio anything. That is between you and him. You've been dying to learn how to fight, anyway. You might not have seen this coming, but ever since I met you, I knew a gun wasn't gonna be enough for you."

"You're right, Jim. I'll get on it. Right now, I'm hungry."

Back to whispering, Alice said, "Later, if you're a good boy, I'll explain torts to you. Torts are wrongful acts that lead to legal liability."

CHAPTER 7

PAUL

Isabella Goodwin became New York City's first female police detective in 1912, under Police Commissioner Theodore Roosevelt. In 1957 Police Detective Sandra James dreamed of becoming New York City's first female police commissioner.

Detective Sandra James called Paul Zanetti.

"Hey, Pauly, I am going to be late helping you with your mom. I have some errands to run. I'll be there around lunchtime. How about I bring us something to eat from Etta's candy store?"

"That'd be great," Paul said. "I'll have to decide for my mom. How about soup for her and tuna on white for me?"

"Good, and I'll get a burger for myself."

"I'll pay you back."

She said, "I'll be there as soon as I can."

"Okay, Sandy. See you later."

"Paul, before you hang up, I want to ask you something."

"What?"

"Paul, how do you feel about me? You're my boyfriend, but we never do anything about that, you know what I mean. Do you love me?"

"Sandra, I do love you, but not the way you mean."

Sandra said, "I feel guilty, like I'm not holding up my end of our relationship."

Paul said, "I should never have let this go so far without talking to you about it. We seem to be using each other to protect ourselves from other people. We're like a brother and sister. You are a shockingly beautiful woman and, if you let them, men would flock to your door, even here in the South Bronx. They would risk their lives to court you. But how many men who feel attracted to you would you let get close? It's not your older brothers they're afraid of, Sandra. It's you. I'm just the 'beard,' the pretend-boyfriend. Thank you for breaking the ice."

"It's all right, Paul, it is. I love you too, but as you say, more like a brother. I'll always be there for you and your mother. I had to straighten this out."

Paul said, "Do you think either of us will ever find someone to be with?"

"Maybe you will, Pauly, but my fate is sealed. I'm going to become New York City's first female police commissioner."

"Sandra, I think you can run a police department and manage a family at the same time."

"That's kind of you to say, Paul, but men find me difficult to relate to. I'm a leg breaker. That's kind of a turnoff to most guys, don't you think? I'm not sure I am destined to be with anybody."

"I wouldn't bet on it."

"Being alone suits me. I'm not gonna join a convent or anything. I love being a detective. I love Louis, my partner. There's so much I want to do. What I do for a living is dangerous. I don't want to leave a husband and children widowed and orphaned. I like things the way they are. If I want to work up a sweat, I go to the gym, kick the heavy bag, jump rope, run laps. I don't intend to be with a man for the rest of my life."

Benjamin Laughlin lay on the couch holding a bag of frozen peas to his bruised face and looking over his new copy of *Mad* magazine.

The sound of the locks opening in the thick metal apartment door made his head turn. He smiled sheepishly at his father. Thomas was still wearing his white butcher's apron splattered with blood from the day's work. He had brought lamb chops home for supper. He winced at the sight of the bag of frozen vegetables pressed against his son's face. He locked the door and wearily put the package of chops down on the counter, exhausted from the long day of standing.

"Looks like you were playing rough at school."

"Yeah, Dad," Ben said without enthusiasm. "I ran into a door."

Thomas said, "I've done that a number of times myself."

"Dad, I want to stop going to school. I hate it. I'm not doing good in any of my classes. School's a complete waste of time. I don't have any friends there, anyway. I want to stop going out of the house, period. The street is dangerous. I have everything I need right here."

"Son, think about it. Staying home may seem like a solution to your problems, and I don't blame you for wanting to lock yourself up in here, but it is not a practical option. You are going to have to walk the streets for the rest of your life or you will starve to death. I'm not gonna live forever. You will have to get a job, even if it's digging ditches. You'll have to shop for food. And, if you want a better job, you'll have to get better grades. If I could do it for you, I would, believe me, but I can't. Am I getting through to you?"

"Yeah, Dad. I understand. But I hate my life."

"Son, I love you. I know I haven't been the best father I could have been. There is no excuse for that. Not your mom dying. Not the war."

"Dad, you've been great. Anybody would have been down after all that happened to you. I'll try harder in school. Forget what I just said. I'll learn to take a punch."

"Son," the father said. "I have let you down. I'm sorry."

Benjamin said, "Dad, couldn't we move somewhere else?"

"My business is here. Please tell me you're joking, Benjamin."

"Yes, Dad, I am joking, I am. Deep down I always knew this day would come."

"My God, boy. Your mother would be so angry at me for letting things get this bad. There's a whole beautiful world out there. I can't let you stay locked up in this apartment. Not to mention, there's an army of women who will hurt you in ways you can't imagine. You definitely do not want to miss out on that. If you think the street is tough, wait until a woman gets hold of you and tears your heart out."

"Is that what happened with mom?"

"Ah, shit, boy." A tear escaped the father's eye. "You know . . . yes, that's exactly what happened. I fell in love with her, worshiped the ground she walked on, adored her, gave her my heart on a silver platter, and I was happy to do it, so happy. Then, she went and died."

"I'm sorry, Dad."

"It wasn't your fault. These things happen. And she did me a favor. She gave me a precious gift. A baby son. You. A beautiful boy for me to take care of, to protect until you could protect yourself . . . and your family when you get older. I love you, boy, but I think I went too far on the protection part. I let you down. You're not stupid, either. If you ever want to be a lawyer, like this Perry Mason you read about all the time, you are going to have to get your grades up."

"I'm just nowhere near smart enough to be a lawyer."

"How do you know if you don't try?"

"What's for supper?"

"Lamb chops."

"Bless us, Oh Lord, and these Thy gifts, which we are about to receive." Benjamin opened his eyes and lifted his head.

"Amen," they said in unison.

"Dad, why do we pray before we eat?"

"Gee, I guess this is a night of tough questions. Son, look at all we have: food, shelter, each other. God delivered you safely from your sweet mother before she died. He got me through the war. A person pretends not to believe in God until men are coming after him, to kill him. You're gonna have to come to your own conclusion about things like that. Your mother believed in God more than I did. She made me take her to church sometimes. I just like us to say grace before we eat on account of her."

"Did you blame me for her dying?"

"What a question, boy. You are pretty smart. I don't think so. I love you as much as I ever loved her, now, but I'd be lying if I didn't say I thought crazy things when I got as sad as I did after she died. I'm not gonna lie. You were just born. I didn't know you very well and she died. I knew her. I wanted her. I loved her very much. God, man, I loved her more than life itself, more than my own life, let alone yours. But when the pain eased up, I realized you were a part of her and me together that I could hang on to. Now when I look at you, I think I may have held on too tight, but we can fix that. Somehow, we are going to fix that, you and me together."

CHAPTER 8

BUDDIES

"Come on, man, get up."

Thomas Laughlin tugged on the collar of his friend Hal's frayed jacket. Hal Ferragamo was a forty-two-year-old, heavy Italian. He lay on his back in an alley. He had vomit on his shirt and urine soaking through his pants. He smelled like a portable toilet on a construction site that hadn't been serviced in a long time.

Thomas had no idea how long his friend had been lying there.

"Hal, buddy," Laughlin said to his half-conscious friend. "You gotta find something more fun to do with your nights."

Hal squinted. "No, Tom. You gotta stop coming after me. I should never have given my landlady your phone number for emergencies. Let's face it, I'm gonna die of this stuff and there ain't a thing anyone can do about it. The booze used to do me a world of good. Now it's killing me. I've seen it before. Don't break your heart over this. Let me go."

Laughlin said, "C'mon, man. Let's get you home, and, phew, you gotta take a shower. Then we'll get some food into you."

"Tom, you don't understand." Hal felt around his chest and pants for his pack of Luckys. Amazingly, they were dry. He tried to open the pack, but his hands were too shaky, so Laughlin did it for him.

Laughlin said, "How about the meetings, my brother?"

"You can't be serious. They are no good. I heard they give you bad coffee and stale donuts and talk your ear off. You know how many guys around here died going to those meetings? Might as well put me in a box. I am a dead man!"

"Don't say that, Hal. I won't give up on you. I don't care if I have to close my shop and take you up into the mountains to dry you out."

Hal said, "Don't waste your time, Thomas."

Laughlin said, "Waste, Hal? I remember screaming at you to leave me, but you wouldn't. You remember? I was a dead man too. Shot to hell. You wouldn't listen to me. You wouldn't let me be. I begged you to get out of there and save yourself. Patsy was dead. The baby was with my folks. They would done a hell of a lot better raising him than I did. That's for sure. But you wouldn't let me go. You slung me over your shoulder like a side of beef. By the way, that hurt, you baboon. You could'a put some padding up there. If the bullet holes didn't kill me, I could'a died listening to your monotonous voice telling me not to die."

Tears filled Laughlin's eyes.

Hal said, "Quit your bellyaching, Thomas. We made it out of there, didn't we?"

"Hal, you and me have the exact same problem. So many times since the day you carried my bleeding body to the medics, me bitching every step of the way—I know, I'm sorry—but so many times since then I have wished you had let me die. We are two of the most messed-up human beings that ever lived."

"Geez, Thomas. I guess I owe you an apology. All these years I thought you were happy, sitting there on easy street with your butcher shop and your son by your side. Beautiful housewives flirting with you and asking you for meat. It never occurred to me you were feeling as bad as me."

"That's all right, Hal. That was a fantasy. You want to make up for it? To show me you're sorry for saving my life? Go to the meetings. I hear they get drunks to laugh again. Then you can teach me. Maybe there's another way. If there is, I never heard of it. Point is, you gotta stop drinking or you're gonna leave me stranded without a real friend in the world, except for Reggie, who I never see. If I'm annoying you now, it's your own damn fault. I begged you to let me die."

"Don't say that, man. I love you," Hal said.

Thomas said, "If you love me, please don't hug me, because you smell like fifteen kinds of crap. I'm not leaving you. If I have to go on living and suffering this way, you do too."

Hal said, "Okay, you rotten, no-good son of a bitch. I didn't think I could feel worse, but you found a way. Now I am twice as depressed as I was before you showed up."

Thomas said, "Now you're talking. Let's get you home and take care of the stink."

Hal Ferragamo took a long, deep drag on his cigarette. The burn in his lungs from the tobacco worked like a tonic. His situation might not be as hopeless as he thought. On the other hand, it might be worse.

Laughlin put on a pot of coffee while Hal was in the shower. The butcher opened the refrigerator and put together a meal. The sound of hot water spraying out of the showerhead sounded good. He could hear Hal humming.

Hal came out of the bedroom looking like a new man in fresh clothes, drying his hair with a hotel towel he must have stolen in his travels. "Thanks, my good friend. I'm feeling much better."

Laughlin got up from his chair, poured Hal a cup of coffee, and refilled his own. "I cooked you some eggs. Sit down and eat."

"Thanks. I am famished. Now that you got me squared away, it's time for me to ask, how're you doin', Thomas?"

"Hal, I won't lie. I told you straight. I wasn't just trying to make you feel guilty for saving me. I am not happy. I think I'm tired of being a butcher. In the war, I couldn't wait to come back to New York and open my own butcher shop. The patrons are all nice people. It's just, I'm restless and moody. And I'm just starting to realize how bad I dropped the ball with Benjamin."

"Thomas, have you given any thought to grabbing you one of those fine-looking women who walk in and out of your shop every day?"

"Hal, I'm not going home with any woman young enough to be my daughter. The ones my age are all married. Besides, I have got to do something about the lad before I even think about engaging with a woman, young or old."

"Engaging? You sound like you're talking about barnyard animals. Now, about Benjamin, I'm telling you, Thomas, let me and Reggie take him off your hands for a couple of weeks. We'll bring him up to the country and make a man of him, or kill him trying, whichever comes first. He'll be drinking, smoking, gambling, and, you know, learning how to be with a woman, by the time we send him home, if he ever comes home. He won't learn anything worth a damn outta books or talkin' to you. Time we're done with him he might not know how to read or write, but he'll surely know how to use his fists, by heaven."

"Hal, have you completely lost your mind?"

"Thomas, think about it. We'll pick fights for him with gorillas twice his size, and then leave him to live or die. We'll get him a woman or two. Oh my God, Thomas. Our kid Benjamin. Under that frightened, sensitive, boyish exterior lies a savage beast just begging to break loose and tear into the sweet, smooth body of a young maiden and her adorable twin sister. With all due respect, Thomas, he's a mama's boy without a mama."

"Hal, that hurts. I've been doing the best I could. Maybe you're right. I don't know. He doesn't want to fight. He doesn't want to study. He never asks me about women. All he does when he's not in school is eat cupcakes and candy bars and read comic books. I think he wants to be a lawyer, but he'll never get there if he doesn't do better in school. And he's getting pushed around at school. Comes home with black eyes. Maybe I should take you up on your offer, because I sure as heck have not taught him how to defend himself."

"I'm telling you, man. Give him to us. We'll whip him into shape, scare the living daylights out of him, turn him into a holy terror. After he gets outta the penitentiary, if he's not too old, he can go to law school and give you some grandkids. Whadya say?"

"Hal, you do not fill me with confidence, but you make me laugh. That's why you gotta take the cure."

"Jesus, man," Hal said. "We should go see Reggie sometime. He's gotta be doing better than us. Last I heard, he was working in a garage."

CHAPTER 9

POSTGRADUATE

It was the dead of night. They were still awake. Alice sat alone on a pillow on the windowsill in her and Jim's bedroom. Jim was in the living room reading Jack Kerouac's *On the Road,* giving Alice some space. It had been an emotionally exhausting day.

After her divorce from Andrew, the uniformed New York City police officer, Alice had sworn to herself that she would never live with a man again, for the rest of her life. One marriage, no matter how brief—and theirs had lasted less than a year—was enough to convince her she was too selfish and temperamental to share a living space or an emotional relationship. Yet, here she was, living with Jim.

She sat alone, nursing a juice glass of whiskey, looking out the open window at the moonlit roofs of neighboring buildings. Laundry fluttered on clotheslines to dry for the first time since last summer.

Jim wandered into the bedroom and approached her gently, almost guilty for intruding on her solitude, but unable to control his urge to wrap himself around her, feel her, smell her, smother her with affection, never let her go. He delicately removed the juice glass from Alice's hand and took a sip.

"You look so much better in the tops of my pajamas, Alice, than I ever did."

"You always say that, Jim."

They kissed, sweetly. He handed her back the whiskey.

Jim said, "Before I withdraw to spend time with Jack Kerouac and his gang, I'd like to ask you to please be careful not to fall out of that window. It's a long drop."

"I will."

The warm spring air foretold the suffocating heat of a Bronx summer.

"You were my favorite graduate today, Alice. I loved the way you flipped your tassel."

"Really, Jim. Did it excite you?"

"I wasn't going to mention it, Alice, but yes, frankly, it did. I enjoyed your friends too, although I couldn't tell you any of their names. Sally, Jill, Susan, Betsy, all you girls were heavily outnumbered by the men, but you were all pretty amazing looking. You're all gonna fill the galleries at your trials. Watch out, Perry Mason. I hear they're coming out with a TV show about him in September. You might want to get a TV to watch him with."

"Isn't that interesting about old Perry?" Alice said. "He breaks the law, tampers with evidence, suborns perjury, encourages his clients to break the law, and did I mention he also forges signatures, yet thousands of men and women have become lawyers because of him. I have read a bunch of his books. Erle Stanley Gardner clearly loves being a lawyer, and it's hard not to want to be a lawyer reading Perry's cases. I'm not joking, he's at least partly responsible for my wanting to be a lawyer. One of my first jobs was as a shop girl at Strawbridge and Clothier in New Jersey. It was a great job. That's when I read my first Perry Mason book. During the war they let me stuff boxes full of clothes and mail them home to my family. Dresses for my mom, shirts for my brother and father."

"Alice, you're crying."

"No, I am not. Yes, I am, a little. It's graduation day, and my brother, Phil, and my father are not alive to see it," she sobbed.

"Alice. I'm so sorry they aren't. I think it's good for you to remember them at a time like this. Without a doubt, they would be deliriously happy for you."

"Jim, you are an angel. I'm not sure I deserve you. My father and Phil would be glad you're here to represent them."

Jim said, "That makes me very happy."

Alice said, "Graduation was pretty boring, wasn't it?"

"Well, Alice, it was great to see your mother again, and your aunt and cousin, not to mention Antonio and Maria. I loved the slow dances with you."

"Oh, Jim. You were so sweet about it," Alice said, and pressed her lips to his cheek. "You were a perfect gentleman. You even ironed your own shirt. I knew you had it in you."

When she had freed his face, he turned and said, "Amazingly, you may not even remember this, but when you were dressing to leave, you taught me another law term: 'detrimental reliance.' Which means that if I do something like sit through your unbelievably long graduation ceremony, except for the part where you got your diploma, in expectation of you doing something in return for me, the courts consider you bound by law to deliver."

She smiled, batted her eyelashes at him, and asked, "So, what is it you expected me to do in repayment for your attendance at my graduation?"

"Not what you think, Alice. I am a gentleman. This would be a fully clothed dinner downtown at a cozy, but expensive, little place of your choosing and a visit to the Pablo Picasso exhibition at the Museum of Modern Art. I have a friend who's a curator there."

"Don't you ever get tired of hobnobbing with the rich and famous? Leonard Bernstein, Rosalind Russell, Julie Andrews, and now a curator at the Museum of Modern Art."

"No, Alice, I do not get tired of it. I started out as a lowly carpenter and worked myself through set building on Broadway to becoming the designer and builder of mansions on country estates. The last house I constructed, however, exploded, killed a doctor, and later burned to the ground. You proved it was murder, saved me from being convicted of negligent homicide. It's been a rough road back to Broadway. Allow me an occasional brush with fame. Besides, you just graduated law school. Who knows into whose company that will take us. You may someday be introducing me to royalty. I am incredibly happy for you accomplishing your dream. Perry Mason would be thrilled."

"I know you're right. I will remind you, however, that being a lawyer means nothing if I don't pass the State Bar in July and survive waiting for the results until October. It's gonna be a long three months. I'll have to think of something to do with myself. For now, dinner and Picasso sounds terrific, although the dinner is going to be here in the Bronx."

CHAPTER 10

LUIGI'S

The aroma of tomato sauce, herbs, fresh-baked bread, and red wine enveloped them as they entered Luigi's Restaurant. This place was not the only reason Alice insisted on living an hour north of downtown Manhattan, where she worked, but it was high on the list.

The warm weather held with it one of the other big reasons Alice loved living here. Near Bedford Park Boulevard was a Roman Catholic church alongside of which were steps down the hillside to a vacant lot. After church on Sunday, women in black set up an awning and card tables to hold wine, anisette, crooked cigars, mozzarella, and sliced tomatoes from the vines in the yards in back of nearby houses. Up on the edge of the sidewalk on the Grand Concourse was a low black fence on which Alice sat for hours watching the old Italian men sip their drinks, talk loudly, and roll their ball, trying to get close to the boccino, the object ball. The team that threw out the boccino went first.

Those men and women were regular customers of Luigi's.

"Ay, Alice, sweetheart, how nice to see you and your boyfriend in here on this fine spring evening. Very romantic."

The restaurant owner's wife, "Mrs. Luigi," as Alice was fond of calling her, was actually named Helena Cantori.

"So, what have you two been up to, Miss White, darling, and Jim, right?" the proprietress asked her beautiful dark-haired customer and the handsome boyfriend.

Jim said, "Right."

Alice said, "Studying."

Helena said, "We have a new red wine for you to try. You'll like it. Ever since you graduated law school, Alice, we hardly see you. Burning the midnight oil, eh? I know. I watch television sometimes, and I see that you have to pass the Bar exam before you can practice. You know, darling

Alice, you could come down here, before we open up, to study. Tell her, Jim."

Jim said, "She's right, Alice. This place smells incredible. This would be a cozy place for you to read the law, and I could meet you here when I get back from downtown. You wouldn't have so many distractions here."

Mrs. C. said, "You could have a booth for yourself and some antipasto, and, especially for you, some peace and quiet. You would at least be around friends. I don't like the thought of you cooped up in that apartment with your books. Think about coming down here. You know what they say about all work and no play makes Alice a dull girl, huh?"

"Oh, Helena, why are you so good to me?"

"Alice, you're an amazing woman. Also, you know how much the 'old gentlemen' love to follow your adventures. They ask about you whenever they stop in for their veal and spaghetti meetings. The crazy things you do, the chances you take, the people's lives you upset just make us all love you more."

Alice blushed. "How sweet of you to say so."

Helena said, "The old gentlemen have helped us out in our restaurant very much over the years we have been open here. Do you remember when the Health Department wanted to shut us down because one of the girls we had waiting tables wouldn't go out on a date with the inspector? They got the inspector to change his mind and give us a triple-A rating, just like that."

Alice said, "I wonder what they did to change his mind. You think maybe they hung him out a window upside down?"

"Alice, dear, I try not to question their methods. They come from a more primitive time and place, and I respect them for it. They just want what's best for us. We gave the inspector a meal after that, and you know, that waitress went out on a date with him after all. She said he was a perfect gentleman. But he was so nervous that he begged her permission not to ask her out again."

"Ha, ha, ha. What a story, Mrs. C. Makes a woman feel protected. Do you ever see Mr. Trusgnich himself in here?"

"Why do you ask, Alice? Very rarely does that man grace us. He carries such responsibility on his back. We deliver to him all the time, with pleasure. He's down by Fordham Road. You take a left on Fordham and a right on Arthur Avenue. The Little Italy of the Bronx, they call it. You need something from him? Tell me. You make him laugh. That frozen face of his hardly ever smiles."

"I need a gun permit, and he's the only one who can persuade the proper authorities to give it to me. Nobody in the government in their right mind would issue me a gun permit. And, if possible, maybe he could have it backdated a few years. I'm going to become a lawyer, and I'm planning to terrorize an entire city, that is if I don't get disbarred for carrying a concealed weapon without a permit."

"Alice, I don't think that's such a big problem. I'm sure Mr. T. will be only too happy to oblige you for the entertainment he and his friends get watching you flirt with death. Since you're not studying tonight, you two need a glass of wine. It'll be on the house. If you don't mind, I think I'll join you."

"You're the best, Mrs. C."

Mrs. C. raised three fingers at Lorenzo, the bartender, to signal three glasses for her and her guests.

"I'll pass the word to our friend, and you'll have your permit, and we'll have a new lawyer in the neighborhood. Armed and dangerous. Meanwhile, empty that pretty little head of yours and relax. A busy lawyer like you're going to be has to learn to relax, even with problems hanging over your head."

"Yes, I expect there's always going to be difficulties in my line of work."

"Yes, there are, pretty lady, and just remember, we expect gossip, plenty of stories straight from the horse's mouth. When you're a lawyer, we'll feed you, but you will have to sing for your supper. Eh?"

CHAPTER 11

ANTONIO

Antonio Vargas, six foot four, two hundred twenty pounds, muscular from hard labor and weightlifting in and out of prison, carefully rolled himself out of bed so as not to disturb his wife, Maria. He snatched the pair of black jeans off the chair where he had put them the night before, slid them on, and went out to the kitchen. He put on a pot of coffee and finished washing the dishes from supper. When he was settled with coffee and involved in the *New York Post*, he was pleasantly distracted by Maria wrapping her arms around his neck and kissing his ear.

"Let me get you a cup of coffee, my angel," he said.

"No, honey. I got it. You just sit there and enjoy your paper. You are *el jefe*. There'll be plenty of time later tonight for you to be up and running around keeping tabs on your people. But, please, give me the funnies."

"Funnies? Don't you want to see the advertisements, look for sales like other women?" he asked.

"Oh, honey. I am not like other women." She smiled at him flirtatiously. "Haven't you noticed?"

"Yes, sweetheart. I have noticed that very much. What shall we do today? It's a big night for me at the clubs. I got a new pair of boots for the occasion. I am paid to protect quite a lot of people. Thanks to your girlfriend, Alice White, getting her young men to investigate my new employees before I hire them, I have an army of dependable people to do most of the hard work for me. That is, unless something happens that requires my delicate touch. I won't have much to do tonight but move from place to place, looking over their shoulders to see if they need help keeping the peace."

"Alice White is not my girlfriend, my husband. I love her like a sister, but she is your girlfriend. I do not mind. As I have told you, you can work up your appetite anywhere you want as long as you come home to eat."

They sat in peaceful silence reading their sections of the newspaper and sipping coffee.

"Honey," Maria said, "I hate to bother a man of your stature with such trivial matters, but we are out of some drugstore items, and I am about to put in a load of laundry. Would you mind walking down and visiting your friend Pedro? Peroxide, aspirin, cotton balls for my nails, chewing gum, and don't forget toothpaste."

"Good. I'll get everything on your list and a quart of milk from the grocery. I want some milk before I start my rounds. It will settle my stomach. Do you think you would like to take a walk before I leave for work later?"

"Yes, my darling. While we're out maybe we can visit the little Spanish place that just opened down the block and sample their food. You never know how long these little restaurants will stay in business, and I heard this one is great."

"It is a deal. You take care of our clothes, and I will break in my new boots walking over to the Pharmacia."

At the drugstore, Antonio waited patiently with his hands full while a little old lady rummaged through her change purse for enough to pay for a bottle of Pepto Bismol. The pharmacist looked at Antonio over the woman's head and rolled his eyes in helplessness for the delay. When she was gone, he said, "Antonio, my friend. *Como estas?*"

"Good, Pedro. Very good. Just getting exercise before the night's work. Last night was no picnic. People like to blow off steam after work."

"Ah, my friend. After all your success in the security business, you still get your hands dirty, eh?"

"Not so much anymore. I have young college guys now, helping me get reliable help. One of my crew is a woman."

"I know her, Antonio. Lorna Doone. On account of her name, they call her 'Cookie.' She comes in here once in a while. Nobody bothers her. She's got a look about her and a reputation."

"Yeah. She's one of my best employees. Smart, strong. A peacekeeper. She almost signed up with the police, but I made her an offer that was hard to turn down and she said yes. Don't get me wrong, I get along great with the police, but they would have been too much discipline for her. She's a street fighter, which is what working for me requires."

"I'm happy for you, Antonio."

"What's wrong, Pedro? I see it in your eyes. You can tell me."

"What?"

"You never gossip with me like this, Pedro, unless something is bothering you. You are scared. You are worried that, whatever it is, it will upset me. You are right. An enemy of yours is an enemy of mine. Spill it. I'll decide if I'm going to kill somebody."

"Antonio, I hate to bother you with such a small matter."

"Don't be silly, my friend. Whatever it is, we'll find a solution. How long have we known each other?"

Pedro said, "Long time, amigo. But you're always looking after me and my family and I can never pay you back. Why should I burden you with such a tiny matter?"

"Hey, I'm just big is all. That is not my fault. When I hit something, it breaks. It's very interesting. We all have our skills. Violence is mine. If you were my size, you know you'd be kicking the ass of anyone who came around bothering me. So, tell me what is up?"

"A Gypsy, Antonio. A skinny, black-haired Gypsy. Mean as a maggot, Antonio. The rumors about him are not good."

"He's been in here, Pedro?"

"Yes, Antonio, but he didn't do anything. He just talked."

"What did he talk about, Pedro?"

"My wife and my children."

"I can see why you didn't want to tell me. That makes me very angry. I heard about him. It was only a matter of time before him and me would tangle. I will straighten this out. Thank you for telling me. I'm not against selling protection. That is what I do for a living. I just do not sell protection from myself, like he does. That is robbery. Do not pay him a thing. Tell him I said so. Sometime soon, he will cross my path. Of that I am certain."

CHAPTER 12

GANG FORMS

Earl Jones was a longshoreman, a union member in good standing. He was thirty-two, five foot eight, two hundred pounds, with a large belly and a black-stubbled face. He was strong as an ox and ruthless.

"I am getting a crew together," the Gypsy said.

They were sitting at a waterfront bar, a place popular with longshoremen.

He went on, "I heard you were a man I could trust. Strong, respected. Maybe you have run a crew or two in the past. I think maybe you have. I want your help."

Earl said, "If you don't mind, let's step outside for this conversation."

Montes said, "Lead the way."

Jones walked through the nearest exit out onto the wharf. It was no longer daylight, but men continued to move freight.

Jones said, "You can see why I take jobs besides working on the waterfront. I am willing to strain under the weight of cargo, for whatever living I can make, but I need a score once in a while so I can breathe."

Montes said, "Good. We're in the same place."

Jones asked him, "What are we talking about? A crew sounds like a big job. I heard about you too, Mr. Montes. You don't usually do this kind of work."

"Yes," Christos Montes said. "I understand what you are being too polite to say. That I am a penny-ante thief, a pickpocket, a two-bit hustler, a window-breaking, paint-splashing seller of protection. That a big job is out of my league. This is a bank robbery. I'm talking about over a million dollars."

"No insult intended, Mr. Montes," Jones said, "but, before I agree to risk hard time if things go south, the electric chair if things go far south, like to hell, I like to know what I'm getting myself into and who I'm getting into it with."

"You are already living up to your reputation, Mr. Jones. You speak the hard truth," Montes said. "That truth is enough to weed out the weak of purpose. That is not what I am."

Jones said, "I face facts is all. No use kidding ourselves, a big robbery means lockup for who knows how many years, depending on how the judge and the jury feel the day you're sentenced. As long as you understand that and you're not fooling yourself that this is gonna be easy to pull off, I'll talk to you."

"I do understand," Montes said with an edge of irritation. "Can we get down to details?"

Jones said, "Hey, don't get bent out of shape. This is why you want me. Sometimes facing the penalty for failure gets it done right in the first place."

Montes said, "You are right. I apologize."

Earl Jones said, "Now that's out of the way, why should I help you?"

Christos Montes said, "You said it yourself. You should help me because you are living a hard life here on the docks. You ask for work every day, and it's not a sure thing that you'll get it, and, if you get it, it's not a sure thing you will be paid what you were promised. I've talked to men who work here. You are a hard worker, a good worker, and smart. You deserve better. I need you to help me organize the job and the crew. I do not want to miss anything."

"You want me to put together the whole crew?" Jones said.

The Gypsy said, "No, I don't. Organization and muscle is all I need. I need control of customers and the people who work at the bank. I need the same men to help with the heavy lifting. I figure just two men, trustworthy, strong, maybe dockworkers. They have to be handy with a gun. I already have a wheelman, who will double as a lookout, and I have an explosives pro, who's also a toolmaker. He'll handle blowing the vault door and getting into the safe-deposit boxes. I want to keep the number of guys low. Less chance of a leak and the bigger everyone's cut is. That'll be six of us. I figure a million and a half, six ways. A little extra for the driver since he starts work the night before. Your guys will handle the guard, the tellers, and any pain-in-the-neck bank people that suddenly get brave. What do you think? Is that going to be enough men?"

Jones said, "We can do it. You are right about keeping the crew manageable. I have the men for the job. We're going to have to case the place at least once. Opening time, guard placement, layout around the tellers' windows, the vault. In ones and twos, not all together like some kids' class at a museum. If we do it in a group, we might as well announce the date and time of the robbery. Gun practice at a range before. Alibis. I'll do my guys. You take care of the driver and the explosives guy, Mr. Montes. How long we got to get ready?"

"Not long. Less than a week. Is that good with you?"

Jones said, "Yes. The boys are gonna want some time with their girls in case they don't make it out alive. That's one full day. Two days to watch the bank open and close and walk through the layout twice each in shifts. The driver will need to case the neighborhood and traffic patterns, time to get a car and plates together the night before, and maybe the day before that. An afternoon at a gun range for each of us. Pick a few ranges and don't go in more than two at a time, so we don't bunch up in the same places. Start now on solid alibis for everybody, you included. If I think of something else, I'll let you know."

Montes said, "Very good. I'll pass this on to my guys."

"So, tell me again, Mr. Montes. You told me why you thought I should want to do this. After all I just told you, why would YOU want to take this incredible risk?"

"That's a fair question. I'm tired of my life the way it's been. I'm sick of throwing stink bombs, threatening business owners and their families. I can't do this anymore. I won't do it anymore. I want to get out of here with a bankroll, and I am willing to die trying, if I have to."

"Is there someone else in on this that I should know about? A silent partner?" Earl Jones asked his prospective employer.

"No. There is no one you should know about," Montes said in a manner that invited no further questioning.

"Good deal. Whatever you say. Just so you know, I don't really care if there is someone," Earl Jones voiced his suspicion.

"It's good we understand each other," the Gypsy said.

Earl Jones said, "I'll give you this. You have guts to even think about doing a job like this. If this was easy, everybody would be robbing banks."

"I'm glad I found you," Montes said. "You did good, laying it out. I appreciate that."

Earl Jones said, "It sounds good. Six guys. Less than a week from now."

"Right."

Jones said, "I just want to say this one more time, then I won't say it again, Mr. Montes. There is so much that can go wrong. The guys will all have to be armed. Bank robbery is about life and death. This is not a cash register in a grocery store. People feel different about banks than they do about businesses. They defend banks with guns. They have alarms. They expect crooks to try to steal their cash and valuables, to blow their vaults. There are family heirlooms in those vaults, documents, jewelry, gold bars, diamonds, and works of art, like paintings and statues. Insurance companies will come after us hard. Law enforcement will come after us also. They're not gonna give up without a fight. They're prepared to kill to protect their customers' property. We are going to blow the vault door and people could get hurt, even us, in the explosion. I don't care how good your explosives expert is."

Christos Montes said, "You're not telling me anything I haven't already thought about. You got more?"

Earl Jones continued, "Yes. Please bear with me. I don't know you that well, or really at all. Let me make sure we completely understand each other before we do this, because there'll be no time afterwards."

"Okay," Montes said.

"You know about guns, don't you?" Jones said. "They go off, sometimes on purpose, sometimes by accident. That adds prison time if we get caught. That's maybe a ten-to-twenty-year stretch up the river, in Sing Sing, which can shrink down to a year or two in isolation on death row if things go really wrong, usually followed by being strapped into 'Old Sparky' where the electricity catches your shirt on fire, and you crap your pants before you die. You still want to do this?"

Montes said, "Yes. I don't want to live this way, shaking people down for pocket change. There's this old guy, a butcher. He disrespected me. I hit on him for protection money. He served in the Pacific. I heard he was on Iwo Jima, that's how old he is. Doesn't matter where he served. This guy wasn't going to be pushed around. I felt ashamed. I never want to feel that way again. We're gonna score big. Then I'm gonna find a way to teach that butcher a lesson he'll never forget."

"Okay, man. I just had to make sure we were both all in on this. You convinced me. Sorry about the vet. Iwo Jima, huh. I'm surprised he's not living at the Salvation Army. A lot of those vets fell into the bottle or worse when they got home, and they never climbed out. It's sad. They're all over the streets."

"He thinks he's still a soldier, invulnerable. I'll show him."

Earl Jones asked, "You said less than a week. When exactly are we doing this?"

"Friday morning, nine o'clock sharp," Christos Montes said. "The sooner the better. We go in. We come out with the money. It's over."

"Let's do it," Jones said. "My mother's gonna kill me if she finds out. That's if I'm not already dead by that time."

Montes said, "Write down your number. I'll stay in touch. We got to check off all the stuff you said. You start your guys off with their women so that's out of the way. Then we'll start casing the bank, making alibis, and hitting gun ranges. See, I paid attention."

CHAPTER 13

THE DAY BEFORE

Earl Jones spoke to the two stevedores he had recruited.

"You saw the layout, the teller windows, the offices in back, the vault, and the guard. There's only one guard and he stays over off to the right of the windows. The stands in the front of the bank have deposit slips. Customers could stop there when they come in. It shouldn't be all that crowded at opening time, but there could be some customers, so keep your eyes open. If there are, we move them to the side of the teller windows where the desks are for people to sit when they apply for loans."

Jones and his men were on Rockwell Avenue in Washington Heights at the northern end of Manhattan. The men's names were Arty Watts, who was from the Bronx, and Harry Walker, from Brooklyn. The three of them were standing in an alley alongside one of the hundreds of neighborhood bars in the city. It was Thursday night.

Earl asked them, "You shot a hundred rounds each at the gun range, right?"

They nodded in the affirmative.

"You got alibis set up?"

Again, they nodded.

They were, all three, heavily muscled from lives of hauling freight. Anabolic steroids were new to the Olympics, to combat the Russian weightlifters' use of testosterone. All three of these dockworkers looked like they had partaken. It hardly mattered because, with or without steroids, these were the hardest of a breed of hard men who had been eking out a living loading and unloading oceangoing freighters since the beginning of time. They had earned their bulk the hard way.

Arty Watts from the Bronx asked, "We're strictly crowd control, right? We haul some stuff out of the vault and we get a full cut, right?"

"Right," Jones said. "Just keep your eyes open and your mouths shut. The less witnesses have to identify us with, the better. Watch the tellers. We don't want them setting off any alarms if we can help it, but we may not be able to stop it. That's why we got to keep the time in that bank as short as possible. And, don't forget, let the bank people see your guns. Try not to shoot anyone if you can help it."

Harry Walker from Brooklyn said, "I'll take the guard?"

"Good," Jones said. "Let's hope he's not into committing suicide. Nail him down first thing. Take his gun. Check him for walkie-talkies and remote alarms. Just take it easy, both of you. Robbing the bank is the only thing we're there to do."

Arty Watts said, "You're the boss."

Jones responded, "You just stay quiet and look mean, unless me or our fearless leader, the Gypsy, tells you otherwise. Straight in. Straight out. The faster the better. Stay alive. You don't get to spend a dime if you're dead. We all have tattoos on our arms, so tape over 'em. This'll be the easiest money we ever made."

At the same time, Christos Montes conferred with his two specialists. They stood around a pool table in a closed pool hall. Each sipped a bottle of Schlitz.

"I picked you guys because you're the best at what you do," Montes said.

Jimmy Cage, the toolmaker and explosives expert from Detroit, said, "I saw the vault today. It shouldn't be a problem."

Montes said, "Thank you both for coming to New York. I'm thinking we will all be well paid for our trouble."

Richy Anderson, the driver from Cincinnati, spoke. "I looked at the neighborhood around the bank. It'll take me some time to set up. I figured a way to make us disappear, after we leave the bank, that you will love."

Montes said, "There's two heavyweight dockworkers and their handler that'll keep people in line, Jimmy, and help carry the loot. They'll take care of the bank guard, the tellers, and any customers that show up. I'll help carry stuff if you need me."

Richy Anderson, the driver, who was going to also act as lookout, said, "I'll be up most of the night collecting dependable wheels. I'm gonna work on the engine and get license plates. By tomorrow morning

I'll be ready to ride. It'll all be set up. I'll get a nap in when I'm done, then pop a handful of bennies."

Montes said, "You guys have your work cut out for you. Again, thank you for showing up."

Montes turned back to the driver. "Mr. Anderson, they said you were a magician. I'm looking forward to seeing you in action. We're putting our freedom and our lives in your hands."

Richy Anderson responded, "Gentlemen, be prepared for the ride of your life. I'll have you off the streets maybe even before the police know the bank's been robbed."

"This I gotta see," Jimmy Cage said, taking a swallow of beer and a deep drag off his cigarette.

Anderson added, "I'll keep watch outside while you all make your withdrawal. You boys do your magic inside, especially you, explosives guy."

He smiled at Jimmy.

Anderson spoke again, "Show me you can blow a safe without bringing down the whole building on your head, and I'll show you I can make you vanish into thin air, without a trace."

"You're both carrying .38s," Montes said, "like the ones you shot on the range. Fresh ones are being delivered to my place tonight. I carry my own gun. The other guys will get .38s too. Everyone turns their weapons over to you, Anderson, on the drive out of there and you'll wipe them off, break them down, and get rid of 'em like I told you."

"What time we meet?"

"Seven a.m. My place, 1158 Watkins Street, not far from here. Apartment 4G. Don't write anything down. No ID in your pockets. Tattoos covered. You'll get cash before we split up. Full cuts later. Bandanas and guns at my place in the morning. Get some sleep if you can even think about sleeping."

CHAPTER 14

7 A.M., THE DAY OF

The tall, dark-haired Gypsy, Christos Montes, sat in apartment 4G on a stool at his kitchen counter. He had a cloth spread out with the pieces of a Belgium-made Browning Hi-Power 9mm automatic on it. He ran a brush with solvent through the barrel, then a torn piece of white undershirt to wipe out the solvent and satisfy himself it was clean, then another rag with gun oil to finish the job. He cleaned and oiled the body and the slide and reassembled the weapon. Last, he rubbed the whole gun down with a clean towel, slid a magazine with thirteen 9mm bullets into the grip, racked the slide to put a bullet in the chamber, left it cocked, and put the safety on. It was, in gun parlance, cocked and locked.

He slid the gun into the holster under his left arm.

The coffee on the stove finished perking. The smell was intense. Christos removed the basket and threw it into the sink, turned the burner to low, and poured himself a cup and took a swallow. From a kitchen drawer he retrieved his lockpicks.

Out the door he went, and up the stairs two at a time to the roof. It was overcast, threatening to rain. He walked across the tarred surface to the housing of the elevator shaft. With a pick, he found the pins and popped the padlock open. Inside the shaft, on the walkway around the cable mechanism, he found the bundle right where he'd left the cash the night before. He unwrapped it and inspected the .38 Special revolvers and rewrapped them.

Downstairs he filled the cylinders in each of the guns from the carton of bullets he had bought days earlier. Then he laid the guns out on the counter and sat down to sip his coffee and read the paper. He was nervous. He couldn't focus on the newsprint, so he looked at the pictures. He most certainly could not sleep. He had not been all that unhappy hustling business owners for protection. It was a dirty way to make a living, and he was ashamed of himself for doing it, but the chances of dying in the act, or prison, or death in the electric chair, were a lot lower than with robbing a bank.

Earl Jones arrived with his two fellow dockworkers: Arty Watts from the Bronx, five ten, two hundred twenty pounds, and Harry Walker from Brooklyn, six foot even, two forty. The burly Earl Jones and his men all wore oversized denim jackets and pants.

"Help yourself to some coffee," Montes said over the top of his paper. "You guys set to go?"

Jones replied for the three of them, "Absolutely. Those our guns?" He nodded at the counter.

Montes replied, "Yeah, they got here, and they look good. I put bullets in them. Help yourself."

The men took a revolver each. Earl took a cup out of the dish drying rack by the sink and filled it with coffee.

Earl introduced his men. "Meet Arty Watts, from the Bronx."

Montes nodded. Watts gave him a two-finger salute.

"And Harry Walker, from Brooklyn."

Harry said, "Pleasure to meet you."

Earl Jones asked, "What about the out-of-town talent?"

Montes said, "They should be here any minute. One of them spent the night fixing things up for the getaway. He's supposed to be like Houdini at disappearing us practically when we hit the street. Let's hope he lives up to his reputation."

On cue, the door opened and Jimmy Cage, the explosives expert, walked in. Rich Anderson, the driver, was right behind him.

Montes said, "Lock the door."

Jimmy did.

"You all can smoke if you want," Montes said.

With everyone crowded in the small kitchen, tension rose as the seconds ticked by.

Richy Anderson went over and helped himself to some coffee. He lit up a smoke and sat down. He had been up all night, and the fumes of his adrenaline were fading fast as everyone else's were just kicking into gear. He put his coffee down on a side table, his cigarette into an ashtray, slid down in his chair, closed his eyes, and he was out like a light, into a deep sleep.

Twenty minutes later, Anderson woke up. He popped a handful of bennies—Benzedrines—into his mouth and washed them down with the remains of his coffee.

Christos Montes slid his Browning Hi-Power automatic out of its holster and checked it over.

Thirteen rounds in the magazine was more than most. "Nobody ever got into a gunfight wishing they had less ammo," the guy who sold the gun to him had said. He looked at the men he was about to stick his neck out with. All the help in the world was not going to stack the odds in their favor.

The minutes ticked by. At last Montes looked at the clock on the wall and said, "It's time. Mr. Anderson. Go get the car and we'll meet you around back of the building."

Richy Anderson jerked to a stand. The handful of bennies had apparently kicked in. He stubbed out his cigarette, took the car keys out of his pocket, and headed out the door.

They were all anxious to get this over with.

Montes told the remaining men, "Grab bandanas on the way out. Tie them around your necks, but don't pull them up until you're walking through the door into the bank. We don't want people in traffic seeing a bunch of masked men headed into a bank. It might give them the idea we were there to rob it."

On the stoops of houses all over Manhattan, men and women sat sipping coffee, smoking cigarettes, guessing at the makes and models of cars in the traffic going by. Everyone relaxing before the onslaught of another workday. At least it was Friday. The weekend was so close they could taste it. Tonight, they would party.

In Washington Heights, out of sight of the street, men filed out the back of Christos Montes's building and into a souped-up black Buick.

CHAPTER 15

THE JOB

"Jim, I'm leaving early to deposit my paycheck before I go to work. It's not a long walk to Nassau Street from the bank."

Jim said, "Why don't you open an account at a bank up here in the Bronx?"

"It would be a waste, Jim. I almost always make deposits on my lunch hour."

Jim said, "Okay. You go on ahead then. I'll ring you if I have time to meet for lunch."

Alice said, "I'm going to need a whole new wardrobe when I start practicing law. I'm assuming I'm going to pass the Bar in July and be licensed in October. That's what I'm saving up for."

"Alice," Jim said. "You know, what's mine could legally be yours. Just say the word. I'll speak of it no more."

Alice laughed. "You do that, smart aleck."

She kissed him as she was leaving.

Alice strode purposefully down Wall Street, in a skirt and the black high-top Keds she would change out of into dress shoes when she got to work. She was anxious to make her deposit at the First National Bank and get back to her office before the deluge it looked like was about to begin falling from the sky.

The temperature was rising inside the car. The black Buick was starting to smell like the locker room of a losing team as the gang sat parked at the curb on the corner of the bank. During the night, Richy Anderson had "found" the Buick in the employee parking lot of an all-night diner. He had checked the tires, switched the plates, severely tweaked the engine for maximum performance. It sounded like a hot rod. The gas tank was full. His hands were rock steady, fueled by professionalism, amphetamines, and the thrill of the precision high-speed drive he was about to undertake at the conclusion of the robbery.

The silence inside the car was briefly broken by the spinning of cylinders, the last-minute check to see that they were filled with bullets. Then there was just the sound of breathing.

Anderson had pulled the car into a position so the gang could slide into and out of the bank with minimum exposure to the view of passing traffic.

Christos Montes leaned in toward Richy Anderson and said in a whisper, "You keep a sharp eye out for trouble and get us the hell out of here when it's done, and you'll get a hefty bump in your take from me personally. Understand?"

Richy said, "Excellent. I'll be here when you finish the job. You can count on it. Meanwhile I'll be your alarm system. Anyone headed in, I'll throw gravel hard against the front window. Bad trouble, like the cops, I'll fire my gun. Meanwhile, you just take care of yourselves inside. When you're done, I'll make you disappear like smoke up a chimney."

The leader, Christos Montes, the ramrod, Earl Jones, Jimmy Cage, Harry Walker, and Arty Watts sat waiting for the bank to open. Their driver, Richy Anderson, got out of the car alone, unmasked, looking like an innocent pedestrian. He lit a cigarette

and took his place near the fountain, like a
businessman waiting for the bank to open.

At exactly 9 a.m. a middle-aged woman in
blouse and skirt appeared inside the heavy glass
entrance door. She squatted down and used a key to
raise the bolt projecting from the bottom edge of the
door into a hole in the floor of the bank.

As she turned and moved back into the
bank's interior, Montes said, "Let's go to work, men."

Richy stood at the fountain and whispered to
himself, "Go get 'em, boys."

Montes led his men single file at a rapid pace
in through the front door of the bank. As they crossed
the threshold, they each raised their mask. No one
was hanging around the stands in the front where the
deposit slips were stacked.

Morning traffic was moving lazily along Wall
Street. The skies opened up, and a drenching rain
began to fall.

Montes spotted the vault door on the back
wall and waved Jimmy Cage toward it.

Earl Jones silently directed the two dockworkers, guns in hands, to spread out in front of the tellers' windows. An older, uniformed man came ambling out from the back with a cup of coffee. He had a revolver strapped into a holster on his hip.

Harry Walker was on him, like he said he would be. The guard raised his hands. Walker relieved him of his gun and patted him down, found a pack of cigarettes, some keys, and a handkerchief. He took the cigarettes and gave the guard back the rest.

"Don't you know these things will kill you?" He held the pack up to the man he had taken them from.

The handsome woman who had unlocked the front door for them arrived at her place behind one of the windows and panicked at the sight of masked men with guns. Montes approached her, and the woman's eyes darted toward the edge of her counter.

"Don't do it," the gang leader told her, his accented words clear. "Don't touch the alarm or I will kill you where you stand."

The woman's whole body began to shake visibly as she gave a wide-eyed nod of assent.

The teller in the next window, a young man, looked on, clearly frightened.

Montes pleasantly asked the female teller, "What's your name?"

"Margaret," she said. "Margaret Hopkins."

"Okay, Margaret. You are doing good. Now, fill this bag with the cash from your drawer. We aren't here to hurt anyone. We're here for the money. Nice and easy now."

He slid a carpetbag under her window.

She opened her cash drawer and began filling it.

Montes said, "That's it. You're doing fine."

Then he said to the young man at the next window, "You're next. Get ready."

Executive vice president of the bank Samuel Evans stirred a tiny tablet of saccharine into his second cup of coffee of the day. He marveled at what a great job he had. He held a position of responsibility and respect, while doing nothing to earn either. He pretended to supervise the staff and made inappropriate advances on the prettier female employees. How did he ever get so lucky? He sat down to read the morning edition of the *Daily News*. He never knew if there was going to be a picture of a dead gangster lying in a puddle of blood outside a restaurant. Sometimes there were pictures of boxers after successful bouts or baseball stars who had just broken records. Marciano, Mantle, Maris, Ford, Berra were all seen exhausted and smiling for the camera.

A shrill solitary voice pierced the usual quiet of Samuel Evans's sanctuary. Evans could not make out the words, but he had no doubt that the bank was being robbed.

This was his big chance to make it to the front page. He could see it now. A picture of him smiling down at the dead body of a bank robber on the floor of the First National Bank on Wall Street. A quote of him saying, "It was no big deal. That's what I get paid for. Saving lives and protecting depositors' money."

He walked over to the sideboard in his office, where his prize possession was proudly displayed in a glass case. A Smith & Wesson .44 Russian revolver from the previous century. Evans's brother-in-law worked for Mayor Robert F. Wagner, Jr., and had arranged for the gun to be permitted.

Alongside the display case sat a cardboard box of cartridges he had never intended to use. The danger of pointing a loaded gun at a gang of armed bank robbers never entered his mind. He was lost in a dream of invincibility and fame.

He ripped open the box of bullets and filled the chambers of his magnificent weapon. He dumped the rest of the ammunition into the outside pockets of his suit jacket and moved to the door.

He listened. It was quiet. He sensed this was his chance to take the robbers by surprise. He imagined they were preoccupied with the vault.

He could see the caption under his picture in tomorrow's newspapers.

EXECUTIVE VICE PRESIDENT SAMUEL T. EVANS, OF THE FIRST NATIONAL BANK OF WALL ST.

And the copy.

"Certain that a robbery was in progress, at great risk to himself, Mr. Evans emerged from his office, his prize .44 Russian revolver in hand. Scanning the bank, he spotted the leader aiming a gun directly at him. Before the ruthless gangster could pull the trigger, Evans shot and killed him, thus thwarting the robbery and preventing harm from coming to his fellow bank employees and customers."

In actuality, Evans scanned the area in front of the counter and confirmed that a robbery was indeed in progress. Guns were visible in the hands of masked men. Almost immediately, a gunshot was fired, and he was hit in his neck. From his time in combat, he recognized it was only a surface wound and reflexively fixed his weapon on the masked gunman who had shot him, pulled the trigger, and hit him square in the center of his forehead.

Arty Watts, of the Bronx, lay dead on the floor of the bank. The gang leader, tall, thin, also masked, lifted his Hi-Power 9mm Browning automatic and shot the bank executive through the heart. Samuel T. Evans, Executive Vice President of the First National Bank on Wall Street, was dead before he hit the floor.

The morning quiet of the bank was shattered by the two shots. This put everyone, gang members and bank employees, on edge. The stakes had just risen dramatically.

Outside the bank, the sound of the shots reached the driver, Richy Anderson. The rain was coming down in earnest, drenching him as he absorbed the horrible reality of the gunfire and how it might affect his future place of residence.

Alice White approached her savings bank with an open umbrella. She couldn't hear anything except the sound of the rain and the splash of tires plowing through water in the street. She was ignorant of what was happening in the bank, but she certainly noticed the incredibly handsome man, with wet brown hair and dripping rimless glasses, who had pulled the door handle and was holding it open for her. From somewhere in the rain she was vaguely aware of the sound of pebbles bouncing off the bank's front window, but it was raining too hard for her to bother looking for whatever fool had thrown them.

The shower of pebbles got Christos Montes's attention and he turned to see the couple entering the bank. They looked like lovebirds. He recognized the butcher and understood it as a sign from God that this was the perfect time to kill him.

The smell of fresh gunfire, with which both Alice and the handsome stranger were familiar, reached them, and they stopped in their tracks. They looked at each other in mutual recognition of their situation. The tall, dark-haired, masked man leveled his gun at them and closed the gap. He nudged his gun up twice and they both raised their hands. Laughlin recognized the Gypsy.

Montes said, "You both just stand here. Stay put until we clear out."

He went and told Harry Walker to watch the couple up front.

Behind her teller's window, Margaret Hopkins, still visibly shaking, finished emptying her cash drawer and passed the carpetbag to her fellow teller for him to do the same. Then she raised her hands.

Christos turned back to Margaret. "Everything is all right, young lady. We'll be out of here before you know it."

Jimmy Cage fast-walked away from the vault and yelled, "Everybody, hold your ears!"

Everybody, including Alice and Laughlin, did so.

BOOM!

Margaret watched the man run back toward the vault. He pulled the door open and went inside with two empty canvas duffel bags and long tools that looked like crowbars. Earl Jones took over covering the two customers and the interior of the bank. Harry Walker and Christos Montes followed Cage into the vault.

Montes yelled, "Let's be quick. We don't have all day."

Montes and his men came out of the vault with bags full and arms loaded.

"We'll sort it out later," Montes said. "Let's get the hell out of here." He led the way.

The robbers started to exit the bank, past the pretty dark-haired woman and the stud. Earl Jones hung back to see if Montes needed his help. He kept his gun trained on the two customers.

Montes, his arms full, was last out, clearly conflicted about killing the butcher. He stopped to stare into Thomas Laughlin's eyes and put his load down on the floor.

Montes said to Earl Jones, "Take off. I got these two."

Earl holstered his gun and prepared to unmask as he headed out the door of the bank.

Laughlin was certain that, after surviving the hell of Iwo Jima, he was about to die here, in a bank in civilized New York City, because he was too lazy to make a night deposit.

Montes pulled his gun.

"I told you I would make you pay for your arrogance, Mr. Laughlin. Say your prayers."

Montes took aim at the butcher's chest. Alice White pulled her gun and pointed it at Montes's head.

"Pull the trigger," she told him, "and it will be the last thing you ever do. All that money and you will never get to spend any of it."

Montes nodded in acceptance. He re-holstered his weapon and picked his load up from the floor.

"Shoot me if you want," Montes told her.

Alice said, "I shoot you and your men will come back and shoot me. I'll pass. You got what you want. Leave now and we'll call it even."

The Gypsy nodded at her and continued on his way out of the bank.

Laughlin gave Alice a smile. Maybe it wasn't his time to die after all.

"You saved my life. I owe you."

She said, "You would've done the same for me, I'm sure. I'd love to take credit for being heroic, but he didn't leave me any choice. You're welcome though."

Alice and Thomas looked through the window and watched the masked men stuff their loot into the trunk of the Buick, while the unmasked driver ducked in behind the wheel. He moved too fast for them to get a good look at his face. The loudness of the exhaust, even muffled by the glass at the front of the bank, and the squeal of the tires spoke of a mechanic's tampering with an ordinary passenger car off the line in Michigan. The license plates were a blur.

Richy Anderson drove up the street like it was the Indianapolis 500, passing cars like they were standing still, running red lights, and causing horns to blare and tires to screech. There was a hostility about the car's movement that no sane person would have challenged. Cars moved out of his way if they could, and drivers shrugged it off as this being New York City, so what could you do?

Three blocks north of the bank, Richy cut a hard right into an alley, drove the car up parallel ramps into the back of a tractor trailer. Up and into the truck he took them, then turned off the ignition and engaged the emergency brake.

Anderson said, "There's a canvas bag on the back floor of this car. Put your guns in it and leave them for me. I'll wipe them clean of prints, break them down, and get rid of the pieces."

He exited the Buick, left his jacket on the seat, and dropped down out the back of the truck. He slid the ramps in alongside the car. Then he shut and bolted the doors and walked around to the driver's door of the truck. He opened the door and put on the Yankees baseball jacket that was lying there waiting for him. He climbed into the driver's seat, put on the baseball cap and sunglasses he had left on the dashboard, pulled the door shut, and started the truck's engine. He moved the gearshift into first, let out the clutch, and drove straight ahead, out the far end of the alley, merging into morning traffic. The rain had stopped and the sun was out. It was turning into a pretty nice Friday morning in Manhattan.

CHAPTER 16

COPS AND ROBBERS

Bam thud, bam bam, thud thud. Bam bam bam! Fists, elbows, knees, and sneakers slammed into the body bag suspended from the ceiling of Detective Sandra James's living room. Sweat streamed from every pore of her body.

Ring . . . ring . . . ring . . . She'd been at it for thirty minutes. There was something about the sound of the phone that told her she was done for the day. She bit the end of one black Everlast glove, pulled her hand out of it, and spit the glove out onto the floor. Then the other. She reached for the telephone on her coffee table and lifted the receiver.

"I catch you at a bad time, San?" her partner and mentor, Detective Louis Maraglia, asked.

"Saved by the bell. I was killing myself, Louis. Whadya got?"

"Bank robbery and double homicide on Wall Street. First National Bank. You just got time for a shower. When you're dried off, come outside and lock your door. I'll be parked on the street out front, reading the paper and smoking a cigarette."

She took the pitcher of ice water out of the fridge and had a glass. No one would guess a woman had been within a mile of this place for years. She was the only girl, the youngest of five children, in an Italian household. Her older brothers had taught her to live like a slob.

When she was in the car, Louis said, "Sandra, all that working out is paying off. You're in terrific shape. You still swallowing them raw eggs in the morning? No offense, partner, but the thought of it makes me gag. I don't know how you do it."

"It's an old training ritual, Louis. I'm superstitious," she said. "How're we getting to Wall Street?"

"Down the Major Deegan. It'll get us off the streets. Past Yankee Stadium. Then the FDR. It should take about an hour, but I can make it in way less time if I put my mind to it. I'll save the lights and siren for if we get stuck."

He said, "Hey, Sandra. I stuck my head in the gym the other day and saw you flip a young guy over your head. Over your head! I almost cried it was so beautiful. He had at least six inches and fifty pounds on you. It was magnificent. If I live to be a hundred, I'll never get over it. David and Goliath. I love it."

She said, "Whoa, there goes Yankee Stadium. We're flying, Louis. What's waiting for us?"

Louis told her, "There were only two customers in the bank who came in when the robbery was already going down. Before they got there, a bank executive killed one of the robbers with his Russian .44 revolver, and one of the gang members, maybe the leader, put a bullet into the banker and killed him."

"It's gonna be a hot time in the old electric chair tonight," Sandra said tunefully. "These guys are amateurs. Their leader, if that's what he was, should've shot the banker in the knee, not killed him, for God's sake. Small time. A robber getting killed may be homicide for the others, but everyone knows that the penalty is worse for murdering the banker. That gang leader just bought them all a ticket to fry in Old Sparky or, at the least, life without parole."

Louis said, "A couple of tellers were out front, unharmed, a woman and a young man. The guy is okay, but the woman is in shock. She had to be taken to the hospital for sedation and observation. There's no accounting for people's reaction to being held up at gunpoint. Two tellers who were about to begin work when the robbery started hid in a utility closet in the back. One of 'em was deafened by the blast that blew the vault open, but she can read lips."

"Okay, Louis. We're almost there. At this speed you're gonna have to pump the brakes a block before we get there. What about the two customers?"

"A man and a woman," Louis said. "They're being held for us to question. The man's a local butcher who was there to deposit yesterday's receipts. He closed his shop late last night and was too tired to run it over to the night deposit. The woman's a legal assistant and investigator for a small law firm on Nassau Street. She was there to deposit her paycheck."

Detective James said, "Maybe one of the customers saw the getaway car. The plates had to've been stolen. It's gonna be a long day."

"We found these two hiding inside a storage closet in the break room," a uniformed police officer told Detectives James and Maraglia. He introduced them to a couple of nervous young women in business attire. "They're tellers. They were just about to come out front to start work when the robbery began. They're not going to be much help. They saw nothing from inside the closet, but they thought they heard a loud threatening voice, gunshots, and, finally, the explosion. This one lost her hearing in the blast, but she can read lips enough to answer questions."

"Good job," James said. "Where's the guard?"

"He's sitting in the break room. He says they took his gun first thing."

"What about the two customers we saw out front?"

"Them," the officer said, turning toward the front of the bank. "They're interesting, but I'm not sure they're gonna be much help either. I told them to stick around so you could talk to them."

The man and the woman stood conversing. They looked relaxed, romantic even. Detective James watched them talking, looking at each other, as she approached. She felt a twinge of, maybe, jealousy.

The uniformed officer who had been standing near the couple took a few steps toward the approaching detectives and said to them in a low voice, "These two are not together. They just happened to come in at the same time. He's a butcher. Got his own shop not far from here. Name's Thomas Laughlin. He walked over this morning to make last night's deposit. The pretty dark-haired one is Miss Alice White. She says she just came in to deposit her paycheck. They're both real calm considering what happened here. She does investigations for a law firm on Nassau Street where she doubles as a legal assistant. She carries a gun, a .380 auto; says she's got a permit for it, just not on her at the moment."

"We'll see about that," Detective James said, aware of her own irritability.

"Okay, Jonesy, we'll take it from here," said Maraglia. The officer with the nameplate ARTHUR JONES moved away.

The detectives approached the witnesses. The blond female detective said to the good-looking man, "Hello, Mr. Laughlin. I'm Detective James."

He said, "How are you, Detective?"

She asked him, "What did you see?"

He said, "Not much. The shooting they told us about was over before we got here, but I could smell it when I got inside. I wanted to turn and run but they spotted us right away, and the man I believe was the leader pointed his gun at us. When they were leaving, he pulled the gun again and was going to shoot me, I think because he knew I recognized him. He's almost certainly the Gypsy outlaw named Christos Montes. He has tried to sell me protection for my butcher shop. That's how I recognized him behind the mask. He was really going to do it, shoot me, I mean. He would have too, if Miss White here hadn't pulled her gun and told him if he killed me, she would kill him. She was amazing. He could tell she meant it. So he just picked up the loot and left."

Laughlin finished, "Other than that, I didn't see anything, really. Oh, except the getaway car was a Buick, black."

"That's all for now, Mr. Laughlin, but you've been very helpful. Thank you."

James pivoted toward the attractive dark-haired woman, Alice White.

"Hello, Miss White," the detective said. "Did you see or hear anything your friend didn't mention?"

"With all due respect for Mr. Laughlin, Detective, he is not my friend, but I was happy to stop that guy from shooting him. I never met either one of them before in my life," Alice told the blond police officer. "He is, however, a very nice-looking person, and, if I didn't have a boyfriend, I would be tempted to make an improper advance on him."

"You pretty much don't hold anything back, do you, Miss White?" James said.

"Believe me, I'm working on it."

"I'm almost afraid to ask, but do you have anything else to add?"

"Well," Alice said. "I saw a man out front through the window, but I couldn't identify him because he was mostly looking away from me, toward the street. There was the big black Buick near him, the getaway car, I assume. The driver's door was not completely shut. When the robbery was over, they threw their takings into the trunk, piled into the passenger seats, and took off like a bat out of hell."

Detective James said, "That's helpful. Thank you. You didn't happen to get a license plate, even though it was probably stolen?"

"No, sorry. I did not. I looked, but it was a blur."

Detective Louis Maraglia watched and stayed quiet during the questioning of the witnesses. Now he said, "You did good, both of you."

Detective James said. "We have your names and addresses. I'm gonna want a copy of your gun permit, Miss White, when you get a chance. Here's

my card. We'll be in touch if we have any further
questions. If you remember something else, please
call."

The rain was over. Alice and Thomas stood
together in the sunshine on the sidewalk in front of
the bank. They had both experienced more violence
in their lives than most people. The bushes were wet.
There were puddles everywhere. It was shaping up to
be a nice day.

The butcher asked, "You okay?"

"Yes," Alice said. "I'm fine. You?"

"I guess. Thank you again for saving my
life."

"You know, Mr. Laughlin, Thomas, I noticed
that blond police detective was having difficulty
talking to you. She seemed awfully annoyed by you."

Laughlin said, "I noticed that too. I have no
idea what I did to upset her."

"Nothing. I think she liked you. I think she
felt threatened, vulnerable."

Thomas said, "I think she came close to
actually striking me."

Alice said, "You're lucky she didn't shoot you. I'm telling you, as one woman talking about another woman, behind the other woman's back, Mr. Laughlin."

Laughlin said, "Amazing. I'm the one that was threatened."

"She felt an attraction to you that she wasn't comfortable with. Just watch yourself if you're ever around her again."

Laughlin said, "Thank you for warning me. Now it seems that you may have saved my life twice in one day. It was a pleasure meeting you, Miss Alice White. Let's never do this again."

"Flattery will get you everywhere, Mr. Laughlin, but I agree this was not a happy event in either of our lives. Two men dead. You take care now. If you ever need legal advice, look me up. Here's my card. I just graduated law school, so I'm not licensed yet. My firm has excellent attorneys who will back me up for the months until I am."

She reached into her pocket. "If I'm not there, they'll give me your number and I'll call you back. Oh, and I have a piece of advice for you."

"What's that?"

"After this robbery investigation is over, find that blond detective. I have a feeling she is worth risking your life for. Ask her out on a date and then duck."

"Are you crazy?"

"No, I'm not kidding. Something tells me she could take your head off with a single swipe, but you seem up to the challenge. The good ones are worth the risk. The fact that she disliked the sight of you that much in there, I found quite stimulating. I suspect you did too. You have to take my word for it. I know we women are not easy to read as a species, but believe me on this. She may not know it, but she's crazy about you. Me, I'm leaving work early today to find my boyfriend and rent a room somewhere. I can't take this kind of experience without finding an outlet for the excitement, if you know what I mean, and I think you do."

"Gosh, Alice. I don't think I ever met a woman quite as outspoken as you are. Even the detective was impressed, and she carries a gun too. I hope I see you again sometime."

"That would be nice. I have two words for you," Alice said.

"What're they?" the butcher asked cautiously.

"The blonde."

CHAPTER 17

THE CONCOURSE

Jim felt Alice's hand on his shoulder. He opened one eye, saw it was still dark outside, and closed it again to await further developments.

"C'mon, sleepyhead—time to get up. I'll make the coffee; you get in the shower. Then we'll switch. You don't have to speak. Just give me a sign."

With his eyes closed, Jim rolled over on top of her. His eyes opened. "I'm awake. You have yourself a deal, unless you want to share the shower with me."

"That would be wonderful, Jim. Personally, I have all the time in the world. You, on the other hand, are on the clock this morning. Soaping each other up will take us places you may not have time to go. I am perfectly willing to visit those places with you. You, on the other hand, have an appointment downtown to make money doing what you love to do. I was planning to meet Elaine in front of the building and catch up on some gossip before I buckle down to study some more for the Bar. It's your call, big fella."

"Gee, Alice. You are so grown up. I'll meet you in the kitchen after I shower . . . alone."

He pushed himself up, off her, and Alice slid out from under him. She grabbed a bathrobe and headed to the kitchen.

He turned on the hot water in the cramped, broom-closet-sized stall shower, fitted into the tiniest bathroom in New York City. The building had been erected in 1936. The bathroom was a cutesy feature built into the wall of the master bedroom that only fit one person at a time, unless one was in the shower. Until Pearl Harbor, the front door of the apartment house had been attended day and night by a doorman. In December of 1941, most such art deco structures along the four-mile stretch of the Grand Concourse lost their doormen to military service.

While Jim waited for the hot water to make its way up from the boiler in the basement, he quickly brushed his teeth, troweled Burma-Shave onto his face with his hands, and dragged a razor through it, until it looked respectable. Then he got into the hot shower for a working day's soap-and-rinse and was done in but a few minutes.

The smell of freshly brewed coffee hit him.

"The shower's all yours, Alice."

"That was fast. I'm leaving you in charge of breakfast while I shower. Please turn off the light under the coffee when it's finished making noise. There's bread I picked up from the grocery store yesterday, for toast, and plenty of eggs, so help yourself. Don't wash the pan. I'll use it for my own eggs when I get back."

Jim went to the apartment door and retrieved the *New York Post,* delivered in what must have been the middle of the night. Newspaper boys were not paid enough, he thought.

A short time later, Alice returned in a bathrobe and with her hair in the twisted turban of a white towel that Jim loved the sight of. A plate of scrambled eggs and toast was on the kitchen table waiting for her, and the frying pan was washed and in the dish drainer.

"Coffee?" Jim asked.

"Absolutely. Thank you for the eggs."

Jim poured her a cup and refilled his own. They ate in silence for a while. Jim perused the paper.

"Who exactly are you meeting today, Jim?"

"A new client. One of the producers of the show gave my name to them. It's not theater work. It's a home remodeling job down in Manhattan. Most of an entire mansion. It's the closest thing to building a house from scratch. I promised myself I would never do that again after the last house I built blew up and killed the doctor."

Alice said, "That's how we met, honey. An explosive love story, Mr. Peters. I'm so glad it brought you back to Broadway. You seem so much happier than when you were living up the river in Stanton, building that house for a demanding, ungrateful couple."

"Alice, there are always gonna be those types of problems. The big difference is not what I do for a living. It's who I live with when I'm not working."

"Isn't that the sweetest thing I ever heard."

"Alice, please. I can't stand it when you smile at me like that when I have to leave."

"Every woman I respect does the same thing. What good is having a man if you don't drive him crazy? Tell me more about your project."

"It'll take a month, give or take. I'll be done before you take your Bar exam. Everything is in pretty good shape at the theater. The stage sets are progressing. The guys and women working for me don't need me breathing down their necks all day. They're doing an excellent job."

"I'm happy for you. Take a break from the theater. See if you like working on a house again. My studying is gonna escalate from now until July, so I'm glad you'll be gainfully employed for a good chunk of that time."

"Really, Alice, it's not pocket change they're paying me. We're talking big money, which is what I will need to pay for the graduation present I'm planning on buying you after you take your exams."

"Jim. My gosh. What could possibly cost what you will make for remodeling a private home in Manhattan? That must be some kind of a gift you have in mind for me, mister. Let me see. It's more than dinner and a show. Is it an animal, a vegetable, or a mineral? What am I going to do with you?"

"You know I'm not gonna tell you. The next few months are going to be a nightmare for me because you are gonna torture me to find out."

"What can I possibly do to thank you, my dearest angel?"

Afterward, Jim got dressed, again, and called his new clients to tell them he had been held up by a family emergency. He kissed Alice and left.

Alice instantly missed him but busied herself doing the dishes. She needed a run.

After putting the bread back in the wooden bread box on the counter, shaking the crumbs out of the toaster into the garbage, and putting the butter back in the refrigerator, she brushed her teeth and put on running shorts and sneakers.

She ran all the way up the Concourse to Jerome Avenue, and along the elevated train line to Zabronski's butcher shop under the tracks. She gossiped with Mr. Zabronski about his family and replaced her depleted stock of meat with steak and lamb. When she got home, she squeezed the meat into the freezer and took her five-and-dime beach chair out of the coat closet. She rode back downstairs in the elevator to the art deco lobby. She exited through the ornate front doorway to the sidewalk in front of her building for some girl talk. She sat alone for a while, still in her running shorts, looking lazily out over her precious neighborhood. She watched passing cars and buses on their way south toward Fordham Road and north toward Yonkers. Pedestrians headed into local businesses on the next block, most of them going to the supermarket on the far corner. At least Jim hadn't taken her away from this wonderful neighborhood in the Bronx she had been calling home since the war. She'd never felt so genuinely happy.

"Alice. Oh, Alice. I'm so glad to see you." It was Susan Atkins, who she had helped out of a jam a few months ago.

"Susan, how wonderful it is to see you too. You look great. What have you been up to? Tell me. I need to be entertained. I'm on a break from studying for the Bar."

"I was going to call you, but now I don't have to."

"What about," Alice White asked.

"I wanted to see if the offer you made is still open for me to work in your office."

Alice said, "What prompted this momentous decision, Susan?"

"I finally had enough."

"You mean you and your infamous boyfriend, Stanley Kramer, are splitting up?"

"No, Alice. We're actually doing quite well, Stanley and me. If he opens a hundred more doors for me he wins a set of steak knives. No, it's just that I'm done being humiliated by the lecherous Greek owner of the diner I waitress in."

"I've been wondering how your personal life was working out."

"Stanley is behaving himself. I've never been treated so well. He's a new man. Sooner or later I'm gonna have to forgive him for the pain and suffering he caused me, though it's been so much fun punishing him. I decided he's a keeper. I realize I was as much to blame for what happened as he was."

"Gee, Susan," Alice said, "you sure are growing up. It'll be fun having you at the office. I'm pretty sure I can talk my bosses into hiring you. What's Stanley gonna do?"

"He is one lucky man. That furrier, the one he was helping Michael Pope to fleece, took him under his wing. He's going to go to medical school after all. That's what he was planning to do before he became an apprentice con man and a sexual predator."

Alice said, "That sounds promising, just don't look to me for relationship advice. I am a slave to my desires. Women make plans to live independent lives and then end up selling themselves for a little physical affection. Then out comes the dustpan, the broom, and the baking powder. Men don't have a monopoly on bad judgment."

"Alice, you saved my life. You taught me to respect myself. You dressed me up for that meeting with Stanley. You did my mascara, my nails, perfumed me up like some high-class prostitute and showed enough leg. I might as well have taken a baseball bat to him in front of the crowd at the ice cream parlor where I agreed to meet him and allow him to beg for my forgiveness. It was perfect. It very nearly killed him. I was so angry. I had to work it out, and you helped me do it. It was so dramatic walking away from him in front of all those people. If I don't make it at your office, I'm considering a career on the stage."

The Bennetts made their way slowly out of the front entrance of the building to where the two women were chatting. Andy took the beach chair he was carrying and opened it next to Alice.

Andrew said, "Okay, Elaine. I'm leaving you in Alice's capable hands. You two behave yourselves." He introduced himself to Susan. "My name is Andy Bennett."

Alice said, "Susan Atkins, this is my neighbor, Andrew. Andrew, this is Susan, a woman I assisted in recent times."

"Pleased to meet you," he said.

"Likewise, I'm sure," Susan said.

Alice asked Bennett, "Detective, do you have anything to do with the investigation of the bank robbery on Wall Street, Friday?"

"No, Alice, I have nothing to do with that investigation."

"You know, I was an eyewitness. Two men were killed, and the thieves got away with over a million dollars in cash, artwork, and as much of the contents of the vault as they could carry."

"I know all about you being there. This accident of fate has your name written all over it. Guns, executions, a good-looking Marine veteran who just happened to walk into the bank arm in arm with you. You have a reputation, Alice, and now I do too. All the way in Manhattan people know we're neighbors."

"Did they ask you about me?"

"Yes. I told them if you offered to help, they should run for their lives."

"Humph."

"I'm joking, Alice, no offense, I would be disappointed if you did not find a way to insinuate yourself into the middle of this."

"No offense taken, Andrew. I will try my best to stay out of it, really, I will, regardless of my hard-earned reputation as a busybody and a lunatic."

"All I'm saying, Alice, is that the perpetrators of this robbery are not people you want to fool around with. Even with the help of the Italian mobsters you somehow seem to have become friends with, and your buddy Antonio Vargas, the terror of the New York City security industry. Ordinary people do not go around robbing banks and shooting bank executives. And they certainly don't cotton to people like you, private citizens, butting into their business. So please, be careful."

Alice said, "What makes you think I have time to do anything but study for my exams?"

"Intuition, Alice. I'm a cop, remember, and you are not exactly a sphinx. You have trouble written all over you. You might as well have it printed across the back of your shirt."

"The detectives on the case seem quite competent. They'll have these guys locked up in no time. They don't need my help."

"Alice, that woman, the blonde, will chew you up and spit you out if you so much as talk to anybody about what you saw or heard. She's ambitious, ruthless, and one of them Oriental fighters who will pound you into the ground if you aggravate her half as much as I know you're capable of. I'm sure she was as charming and polite to you as a boa constrictor can be to a chihuahua. You, of course, being the chihuahua."

"Thank you for your warning. I will take it under advisement."

"Don't thank me, Alice. This is all to save me trouble because, if you get in her way, she will track you back to me."

"I promise I won't do anything to upset her."

"Try, Alice," Bennett said.

"I sensed a connection with her the moment I met her. I saw the way she lit into the other witness to the robbery, the butcher, like an angry dog. A sister in arms. I have intuition too, you know."

"Well, okay then," Bennett said. "I gotta go. You and Elaine look mighty cute together. If either of you crosses your legs when the light turns red, you'll cause a major traffic accident."

"How sweet of you to say so," Elaine told her fiancé. "I'm about to have a baby, so I'm not capable of crossing my legs, but the sentiment is so sweet. Bend down here and give me a kiss."

Bennett did as she requested and planted one on his soon-to-be-wife's cheek.

He said, "Alice, you'll call me if anything happens, with the baby, right?"

"Aye, aye, sir," Alice gave him a salute. "I take it Elaine has your number."

"I do," Elaine said with a coquettish lilt.

"You know, I'm going to have to study this morning for the Bar, so, if it's all right with both of you, I'll bring Elaine up to my new, larger apartment for coffee and maybe even a nap if you want, Elaine, until Andy gets back."

"That's fine with me, Alice," Andy said. "Your number I do have. Thank you for your hospitality. With that, I'm off. I'll track you down, Elaine, when I get back."

Alice said goodbye to Susan Atkins and promised she'd stay in touch about Susan's application for employment.

At Alice and Jim's kitchen table, the two ladies sat nursing coffees with cream and sugar. Law textbooks lay out on the table, unopened.

"Elaine, you are looking so good. I'm not kidding. You're a walking advertisement for pregnancy."

"I guess I do feel pretty good, all things considered. I never thought Harry and I could make a baby. Then Harry was killed, and I turned up pregnant with his child. Alice, I won't lie, I'm scared stiff. And I'm so, so sad about Harry not being here to welcome this baby into the world."

Alice's eyes teared up. She was too choked up to answer.

Elaine struggled to get a handkerchief out of the pocket of her dress. She handed it to her friend.

"Wipe your eyes, Alice. You know you don't look so bad yourself. That man of yours must be treating you mighty good, huh?"

Alice went from tears to blushing intensely. "Please, Elaine. You know how private I am about personal matters, but, without elaboration, yes, he is."

"Alice, I believe you. Your face is beet red. I'm jealous. Have you given any thought to having a baby yourself? You're beautiful, smart, funny. You've got a great guy who loves and, let's face it, worships you. What more could a child ask for?"

"How sweet of you to say so, Elaine. Yes, I've given thought to that idea, and I've rejected it. I honestly don't think I was cut out for motherhood. I'm older than you, and it's relatively late in my life to have a child. It's not just that. You have met my mom. She raised me and my brother, Phillip, like we were both boys. She didn't set out to do that. It's just that Phil's friends were my friends. I tagged along with them, and I learned to roughhouse on some of the most dangerous streets in New York City. I jumped from high places. I picked the locks of cars."

"So what, Alice. Those things would only make you a better mother. You understand kids because you are one, with all due respect."

"When my brother died, I was already working with these lawyers, Jack Bryce and Rich Adams. I thought my mother and I would die from the nightmare of Phillip being killed in Korea. I was very depressed. He was my world."

"Compared to you, Alice, I have lived a very sheltered life."

"Jim already has a daughter, Beth, who lives upstate with her mom. I love her like a daughter of my own. Her mother, not so much. Being Beth's stepmother is as far as I'm inclined to go toward motherhood at this time."

"I understand, Alice. You must be excited to finally be starting your new career."

"Elaine, I thought I would be thrilled, but I'm not sure I am."

"What could be so awful that it's spoiling what you've worked so hard to achieve?"

"Jim is now this big shot on Broadway. Important people are fighting over who gets him to work on their next show. They look at me like I'm some pretty little thing, too cute to be taken seriously."

"Alice, will you listen to yourself. A lot of women, including me, would kill not to be taken seriously. That's every woman's dream."

"It's not exactly an asset in the courtroom. Maybe I'm not good enough to make it in law practice. And I carry a gun, which is hardly ladylike. The permit is being dated retroactively with the help of the underworld, which seems to adore me. Let's face it. I'm despicable."

"Maybe you are a little more uncivilized than the average woman. Forget I said that. You know what I mean. You would be an excellent mother. Just think of all the damage you could inflict on society by teaching a little girl to follow in your footsteps. Courageous, loyal, engaged. That's not such a bad thing to pass on to a child."

"You're the one who's about to give birth."

"Alice, you're under a lot of pressure. Let's face it."

"I appreciate your love and support, Elaine. Have you come up with a name for the baby?"

"We thought we'd wait and decide at the hospital."

"I'm so looking forward to your wedding, Elaine."

"Me also, Alice. As you can easily see, it won't wait another minute."

CHAPTER 18

RAID

The detectives conferred before dawn. Time was wasting.

Sandra James told her partner, "Montes is dug in so deep, we'll never find him."

Detective Louis Maraglia said, "There's a bunch of people out combing the streets. We'll find him. I got troops lined up and ready to go once we get an address."

Ring, ring.

Louis lifted the receiver of his desk phone.

"Yeah. This is Detective Maraglia."

"Detective, this is Adams. I figured you'd be there at this hour. I got a location on your man."

"Spill, Adams."

"Arty Watts was being tailed. He was into some nasty people for big money. That's probably why he agreed to the heist. He was followed to a building the morning of the robbery. Next thing anyone knows, Watts is dead, but we got the address where they met up, and an apartment number, from an anonymous source."

'Beautiful."

"1158 Watkins, 4G."

"Thanks, Adams. I won't forget this."

Louis hung up and said, "We're set, Sandra. Too bad we didn't bet on it. 1158 Watkins, apartment 4G."

"Let's go get this pond scum before he gets away," Sandra said.

"Let's be careful," Louis said. "These guys are facing the death penalty. They got nothing to lose. They're running scared. And they have money. They took well over a million dollars for half an hour's work. The younger teller counted five of them inside the bank. That doesn't include the driver. That's more than two hundred grand each. Watch yourself, Sandy."

It was just getting light out. A team of uniformed police officers made the leap, single file, from the next building on the block to the roof of the apartment house where Christos Montes was supposed to be holed up. There were more police squatting on the street side of the cars parked in front of the building, and in the lot out back. They weren't taking any chances. The building superintendent was hauled out of bed and sleepily showed a bunch of them to the basement, where an emergency staircase opened from the floors above. The fire escape from the Montes apartment was covered above and below. This man and whoever might be with him were not likely to go down without a fight, but they were not going to get away.

Louis Maraglia raised his fist, and the raid began. In through the building's main entrance. Up the stairs from the lobby. Down the inside staircase from the roof. Up and down the fire escape.

Bang, bang, bang! "Police. Open up."

Everyone in the building woke up, got out of bed, and raised their hands in the air. This was not the classiest neighborhood in Manhattan.

Nothing from inside Montes's apartment. Not a sound. The police on the fire escape saw no lights coming from inside. They raised the kitchen window and climbed in.

The super unlocked the door. Officers streamed in, guns drawn. The bed was unkempt, but empty. Dirty dishes filled the sink. Garbage spilled out of the can. A couple of pieces of ratty furniture remained. Cigarette stubs filled the ashtray on the coffee table.

"Nobody's here, Detectives." One of the cops stated the obvious.

Louis Maraglia said, "Don't anybody touch anything. Back out of here and tape the door. Let's get the lab boys to go over this place with a comb. Maybe they'll catch a clue as to who they all are, besides Montes, and hopefully where they went."

"I now pronounce you husband and wife," Judge Joshua Ogilvy, Justice of the Peace, told Elaine and Andrew Bennett. They were at the Bronx County Hall of Justice on 161st Street.

Elaine bent over her advanced pregnancy and shared a kiss with her new husband.

One of Andy's police detective friends, Sidney Shapiro, had reserved a room at a local caterer for a small reception.

Alice White made her friend comfortable in a soft, upholstered armchair. Jim went to get refreshments.

A man in his mid-thirties, wearing one of those gray detective business suits, came over to the little group.

Bennett said to Elaine and Alice, "May I present to you my good friend Sidney Shapiro. He's the one who got us this room. Also, Alice, he's the detective who helped find you and your friends when you were kidnapped not long ago. I invited him to be a witness today, so please don't either of you leave without signing the marriage certificate."

Alice said, "Pleased to meet you, Detective Shapiro. Thank you for your assistance keeping me alive during my recent troubles."

Shapiro said, "It was my pleasure, Alice. You're an extraordinary person. I have read about you in the *Post*. I love Franklin Jones's column. I suppose you know he's got a crush on you. Now that I've met you, I can understand why."

"How nice of you to say so."

"It's not flattery. I'm just stating the obvious. Jones calls you a champion of the underdog at great risk to yourself. High praise from that man. I am also a fan of one of your bosses, Clarence Eaton. Some cops say he's on the wrong side of the law, but I don't agree. If he finds out his client is guilty, I've seen him threaten to withdraw as their lawyer if they don't agree to plead guilty. I learn something every time he questions me in court. That's not always the case with defense attorneys. Mr. Eaton and me have butted heads when he's gotten me on the witness stand. I'm not a lawyer, but I hear you just became one, and I can't think of a better mentor if I was to switch jobs. I have to brace myself for his attack, even when I'm dead right and he's dead wrong. Give him my regards."

"I will, Detective Shapiro."

"Do you intend to follow in his footsteps?"

Alice said, "I haven't decided between defense and prosecution, so don't cross me off your list of good guys just yet. I have to pass the Bar in July and wait till October to get the results."

"Five minutes talking to you, and I'd bet on you passing."

"I've done enough damage as a civilian. I'm not sure New York State is ready for me to represent it in court."

Sidney said, "Whether you like it or not, Miss White, I can tell you with the authority of a detective, you are always gonna be in trouble. You are beautiful, aggressive, a little crazy, willing to risk your life for a good cause. The sky's the limit. You could end up president, or at least governor."

Alice White said, "I gotta pass the Bar first."

Shapiro laughed and said, "You'll never just be a lawyer. But I wish you all the luck with your exam. And I'll be watching the *Post* for news of your escapades after that."

Jim showed up with a tray of champagne, soda, and iced tea.

Elaine announced, "Everyone. There is cake and coffee available, which I cannot eat this close to the baby's delivery, but please help yourselves."

Assorted singles and couples moved toward the carrot cake.

Elaine turned to her new husband. "Take me home now, Andy, and, please, go to a meeting if there is one at this hour, so you'll be free when I go into labor."

"There is one," he said. "It starts in about an hour at St. Phillips. I'll leave the number under our phone, so you can call me if anything happens. Do you realize it's been over half a year since I had my last drink?"

Elaine patted her belly and said, "Andy, it's been closer to nine months if you think about it."

"My name is Andy, and I am an alcoholic."

"Hi, Andy," the group murmured.

"My wife and I just got married an hour ago, and she's due to go into labor any minute, so I'd like to share first if you don't mind. I know I just said a lot about my situation, and I know it's almost a typical story amongst alcoholics to be in such a socially unacceptable situation, but I am not the baby's father. He was killed shortly after conception, and I asked his widow if I could help raise their child as my own. I can't do that if I'm not sober, so here I am. I'm excited beyond belief and I, uh . . ."

"Psst, Andrew," he heard Father Jack Donovan signal before he could finish speaking. The NYPD detective stood up, said thank you, and walked over to Donovan.

In a low voice, the priest told him, "It's that time, my boy. She is in labor. Do not drive fast. She only just broke her water, and you don't want to scare the woman. This is her first child and, if memory serves, it will not go quickly. So, relax, go home, and don't forget the little valise that every pregnant woman packs when she gets close to her term."

"Okay, Father, thank you. I am much obliged."

"It's nothing, my son. It's one of the happier parts of my job, to be there when families usher in new life. By the way, thank you for your help tidying up the structural decay of this church. Your friend James Peters reinforced the walls and had a plumber friend of his, Milton Davis, install new toilets and, most impressive, brought a union electrician to practically rewire the entire building."

"It was our pleasure, Father."

"Now go, get out of here, and bring me back news of a newborn king or queen."

CHAPTER 19

AT THE DRUGSTORE

The heavy plate glass door of Manny Harrison's pharmacy was locked. His was the classic corner drugstore, on the west side of the Grand Concourse at 205th Street. Although it was before dawn, a light was on inside.

Up through the trapdoor in the floor behind the cosmetics counter popped the tall, skinny delivery boy, Augie Russo, being paid extra for his trouble at this hour of the morning. He was only sixteen years old, a good worker, but already he was a heavy smoker and drinker. He came from his home down the hill in the Italian enclave. He talked with a severe Bronx-Italian accent, said, "I axed the guy," instead of "asked." He didn't only run deliveries, but he stocked and dusted the merchandise on the shelves of the store and went out for coffee, buttered rolls, and sandwiches when Mr. Harrison asked him to.

"Ay, MH," Augie yelled to his boss, who was occupied in the back at the elevated prescription bench. "After I put this Kleenex on the shelf, you want I should go over to the luncheonette and get us some cawfee and budda'd rolls? They open at five for the people walkin' to the subway, headin' downtown to work."

"That'd be nice, Augie."

Augie said to Manny, "You know, MH, you been like a father to me since my dad was shot in Brooklyn. My mother told me when I came to work for you, 'Treat that man good, Augie,' she said. 'He was good to your father and me when we was broke after the war. Even after we had money to pay, he gave us formula to feed you. He's got a good heart, that Mr. Harrison, the doc.'"

Manny came down off his bench, pressing a key on the cash register to pop the cash drawer open and slip out a few singles. Then he walked over to where Augie was struggling with the crate of facial tissues from the basement. Augie finished pulling the crate up through the floor and lowered the trap door. He reached over, took the money, and put it in his pocket.

"Okay, MH. I'll just leave these here and run next door. Mind if I stop for a smoke?"

"No, Augie. Take a break. You're a good boy. Thank you for coming in so early this morning."

"Dat's what you pay me faw, MH."

"Still, Augie. Good help is hard to find, and you're the best. I'm a lucky man. How's your mother?"

"Awe, she's okay. She's still working at the laundry. She's making good money at it, especially since after some of the soldiers from the neighborhood went and had a talk with the owner."

Manny did not respond to the remark referring to the overwhelming presence in this community. He owed these Italian immigrants a debt of gratitude for their permission and protection to operate his business, the business that fed his ungrateful children, Marc and Nancy. Those kids drove him crazy with their lack of appreciation for the value of a dollar. They thought money grew on trees. Even so, he loved them.

Manny Harrison was sometimes called upon to render certain services in the middle of the night when someone was dragged in from a gunfight and placed on the Cavuto's Funeral Home embalming table for surgical intervention, off the books. It was unspoken that he would assist old man Cavuto in his surgery and supply antibiotics and pain medication. He had a separate wall phone in the kitchen of his apartment where he lived with his wife and kids. It rarely rang, but when it did, he put on a jacket, left the apartment, and locked the door before he got on the elevator to the basement.

Manny said, "It's still dark out, Augie. Did you wake your mother up when you left your house?"

"Naw, Mista Harrison. She was already up. She gets up in the middle of the night, reads the paper, has her morning cawfee. Mom made me my favorite breakfast, sasage, potatas, and eggs, with ketchup. When I left, she was just cleaning up the kitchen and putting in a load of laundry before she went to work herself. She gave me a kiss, on the cheek, and told me to say hello to you from her. I hate when she kisses me like that. She, ya know, gets my face wet and messes up my hair so I gotta comb it all over again, and then wipe off my face. It ain't easy bein' a son without a father, but somebody's gotta do it, right, MH?"

"You know, Augie, you make me laugh, calling me MH like you do. I like it. You don't have any idea how lucky you are. That woman is a saint, your mother. Tell her I said hi back. Before you finish today, remind me to give you a gift to take home to her, from me. Some perfume from the cosmetics counter. Okay now, get outta here. I'll unpack this box myself and put the tissues on the shelf if you do me a favor and cut up the carton with the box cutter when you get back with the coffee."

"Thanks, MH. Sure ting. You're a pretty good boss. I'll tell my mom you said hello. She's gonna really appreciate the perfume."

The kid squatted down to turn the key in the bottom of the front door and unlock it and went out into the cool early morning air. He looked back and saw his boss relock the door. MH had been robbed at gunpoint by someone from outside the neighborhood with a zip gun one night when there were no customers. Them zip guns was made with car antennas, always going off by accident. Mr. Harrison emptied the register and gave the guy the pills he wanted. A few days later one of the men from the neighborhood dropped by and returned all the cash and most of the pills. Nothing was said about the fate of the robber. Manny preferred not to hear about such things.

Augie tapped a cigarette out of a pack and cupped his hands around the match to keep it from blowing out while he lit it.

Just then his favorite customer, Alice White, who he'd had a thing for since he was a little kid, arrived to pick something up from the locked store, like she often did. She was always showing up after closing or before the drugstore opened in the morning. Augie thought it was her way of keeping an eye on Mr. H., especially after he got held up. MH had a soft spot for her too, or maybe even a crush. It was hard not to. I mean, look at her. "Mamma Mia," he mumbled under his breath. Just thinking about her made him bite his lip. There was no one like her.

"Ay, Miss White," he said. "How ya doin'?"

"Just great, Augie. How're you? How's your mom?"

He turned back and banged his palm on the door of the store to get his boss's attention.

"Good, very good, Miss White. We're both doin' good. I'm headed out to have a cigarette and get some cawfee for me and the boss. You want I should pick you up a cup? Cream and sugar, right?"

"Yes, thanks, Augie. That would be great. Here's a dollar. I'm gonna have to take the coffee and go. I have places to be and people to see."

He put his hand up. "Please, keep your money. You know Mr. H. likes to treat you when he can. This one's on him. If we ever need a counselor, we want to be on your good side." His face flushed. What in the holy heck was he talking about? he wondered. She always made him lose his mind.

"I'll tell my mom I saw you. You're a regular celebrity up here in the Bronx, what with you tryin' ta save the customs guy, Applewood, you know. Too

bad it worked out so bad. And after that, you bein'
kidnapped. You shot a guy, Miss White, you know
when they was takin' you away in the car. Too bad
you only hit him in the leg. You're a Bronx hero. You
sure you ain't Italian? You got a lotta nerve . . . uh,
with all respect."

"Augie, don't embarrass me. Go finish your
cigarette. I'll still be here when you get back."

He turned again to the door and pounded the
heel of his palm against it three more times to get Mr.
Harrison to open up.

Manny came up front, looked through the
glass door into the darkness, smiled at Alice, and
unlocked it. Then he locked it behind Alice and they
walked single file through the narrow store packed
with merchandise, toward the counter.

"Hi, Mr. Harrison," Alice spoke to the
handsome middle-aged man in his white tunic with
the top two buttons rakishly undone, as usual. "You
know you drive the neighborhood housewives crazy
with that getup, Mr. H.?"

"Nice of you to say so, Alice. What can I get
for you this beautiful morning?"

"I'm embarrassed to ask, but we ran out of
toilet paper again last night. I need a few rolls of that
sandpaper you call 'Harrison's Professional' toilet
paper."

"Young lady, a little roughness is good for you. You have to admit, it's the cheapest toilet paper in New York City."

"You are absolutely right, Manny. My boyfriend, Jim, took a roll downtown to smooth out the rough edges of the set he's building. That's probably why we ran out."

"Ha. It's not a bad idea, Alice."

Alice said, "You do know I'm joking, right?"

"Of course, I know you are. To tell you the truth, the reason I carry it, I'm afraid to admit, is that I've never gotten over the Depression. That's why I have my own brand of dirt-cheap toiletries: toilet paper, facial tissues, deodorant like glue that keeps you from sweating by preventing you from being able to raise your arms. My son, Marc, made that up and tells it to all his friends. He has no idea what it was like growing up not sure there'd be food for supper. He's a wonderful kid, though, aside from being spoiled rotten, but it's my pleasure to spoil him and his sister, Nancy. He says he's going to be a doctor. Maybe he will. They're smart kids, mostly, even if they don't know the value of a dollar. I have hopes they won't starve to death when they grow up and move out of the house."

Alice said, "I've met your son, Manny. The apple didn't fall far from the tree. He's a lady-killer."

"Enough about my son, the little pisher. Tell me, what show is Jim doing now?"

"*West Side Story*. Leonard Bernstein."

"Well, isn't that nice? Leonard Bernstein. You guys going to go down and see it?"

"Yes. We have friends upstate. You know. I told you about them. He's a plumber. She's a nurse. When Jim was building houses, they worked together, him and the husband, all the time. Jim invites them to every show he does stage sets for. They became my friends when Jim was in trouble, and I went up there to help him out. Jim was my first case."

Manny walked over and dislodged four rolls of Harrison's Professional brand toilet paper from the shelf, which had been overstuffed by Augie this very morning.

"Oh my goodness," Manny said. "I almost forgot to say congratulations on your graduation from law school."

"Thanks, Manny. It took its sweet time, but I made it."

"Alice, you've been living in that building across the street since before this store was even built. You worked yourself up from a secretary. All of it while living in your one-bedroom apartment. I'm proud of you. So is everybody in the neighborhood. They're all surprised you lived long enough to do it,

what with the chances you take. And, no insult
intended, being a woman was not an advantage. This
is monumental. Alice White, my friend. Please let me
be proud of you on behalf of your late father."

"Oh, geez, Mr. Harrison. You are gonna
make me start crying. Don't force me to have to use
one of your number sixty, coarse, facial tissues.
Please desist. I appreciate your kind words, really, but
I hate to tell you, the worst is yet to come. My Bar
exam is in July, only two months from now. Studying
is going to take all my time until then. You'll see me
on my study breaks browsing your shelves, buying
chewing gum and aspirin."

"It will be my pleasure. Augie's back with the
coffee. I better let him in."

"Ay, Miss White."

"Hi, Augie. Thanks for getting me my
coffee."

"Miss White, the owner of the luncheonette
said you was caught in that bank heist, the one
downtown on Wall Street where the two guys was
killed. You sure get around."

"Yes, Augie. That did happen. How in
heaven's name did anyone up here in the Bronx get
my name?"

"The cop that lives in your building with the
widow, Mrs. Applewood. I seen him in the

luncheonette having breakfast just now. He was talkin' to the waitress about you. I know he always says bad things about you being too brave for your own good, but I think he's proud of you like we all are."

"His wife is not Mrs. Applewood anymore, Augie. As you know, they got married yesterday. She's Mrs. Bennett now, and her husband, Mr. Bennett, still thinks I'm a fruitcake. It was an accident, me being in that bank. I never go there in the morning. It was all some sort of terrible coincidence. I thought it would be good to get rid of my paycheck before I spent it. I don't plan these things, Augie. They just happen. So, tell me, Augie, did he look happy?"

"Yeah, Miss White. He looked awful happy. I walked in and people were saying congratulations all over the place for him gettin' married."

"That's not all that happened yesterday, Augie. I'm a godmother. Last night his new wife had a baby girl. They named her Emily."

CHAPTER 20

COP IN THE SHOP

There were no customers in the Laughlin butcher shop on Water Street, near the Financial District of Manhattan. There was always a chunk of meat on the heavy wooden chopping block to be cut to size for frying or broiling. It was good to have meat back on the table. Even more than ten years after the wartime rationing, most people remembered meat being a special treat.

Detective Sandra James sat with her partner in an unmarked Ford sedan across the street from

Laughlin's establishment, watching the butcher arrange his display case.

"Lou," she said. "If you don't mind, I'd like to question Mr. Laughlin alone."

"Okay with me. Just take it easy on him. I think he rubs you the wrong way. I don't understand exactly why. He's a good enough looking man. Most importantly, he's a cooperating witness and he's given us the best intel we've gotten on this robbery so far. He ID'd the leader. I think you just can't get over coming up empty on the raid. You want my advice?"

"What might that be?" she asked.

"Let the man be. He looks like he's suffered enough. Don't hurt him. And don't deny you've thought about it. You have a tell."

"Really? What's my tell?"

Lou said, "Your right eye. It twitches. I don't know what it is about this guy, but your right eye is like a Geiger counter when you're around him. You're doing it now."

"It's a simple follow-up, Louis, to see if he remembers anything else. That's all."

Louis said, "He's depressed, widowed, a military hero. I think he likes you. I ask you, what is there not to like about him? Something about him spooks you, that's all I'm saying. Do your follow-up and then let's get out of here. He's got nothing else to give."

"Okay. You have any more wisdom to impart?"

"You know, San, you're a lot like him. You're both tough. Both loners. Maybe that's why he gets on your nerves."

"Lou, you are crazy."

"Geez, Sandra. Ignore me. I love you like a daughter, and I worry about you. It's this bank robbery that's got me spooked. These guys are amateurs with their backs against the wall. They got nothing to lose by taking us out, or anyone else, for that matter. I don't want your hormones interfering with your judgment."

Sandra said, "Louis, I feel no attraction to this man." Twitch, twitch. "I'm using him like I would any other witness. Maybe his memory has improved. True, the clock is ticking, but I don't want to miss anything if I can help it. I'm not above using his hormones to stimulate his memory."

"Okay, I believe you. Go butter him up and, then, we hit the street for real."

"Lou, seriously, I don't have time for a guy in my life. Maybe it was the war that broke him. He would be a full-time job for any woman, and I am not emotionally stable enough, mature enough, or patient enough to deal with him."

Louis said, "Your eye stopped twitching. That's all I wanted to see. You can go in there now, missy. I'll be out here smoking."

Sandra punched her partner in the arm and hopped out of the car. She walked across the street. Maraglia turned on the radio, inclined his seat, and lit up.

The bell jingled on the door as she entered the shop.

Laughlin turned from what he was doing.

"God, it smells good in here, Mr. Laughlin. My mouth is watering. I am definitely a meat eater."

"Hello, Detective," the rugged-looking butcher was clearly happy to see her. "Have you gotten anywhere in your search for the men who robbed the bank?"

"We tracked them back to an apartment, but they were long gone. No one knows where Christos Montes is, or where any of the surviving gang members are."

Laughlin said, "He's gotta know I identified him. I've been in close quarters with the guy, here in this store. He's a moody man, dark, threatening. He takes things personally. It's a weakness. He sentenced himself to fry in the electric chair, from what I heard, by killing that banker because the banker shot one of his men. It was stupid. I didn't peg him for a bank robber. He's out of his depth."

Sandra said, "I agree. You'd make a good cop."

He said, "It's situational awareness. They taught us that in the war. It came in handy in combat. You have a conversation in your head with the guy that's trying to kill you and figure out his next move. It only failed me once, and that almost cost me my life. I had a talk with this guy who was firing an automatic weapon at me, a machine gun. I must have misheard what he said. I thought he said he had left, so I came out of my hiding place, and he blasted me full of holes."

"If you want, we'll put a man outside your store."

Thomas said, "It won't help. If he wants me, he'll find a way."

"You know, Mr. Laughlin, Montes doesn't hold the patent on ruthlessness."

"You must be a handful for your husband and children to deal with."

"I'm not married." She looked him coldly in the eye. Despite her best effort, her face flushed and developed a sheen.

He said, "I just assumed, a woman like you . . . I'm sorry."

She said, "I'm not at all sorry. I am way too busy for the distraction of a family. I am quite happy being free to come and go as I please. Before I forget why I'm here, is there anything else you can remember about the robbery that would help us catch these creeps?"

"No, nothing else. I caught a glimpse of the driver outside. I couldn't describe him except for being white and medium height and build."

"Okay then. If you think of anything else, please give us a call. I didn't mean to be so defensive about being single. What about you? I understand your wife died."

"Yes, she did, in childbirth. And, by the way, I don't think every woman needs to have a husband and babies. As for me and women, I don't think I could survive going out on a date, let alone being married again. We have that in common. I have a son, fifteen years old. I've been a complete failure as a father his whole life. After his mother died, I deserted him, left him with my parents so I could be a Marine and go off to fight in the war."

"Well, you obviously survived and, I assume, you've been raising and supporting him ever since."

"I survived. That's true enough. I picked Benjamin up from my folks. I can't say that I did anything to raise him, except to clothe him, house him, and feed him, and that's about all. He knows nothing about self-defense. He's getting bullied at school, having his lunch money taken from him by a bigger guy. It's a sorry Marine whose son can't fight his way out of a paper bag. Can you believe it? Like his father, he can't look a woman in the eye. His grades are poor, and I'm too dumb to help him with his homework. He's overweight. He hides out upstairs in our apartment all day, eating candy and reading comic books. He gets little to no exercise. I'm batting a thousand as a parent. Can you imagine me putting that on a woman?"

"Mr. Laughlin, truly you've got major problems. I'd love to stay and talk some more, but I gotta go. My partner's waiting for me in the car. From the look in your eyes, I'd say you've been through the ringer, losing your wife and then in the war. I am a competitive martial artist, a maniac, unfit to relate with polite society. Maybe we can barter over your son. I hear the woman you entered the bank with is looking to be taught how to fight also. How about I give you, your son, and the woman, Miss White, a single lesson, and you will give me whatever number of steaks you think is fair. For now, I have work to do. We'll talk again."

The Earrings

In the 1920s, Edward Alvarez quit his job as a short-order cook in Abilene, Texas, and moved to Los Angeles. As a young man he had apprenticed at a metal casting factory. In LA he used his skills to design glare-proof costume jewelry, which he marketed to motion picture studios.

During World War II, Alvarez used his factory to cast pieces of airplanes for the military.

Arthur Freeman was an aircraft designer and a flyer. In the war he worked with Alvarez. When he retired from military service, he often bought costume jewelry for his wife from his old friend.

For their twenty-fifth wedding anniversary, Freeman commissioned a copy of the costume earrings they had seen in a movie, only these were made with real gold and priceless pearls. The one-of-a-kind pair were stored in a safe-deposit box in the vault of the First National Bank on Wall Street in Manhattan. They were reported stolen in the deadly robbery.

CHAPTER 21

OLD MUSTACHIOS

"They lost him," Frankie "Windows" announced.

"Lost who?" Roberto Cavuto, the undertaker, asked his friend.

"Montes, the Gypsy," Frankie said, "who robbed the bank, shot the banker, and got one of his own guys killed. The cops raided his place, but he never came back after the job. What'd they expect? He's out there somewhere."

They were sitting in the kitchen of Roberto Cavuto's funeral home on Wilbert Avenue. There was a whole world down here. Southern Italian charm reconstructed in their post–world war immigration home in the United States. A true mustachio was a Sicilian. They weren't all from Sicily, but close enough.

Tomato gardens were planted behind the wood-framed homes that housed three generations: children, parents, and grandparents. There were shrines with statues of the Virgin Mary placed right in the middle of prime real estate with buildings respectfully spaced around them. Even non-Italians knew that the shrines were location markers where black-clad Italian grandmothers had seen visions of the Madonna. No one dared touch them. Fresh flowers were replaced almost daily, with special explosions of color at Easter and Christmas. Candles were often seen burning in them.

The Grand Concourse was the dividing line in the North Bronx. Italians lived down the hill on the west side, the Irish were up on the east side. Jews were in the middle along most of the west side of the Concourse, north of Fordham Road. The ethnic populations lived in relative harmony. Together they fended off roving gangs like the notorious Baldies, who quickly stood corrected of their misunderstanding that the neighborhood was easy pickings for shoplifting and armed robbery. A few widely publicized acts of retribution by the soldiers from Manhattan who guarded their relatives here in the Bronx, and this quickly became the safest neighborhood in New York City, if not the world. Outsiders finally got the message to stay away from this area of the Bronx unless it was to buy from the drugstore or the other businesses in the one block of commercial real estate between 204th Street and 205th Street, on the west side of the Concourse. Young women could walk the streets unescorted at two o'clock in the morning without fear of molestation. Alice White hardly felt the need for a gun on her late-night walks from the subway station to her building after evening sessions at NYU Law School.

There was a pot of coffee on a trivet in the middle of the Cavutos' kitchen table. There was also a large bowl of scrambled eggs, another of fried potatoes, a stack of toast, and a chunk of butter on a plate.

Cavuto said, "Frankie. Why don't you have some real food for a change, you know, put a little meat on your bones. Cigarettes are not food. No offense."

Cavuto was short and powerful. It was said of him that he could carry a dead body under each arm—when no mourners were present, of course. He had the appearance of an undertaker with that fixed dour expression and respectfully hunched back. He served as host to regular meetings of this group of old friends.

"Aye, Roberto," Frankie said. "I'm not offended. I'm a picky eater. I got a delicate stomach. That's why I carry a bottle of milk of magnesia in my pocket like some men carry whiskey."

Cavuto said, "You know, Frankie, my wife made this breakfast special for you, and of course also for our illustrious companion Enzo. She secretly wants to fatten you up for, maybe, one of the neighborhood women. She thinks you have been widowed long enough."

Frankie went through a series of uncomfortable expressions, including eye rolls. Finally, he smiled sheepishly and said, "You know, Roberto, there will only ever be one woman for me. My beautiful wife. She's gone. Rest in peace. I ever tell you she was a reincarnated Indian princess?"

"Yes, Frankie, you did. A couple a million times. So, you're not gonna have eggs and potatoes?"

Frankie put his hands up in surrender and gave his unused plate to the undertaker. "You win. Fill it up."

He took a couple of forkfuls and smiled.

"Terrific," Frankie said. "Roberto, please tell your wife it was delicious and thank her for me. Also, I appreciate her concern about me being alone, but tell her I see plenty of women. Don't forget my hobby. I wash windows and I'm with beautiful women all day long. Course most of them are married, and my machinery ain't exactly in factory condition. I'm not ready to settle down with another wife. First thing any of them want to do is fix my teeth. Can you imagine me with a full set of teeth? I'd look ridiculous. And remind her, I got Tony, outside in the car, for company. He likes my teeth the way they are, and he's got a mean right fist, which comes in handy sometimes, and I never seen a woman who had anything like that."

The patriarch, Enzo Trusgnich, moved slightly in his chair, and his two companions turned their heads to look at him. Trusgnich represented Italian interests in the Bronx and had earned these men's gratitude and respect ten times over. Now in his seventies, he still ruled his empire with an iron fist.

The old man spoke through a weather-stiffened face with a voice like a file scraping metal, "So far, this Gypsy hasn't messed with our business. Angelo Benedetto, in Manhattan, gives him some room to operate in exchange for him doing critical jobs that he's good at like breaking into houses and businesses, picking pockets, cracking safes, and copying keys. Montes usually keeps his personal business small and private. This bank job is outta left field. The kid must have a death wish. He's a loner and he's gonna die alone. As long as he stays out of the Bronx, I'll leave it to our Manhattan associates to control him. The good news for them is that he's stupid, so he's not gonna last too long anyway. Set up a meeting for me and Angelo in our suite at the Waldorf. Lucky Montes didn't touch Alice White when she walked in on the robbery. That would have shortened his life even more."

Cavuto added, "The beautiful Italian detective, Sandra James, was assigned to the case. We'll put a bug in her ear to keep an eye on Alice. They're a lot alike."

Enzo said, "Really? Little Sandra James? My God, now we got two women mixed up in this we gotta look out for."

"Maybe," Frankie said. "Sandra's partner is Louis Maraglia, 'The Bear.' We don't need to do a thing. That Gypsy's gonna wish he stuck to small-time operation. He's in over his head. He's gonna be squashed like a bug. Now he's up for murder. We'll send a priest to visit him in the death house, to give him communion and last rites."

Enzo said, "I'll take bets that our gal, Alice White, is gonna get mixed up in this bank robbery business. She takes everything so personal. I'm glad I got her a license for that gun she carries. She's gonna need it."

"Really, Enzo?" Cavuto said. "She didn't have a license?"

"No. Can you believe it? Now she's gonna be a lawyer, she's gonna have to pay attention to stuff like that. Anyway, my boys took care of it. They convinced some guy to get all the paperwork done and make sure it was dated a couple a years ago."

Frankie smiled that skeletal smile of his with the randomly missing teeth. "I would'a liked to see how they convinced him."

Cavuto let out a deep chuckle.

Enzo said, "We gotta think of something to give Alice for graduation."

"'At's easy," Roberto said. "Shotgun. Twenty-gauge, pump with five in the magazine. Every lawyer keeps one in the wall on their side of the desk."

The Savarin coffee was in a large pot on a table strewn with cannolis, cloth napkins, cups and saucers, and finger sandwiches, compliments of the management of the Waldorf Astoria. Angelo Benedetto and Enzo Trusgnich sat quietly with their cups of coffee on tables beside them waiting for the hotel staff to leave.

The bodyguards sat in an alcove of the room, smoking cigarettes and swallowing finger sandwiches whole. When the last maid left the room and the door closed behind her, Trusgnich addressed his fellow Don.

"This man who did the bank job, did you send him?"

Benedetto said, "No."

Trusgnich said, "Rumor is Gypsies are close to being Catholic. My guys'll send the priest to him, Christos Montes, when he's in the death house ready to die. They make them wait a couple of years before they fry them on Old Sparky. You'd think they would die of a heart attack with that long a wait, but they don't."

Benedetto said, "That's very thoughtful of you, Enzo. I'm sorry I didn't think of that myself. I'm not gonna waste my time looking for him. He was never right, you know? Gypsies are different, and he's even more different than most Gypsies. Stay in touch. We don't want this mess to get out of hand. If it does, we will kill him, save New York State the expense."

Trusgnich said, "There are two women from the Bronx that are mixed up in this that I am responsible for, I should tell you about."

Benedetto said, "That so? Yes, you should, so I can look after them. Tell me."

Trusgnich said, "Alice White. She's a lawyer. She's an investigator too and carries an automatic in her belt. Walked into the bank while they were shooting the bank executive. The banker killed their guy, Arty Watts, a dockworker. See how stupid this Gypsy is? The banker is worth ten times the muscle-head to the law. That's why he's gonna end up in the chair."

Benedetto said, "You're right. It was stupid. The other?"

Trusgnich said, "Sandra James, police detective. Big family. She got put on the case. I wouldn't worry about either of them, much. They're both armed and aren't afraid to pull the trigger, but I just wanted you to know who they were in case they cross your path."

"Thank you, my friend, for telling me about them. I'll do my best to stay out of their way. The guy from the Bronx who was shot in the robbery, Arty Watts, I heard of him. He's married to one of us. I'll go in on whatever you say is right for his family. We gotta take care of our own."

CHAPTER 22

SEBASTIAN LUPO

Sebastian Lupo, aka the Wolf, was a Gypsy of the Romani people. Like Christos Montes, he considered himself a Catholic, although he did not practice any particular form of organized religion. In deference to their nomadic ancestors, shortly after the war, Sebastian and his sister moved from Chicago to New York City. When they got to the Big Apple, they continued their illustrious careers as a team of pickpockets around Times Square and the theater district in general. She was the "bump," accidentally tripping into an unsuspecting stranger and drawing his complete attention to the virtually uncovered bosom spilling out of her blouse. The "mark," the stranger, shocked and ashamed that he could not unglue his eyes from her nakedness, was unaware that

Sebastian, the "dip," was relieving him of his wallet, watch, and jewelry. Lupo passed the goods back off to his sister, who would be gone like a shot with the swag, lest Sebastian be stopped and searched. They pulled this off one too many times and dipped into the pocket of a man named Michael Pope, the head of a confidence gang of his own. He took Pope's wallet, keys, and wristwatch. Pope was favorably impressed by being so smoothly skinned. He used his considerable resources to track the pair down and make them an offer of employment they could not dare refuse, on penalty of long-term incarceration and probable execution in jail. At the same time a police detective, head of the Vice Squad, Sidney Shapiro, became aware of Lupo's situation and simultaneously blackmailed Lupo into his employ as Vice's confidential informant within Pope's gang. The Wolf walked the tightrope with trepidation.

When Michael Pope was executed by the Russian mob, Lupo found himself blessedly relieved of his obligation to Pope, and was offered a position as a legitimate undercover officer of the NYPD, under Detective Shapiro.

"I've got something for you to do. Have a seat," Shapiro told Lupo. "How're you adjusting to working on the right side of the law?"

Lupo said, "It's okay. I still have to look over my shoulder, but it's working for me. What can I do for you?"

"I want you to help me out with the bank robbery pulled off by your landsman Christos Montes."

Lupo said, "I heard about that. He's got a mean streak. He makes all Gypsies look bad. What can I do?"

"Find him if you can. He's out there somewhere, maybe planning another job."

Lupo said, "We know each other from a distance, but we never sat down to a meal together. If it's true he robbed a bank and killed somebody, I would never get within a mile of him now. Bank robbery and murder make a person suspicious as all hell of the sudden appearance of a long-lost cousin. He wouldn't think twice about having me killed."

Shapiro said, "I don't think you have to meet him. Just find him and we'll do the rest. If anyone can do this, it's you. A butcher who witnessed the robbery identified him, even with a mask. Montes's apartment was empty when the detectives on the case tracked him down and raided it. I figure he's either gone underground or left the country. It would be nice to find out which. If he's still here, we'd like to catch him and send him up the Hudson River to death row. Capisce?"

"Yeah, I understand. Like I said, I don't feel any love for him. I was a thief myself and I paid the price. I'll do some snooping around, Chief, under heavy cover. My own mother won't recognize me when I'm done. It would be hard to track a loner like him down, but a bank job needs a crew. The guy who got killed was a longshoreman. Gives me an idea where to start."

Detective Shapiro said, "I would appreciate it if you move fast, like today. If he's on his way out of town, he might want to stop and try his luck one more time. It might be too much for him to resist. More people could die."

"I'm on it."

Lupo left Shapiro and headed to a theatrical supply house for what he needed.

"A beer and a shot," the portly stranger with bad teeth and a beard said to the man behind the bar.

The bartender said, "Coming up, mister. Anything with that?"

"Yeah. I'll have a steak and fries, medium on the steak."

The bartender said, "You looking for work? You don't sound like you're from around here."

"I'm from Canada, Quebec. You hiring?"

"Maybe," the bartender said. "Let me put in your order and get your drink."

The stranger lit a Du Maurier cigarette, made in Canada, named after the British actor Sir Gerald du Maurier. Only in New York City could he have found a carton so easily. He swiveled on the barstool and took in the crowd.

If someone was looking for talent to crew a job like a bank, this is where they would come. He was already making progress with the barman. He was sure he could come up with a whisper before the night was over.

The bartender returned with the customer's drink order and put it down on the bar.

"What kinda work you interested in, Quebec?"

"Crewing. And I don't mean on a boat."

"That's what I thought. There's a fella may be looking to replace a man he just lost on a job. It's risky business. You still interested?"

"Yeah, I am. Breaking my back for nickels and dimes is wearing thin."

"You available now?"

"Now ain't soon enough."

"Let me get your food and I'll give you a number to call."

The blond police detective told her partner, "We caught a break, Lou."

"What?" Louis Maraglia asked.

Detective Sandra James said, "You know Sidney Shapiro at Vice?"

"Of course, I know him. The biggest corn dog on the force. I'm surprised he hasn't knocked on your door yet, San. I'm pretty sure he wants to."

"I am not flattered. The detective has a thing for anyone in a skirt, Louis. He must have gotten

brain damaged in the war. But it comes in handy
when I need something."

Maraglia said, "What'd he give you?"

"You know those people over in Vice. They
live in a world of their own. Yesterday he put one of
his undercovers on the waterfront. In a single night,
this guy comes up with a name and a number."

"Who, San? Give."

"Montes met with a man, maybe a month ago.
A guy named Earl Jones. He's a dockworker, a union
man, but also a recruiter for certain operations. Well
respected. Everyone knows how they keep those
freight haulers demoralized in the morning count. He
gets them extra work so they don't starve to death.
Rumor has it he has run crews on armed robberies,
warehouse jobs, and armored car heists. Jones may
even have been in on the Brink's job a few years
back, over two million dollars."

"Interesting," Louis said. "Good work."

Sandra went on, "Like I said, one night
recently, for just a fraction of a second, Montes
crawled his pointy nose out from under a rock into
this place where a few hundred longshoremen blow
off steam every night, and he got spotted. He's a
Gypsy with a distinctive look. Someone noticed him
in the joint and the undercover found that person last
night. Anyway, the guy told the undercover that

Montes made his way to a small table where this burly guy, Earl Jones, was sitting alone, nursing a beer, waiting like. Short, stubby, tough as nails. They sat a bit, shook hands, Jones finished his beer, and they went out onto the pier to talk. In a million years who could get that lucky? Those guys on Vice have ESP, if you ask me."

Louis said, "You just watch out for Shapiro. He's a lech. He probably broke his neck to get that name for you, which he would not have done for me."

"So, now we have a name to help us track down Montes: Earl Jones. And we have a number to get in touch with him, which they traced to his mother's place. I got her address. Say what you want about Shapiro. I admire him for what he did in the war, and he's easy enough for a lady to manage. He's Jewish. Their mothers torture them into submission to women at an early age. I just have to swat him on the nose with a newspaper and he'll behave."

"Just don't turn your back on him, San, okay? And don't kill him either. Some men just can't control themselves. I wouldn't trust him around my own wife." Louis raised and lowered his eyebrows like Groucho Marx.

CHAPTER 23

ON THE HUNT

"A neighborhood in Washington Heights. It's a converted brownstone," Sandra told her partner.

When they were nearing the house, Detective James said, "I'll be the good cop, if you don't mind?"

"Aye, aye, Your Grace."

They climbed the outside steps to the entrance of what, a hundred years earlier, had been a luxurious, single wealthy family's brownstone. Sandra pushed the button to apartment number 3.

Over the intercom came the raspy voice of an older woman, "Yeah, who's there?" She sounded like a two-and-a-half-pack-a-day smoker.

Before replying, Sandra whispered to her partner a little too loud, "That's what you're going to sound like in a few years, Louis, if you don't stop smoking."

"I heard that," gasped the suspect's mother over the intercom.

"I'm sorry, Mrs. Jones, but my partner is trying to quit. My name is Detective Sandra James and I'm with the New York City Police Department."

"Whadya want, toots?"

"We're looking for your son, Earl. I'm with my partner, Detective Louis Maraglia. He's the one trying to stop smoking."

The foghorn voice blasted out of the speaker, "Earl's been good to me. Why should I help you find him if he don't wanna be found?"

"Mrs. Jones," Sandra James said. "Earl is in a lot of trouble. He could get hurt if he's not careful. Two men were killed during a bank robbery. We think Earl has knowledge of that crime. We're trying to help your son out here. We can only do that if we know where he is and can talk to him. Believe me, you don't want to irritate my partner. He's steamed about the men who were shot. I just want your son safely off the street and out of harm's way."

Louis spoke into the intercom in his gruffest, most official voice, "Mrs. Jones. We don't have much time. If you ever want to see your son alive again, you'd be smart to point us in his direction. A brick wall's about to collapse on his head. He's almost certainly gonna be killed by either a cop or one of the men he's running with, if we don't get to him first. Any way you look at it, it's gonna be ugly for him. Could be ugly dead or ugly alive. It's entirely up to you. Personally, I could care less which way you decide. My partner here is a bleeding heart. You ask me, your son is responsible for two men being killed. That's two widows, two mothers, and kids without fathers. So, you'll forgive me if I don't give a damn if you talk to us or not. Make the decision and make it quick. We have things to do."

Sandra roughly pushed her partner away from the intercom.

"Mrs. Jones, don't listen to this man. I was forced to partner up with this cold-blooded thug. Your son is still alive. I want him to stay that way. The man we think Earl is working for doesn't care about Earl. He'd just as soon they both go out in a blaze of gunfire. If you help us find him, there's a chance we can make a deal to keep him out of the electric chair."

"What's in it for you, honey? Why would you give a rat's backside what happens to a mangy dog like Earl? I think the two of you are hustling me."

Sandra came back, "We're just doing our job, Mrs. Jones. What's in it for me is that I get to go home, alive. If your son lives through this, that's all the better. I've seen enough killing for one lifetime and I'm only a young woman. I just want this over."

"Honey, you sound like a lying, thieving, no-good shyster. You need to take some time off to practice your act."

Louis stifled a burst of giggling and said, "We need Earl off the streets and out of our way, ma'am. It's nothing personal. With or without your help, Mrs. Jones, we're gonna get these guys and throw 'em all in the clink. We're not gonna stop until we get every last one of them. Anyone gets in our way is going to die. Just let us in and we'll talk. If you don't like what we have to say, you can tell us to go to hell and we'll be out of here, no hard feelings."

"You sound like a liar too, mister. I'm on the second landing. You know the number 'cause you rang the bell. Ten minutes, that's all you get from me. Then you're gone. Understand? There's a soap opera coming on the radio, and I am not gonna miss it for lying trash like the two of you."

The old woman buzzed them in.

They moved briskly up the stairs and stopped at the door with the 3 on it. Louis pushed the doorbell, but nothing happened.

"Doorbell's probably been busted for years."

He knocked.

They heard padded footsteps headed their way on the other side of the door.

The door swung open and there she stood. They could have drawn a picture before ever laying eyes on her. She had those big bouffant curlers in her hair. She wore a mangy pink bathrobe with bald spots, like an old bedspread, and matching slippers. There was a cigarette dangling from her inaccurately applied lipsticked mouth. Her breath smelled like a distillery, enough to raise the detectives' blood alcohol levels if they stood there long enough.

The old lady looked at her two visitors, scanned them up and down, and finally said, "C'mon in," with a throaty voice, punctuated by the hawking up of phlegm from deep within her chest.

Louis tried not to show disgust. He tipped his standard-issue gray brimmed detective fedora toward the apartment's resident and ambled past her, their fuzzy pink-slippered hostess in matching robe, standard NYC issue for old bats whose sons were serving long terms in Sing Sing. Sandra James closed the door behind them and followed her partner and the old woman down a dark corridor. They entered what Sandra guessed was supposed to be a living room. It was adorned with a torn overstuffed chair and a sofa, both pieces losing their upholstery through ripped seams. There was an old wooden dining table surrounded by six straight-backed chairs that might once have been a matched set but were no longer recognizable as a set due to multiple repairs— possibly from being broken over people's heads in fights, Sandra thought.

"Have a seat," Mrs. Jones offered with an echo of long-lost hospitality.

"You hear about the bank robbery on Wall Street?" Louis spoke gruffly in the tenor of a fellow smoker.

"Yeah, sure." Hawk, swallow. "Whadya think, I live on Mars?"

Sandra chimed in, "We think your son might have been involved in it. We just want to ask him a few questions, maybe keep him from getting into more trouble if he did have something to do with it."

Momma said, "He ain't been around lately."

"For God's sake, Mrs. Jones," Sandra said. "We canvassed the neighborhood. We're cops. That's what we do. He was seen coming out of this house yesterday."

"I forgot he was here."

Sandra rolled her eyes and continued, "Lying to the police is considered obstructing justice, you know. But we're not here to argue over minor details. We don't want to add to your worries. We're trying to save your son's life. People were killed during the robbery. That makes your son at least an accessory to first-degree murder. It's like he's guilty too. That makes him a threat to whoever did the killing. He's a loose end. Tell us where he is. Let him turn us down. Either way he decides, at least give him a chance to get on the right side of this. We can protect him."

"I don't know," she said, smoke blasting out of her nose and mouth, staccato, with her words.

"Geez. Jonesy, Jonesy," the old lady groaned. "What'd you go and do this time? I'm not a rat. Believe me, I am not a rat."

Maraglia said, "Then you might as well plan his funeral, because we're gonna mow him down if we have to."

"382 Delancey Street, not far from here. It's a house. Don't you tell him I gave that to you."

"Thank you, Mrs. Jones," said Louis. He looked at his watch. "Just in time for your soap opera. We'll be on our way."

"Don't you hurt my boy."

Lou replied, "We'll do our best not to. Just, please don't call and tell him we're coming. We don't want to have to kill him."

"Let's assume she called him. You take the front. I'll take the back," Maraglia said in hushed tones since they were close enough to be heard from within the small wood-sided house.

"Ready?" Louis whispered.

"Ready," Sandra whispered back.

Louis cut across the neighbor's lawn to get behind the house Earl Jones was supposedly holed up in. Sandra took a deep breath and let it out slowly to stay calm. She began her climb up the front steps to the porch. Her partner jogged steadily around to the back. She reached the front door.

Detective James pressed the doorbell. It rang. No movement could be heard coming from inside. She banged three times, heavily. Silence.

At last, a voice said, "Yeah. Who's there?"

"Police," Sandra shouted. "Open up."

"What do you want?" The voice got louder and closer, cautious.

"I am NYPD Detective Sandra James. I want to ask you a few questions about a robbery," she said.

The voice inside responded, "I don't know anything about no robbery. I just got here from out of town. Go away."

James said, "I'm not going anywhere, Mr. Jones. You might as well open the door. I have a warrant."

"All right. Just a second. I gotta put on some pants."

Sandra stood in front of the door waiting.

Blam! A bullet splintered its way through the door and entered Detective James's stomach. She dropped to the porch floor.

Gutshot, she thought. *I'm dying.* She knew she was going to bleed to death. She lay there as the seconds ticked by, feeling the blood pumping through the hole in her belly into her clothes. Lou came barreling through the front door from inside the house like a freight train. He looked down at his partner and protégé lying there, bleeding out. He pulled off his jacket and pressed it into her stomach.

"Hold this tight, Sandy. You're gonna be all right. I'm not waiting for an ambulance. I'm driving you to the hospital as fast as I can make it."

"What happened to Earl?" Sandra gurgled weakly, not believing Louis and certain she was dying.

"He shot you through the door, and if you didn't see him out here, he must've hid in the pantry when I ran through the house to see if you were all right. He's gotta be in the wind."

"He may have killed me, Lou. I'm sorry."

"No, he didn't, baby. Don't talk that way. Hang on."

Sandra was losing a lot of blood. She was getting weaker by the second.

Louis lifted Sandra James in his arms and ran down the steps of the house, then across the lawn to the car. He held the gas pedal to the floor for the whole ride, running red lights, causing accidents.

It was a radio-equipped unit, so he called to have Bellevue notified that they were en route. Cascades of horns sounded in their wake.

Bellevue Hospital was at First Avenue and East 26th Street.

It took ten minutes to get to the emergency entrance. A nurse and an orderly bounded out of the bay with a gurney. The nurse inserted an IV and let it run wide open as they moved into the building.

"Female police detective, thirties, with a gunshot wound to the abdomen," the nurse shouted to the supervisor and the emergency physician. "She's lost a lot of blood. Disoriented. Pulse two fifty and thready. Blood pressure seventy over fifty. I'm running Ringer's lactate wide open into a large bore IV, right arm. Legs are elevated. Starting second IV, left arm."

The doctor said, "Don't bother to type and crossmatch her. Start with O negative in both arms. Keep two more units on hand. Throw a heating blanket on her until I'm ready to operate. Draw a blood count and a chem panel, stat, and you can type and crossmatch that draw. I'll get Dr. Impresario to assist me in stopping the bleeding and running her bowel for holes, as soon as she's stable. There's an entrance and an exit wound, so the bullet is somewhere at the scene of the shooting, or in her clothes. Tell the police. Meanwhile let's do everything we can to keep her from going into shock. Blankets, nurse, then catheterize her to monitor her urine output."

The nurse attending Detective James acknowledged the doctor's orders.

"Right, Doctor. I'm getting the blankets. I'll draw the blood and catheterize her."

Turning toward Lou, the nurse said, "Sir?"

"I'm Detective Louis Maraglia, NYPD, her partner," he answered, nodding at the barely conscious Miss James. "I drove her here."

"Nice job, Detective. You probably saved her life by not waiting for an ambulance. I have some chores to attend to for the doctor, but they shouldn't take long. Then I'm going to ask you a bunch of questions. Is that okay?"

"Anything. Do what you gotta do. I'll do my best. I trained her. My wife and I are like her second set of parents."

"Stay right here. Use that telephone if you need to contact your fellow officers or her family. I'll be back shortly."

"Nurse," Lou said, alarmed. "She's gonna make it, right?"

"We'll do our best."

When he heard on the radio in his shop that Detective Sandra James had been shot, Thomas Laughlin was in a panic. Not knowing how bad it was, if she would live, made it worse. The guy on the radio said she was in critical condition. That wasn't good. She wasn't some mud-caked raw recruit dying on a Japanese island in the Pacific, but, to him, she might as well have been. It wasn't fair then and it wasn't fair now.

Oh God, he thought. *I only just met her. I don't want her to die. Please don't do this to me again. Haven't I suffered enough? I promise, if you let her live, I won't bother her. I won't try to be with her. In the fifteen years since Patsy died, I haven't even looked at another woman. So, help me, if a woman I feel something for dies again, I am going to check myself out. I gotta go see her in the hospital, before I do anything else.*

He called for a cab to Bellevue and locked his shop.

When he got to Information he was sweating, worried, trying not to confront caring this much about what happened to her, a woman he hardly knew.

"Detective Sandra James, please?" he asked the desk clerk.

"Room 319. It's that elevator." She pointed across the lobby.

"Thank you." He gave her a sickly smile.

Riding up in the elevator, he was nervous. Maybe the room would be empty, and she would still be in surgery. If she was dead, the woman downstairs would have known and told him.

319. He looked through the glass window in the door and saw her. She was awake, propped up in bed, IVs in her arms. She looked straight at him through the glass. He was a warrior, but he felt like crying because she was still alive. He couldn't remember crying over the death of his buddies in the war, and here Sandra James was still alive, and he was on the verge. His face flushed when she saw him. He forced himself to push the door open.

The blonde detective said, "Hello, Mr. Laughlin. How good of you to come check on me."

"Yes. It's good to see you too, awake and talking. I heard about the shooting and just wanted to make sure you were okay, that there's nothing I can get for you."

"How very thoughtful. They only did surgery to stop the bleeding and look around in there to make sure the bullet didn't puncture something important, which it didn't. It's all good. Still, they had to give me blood and put me on antibiotics. I'm fine, really."

"I, uh, was concerned. After all, I'm the one that gave you the name of the gang leader. I would never have forgiven myself if it was any worse. I'll uh, be going now."

"Please, Mr. Laughlin. This is what I do for a living. Nothing that happens in an investigation is ever the fault of a cooperating witness. Louis got me here in time to save me."

Thomas Laughlin said, "I only wish there was something else I could do. You're going to need a place, even just for a day or two, to recuperate. Someone to feed you and change your bandage. My son and I have an apartment above the store. You could stay in the bedroom and let us take care of you. He and I will share the living room like we do whenever we have company."

"That's very nice of you, but I don't want to put either of you out."

"Not at all. Are you kidding? Benjamin and I would be happy to do it."

"Okay, Detective James," Dr. Mortimer Peterson said. He was a general surgeon in his sixties. "You can get out of here as long as you have a place to stay and someone to look after you for a few days. There are some pain pills for you, antibiotics, and fresh bandages, so don't leave without them. Go easy on the pain pills. They'll constipate you. Keep taking the antibiotic until it's finished."

"That's it then, Doc? I can't thank you enough for patching me up. I was headed for the last roundup, and I would have made it if it hadn't been for you."

"It's very kind of you to say so, but it was your partner who saved your life. He used his jacket to slow the blood loss. He got you here like lightning. Now, Miss James, don't let anything push against your stomach, and no heavy lifting. I take it this strapping young man is going to attend to your needs?"

"Yes, doctor. He and his son have graciously invited me to stay with them for a day or two. Why they volunteered is beyond me. My Italian family was begging me to move in with them, like old times, which would have driven me around the bend. I'm gonna be a terrible patient and ungrateful as sin. This is Thomas Laughlin."

"Pleased to meet you, Mr. Laughlin."

"It's mutual, doctor," Laughlin said. "Thank you for helping my friend."

"Now, Detective James, please call me if you develop a fever or there's any bleeding or pus coming out of that wound. Or, for that matter, any pain that's not controlled by the pills I'm giving you. Otherwise drop by my office in a week so I can take a look at my work."

"You got it, Doc," Miss James said.

The doctor said, "Remember, the stitches are loose to allow drainage, so there will be some fluid and a little blood leaking into the dressing, but not a lot, so you may need to change the bandage several times these first few days. Any trouble, call my office. Bad trouble, just show up."

Laughlin shook the doctor's hand. "Thanks again, Doctor. I'll do the best I can on my end, if she lets me."

James smiled at the doctor, and a nurse helped her into a wheelchair and rolled her out of the room and down the hall to the elevator.

In the sole bedroom of the small apartment above the butcher shop, Benjamin put fresh linens on his dad's bed. He removed every object from the bathroom that was not screwed down and scrubbed the entire room from floor to ceiling, until it gleamed. He went to the grocery store and got bread, eggs, coffee, tuna fish, apples, sardines, toilet paper, canned vegetables, spaghetti, and spaghetti sauce. His father would bring meat up from his store. He was excited to have a guest staying over. She must be a good-looking woman from the way his father looked when he talked about her. His father was not a man who smiled easily, but something was affecting him, and Benjamin suspected this detective did not look like the principal of his high school, who was heavy and wore one-inch-thick glasses.

He took a bath and put on a white shirt with dress pants and was ready by the time his father got home with the detective.

At Laughlin's apartment, Sandra thanked father and son for their hospitality and said she wanted to go to bed and sleep. She had a headache and was still feeling weak from blood loss.

Benjamin was astonished at the sight of a police detective who was so beautiful. He would not mind being arrested by someone who looked like her.

Sandra awoke in the middle of the night feeling much better and went to the bathroom to take an antibiotic. In her drowsiness, not thinking, she opened the closed door without knocking and was confronted by the bullet-scarred back of Thomas

Laughlin, standing at the sink washing his hands. She winced.

"Oh geez, I'm sorry," Sandra said. "I forgot I wasn't in my own home, Mr. Laughlin. I'll come back."

"No, please. Don't worry. I'm finished. I'll leave you the bathroom. I'm glad to see you up and around. You look better."

He wiped his face and hands with a towel and passed her on his way out.

"Yes, I feel much better, thank you. Your back . . ."

"Yes, I'm sorry. I forgot you were even here, or I would've worn a T-shirt."

"No, not at all. It's your home. It's just that I didn't fully envision what happened to you in the war. I am filled with gratitude and admiration for your sacrifice. I don't want you to apologize. It just caught me by surprise. And, Mr. Laughlin, I am quite upset by how I teased you when you came to see me in the hospital. A man who's been through what you have deserves more respect than I have been giving you."

Thomas paused, then said, "Think nothing of it. You made me laugh. I haven't done much of that in recent years. I owe you. What you saw on my back nearly killed me. My buddy who I hardly ever see anymore, even though he lives here in Manhattan, carried me against my objections, for miles, over impossible terrain, to medical care. It is me who should be grateful. My hat is off to you. It's dangerous work that you do. You're surrounded by the threat of violence for the sake of a mostly ungrateful public, like me and Benjamin, every day. We're glad to help you. I'm going back to bed for another couple of hours. First though, I'm putting on a T-shirt. My mother taught me better manners."

She said, "See you in the morning. Please wake me when you guys get up."

In the morning Detective James awoke to the smell of coffee and bacon. She had hardly eaten for the past two days and was now starving. At breakfast Sandra and Thomas did their best to adjust to the awkwardness of having someone to eat with. Benjamin watched them with interest. He had never seen grown people behave like this. It reminded him of how he felt about that girl, Susan, who he kept staring at in school when she wasn't looking.

"You know," Sandra said to the father and son, "I'm feeling good enough to sleep in my own bed tomorrow night."

Benjamin and Thomas were disappointed at the thought of her leaving so soon.

The son said, "It's good you're staying another day, because we got extra food just for you."

Thomas said, "Yes, I'm glad you're staying another night. I like you being here. You need your bandage changed tomorrow before you leave. I can do that in the morning and then take you home."

"It's not that I don't appreciate your hospitality," she said. "For that I am very grateful. I just don't want our investigation to stall out. I wasn't lying when I talked to that old lady who led us to the guy that shot me. I told her if they plan to strike again, more people could die. Otherwise, I would love to be taken care of by you both for another couple of weeks."

Thomas said, "It's fun taking care of you."

She said, "I can take the subway up to the South Bronx. It's not that far. But if you insist, I'd be happy for your company. Meanwhile, bacon, eggs, toast, and coffee. What more could a girl ask for? What's for dinner?"

"Spaghetti and meatballs with some kind of vegetable," Ben said. "I hope you like it."

"I will, I promise. I guess it's settled. I would like to get out into the fresh air later. I don't play the part of the invalid very well."

"Excellent," Benjamin said.

CHAPTER 24

WORKOUT

5 a.m., kitchen of the New York City Police Department training facility, Manhattan

Detective Sandra James said, "It's early. I know. Get used to it. It's the best part of the day for training. I know you're aware that I just got out of the hospital, but, just as I'm not about to let my current investigation lose momentum, I want the three of you to get some techniques under your belt as soon as possible, so you can get started practicing. Most people are asleep at this hour. Not us. We got out of bed to train our bodies and our minds. You are going to do the things I show you today over and over at home, whenever you have a chance."

Sandra turned to the butcher's son.

"I know you wonder if this is going to change things in your life. I'm sorry to disappoint you, but it will not. School will be the same. Home will be the same. The only thing that will be different is you. We're going to make you smarter and stronger. The world will look a lot better to you, even though it hasn't changed. This is not going to be easy, Benjamin. I won't lie to you. But you're out of options. If you keep doing what you've been doing, you will flunk out of school and be forced to go on public assistance. You'll be doing manual labor, working long hours at a repetitive job for minimum pay, which will probably be taken away from you by ruthless men who make their living preying on the weak. If you're lucky, you can be the superintendent of a building, shovel coal into furnaces under boilers for steam and hot water, and take out cans of other people's garbage. Or you'll be eating in soup kitchens and getting torn-up old clothes from the Salvation Army. That won't be because you're not smart. It'll be because you gave up on yourself."

"My God, Detective. I was depressed before I got here. I might as well end it now."

"Do what I tell you, Benjamin. Keep your head down, like a boxer. In fact, take your father to the fights at Madison Square Garden and spend some time together studying the fighters' moves. There's

still a chance for you to straighten your life out.
You're going to let me help you, frankly because I
need the work to recover from being shot and almost
killed in the line of duty and to motivate me to get
back to my job. I want you to bring your schoolwork
with you next time we meet so I can see what you're
up against. I want you to show me your last report
card. If you don't want to end up digging ditches for
the rest of your life, which, don't get me wrong, I
have great respect for men who do such work. But
you have dreams that you will never realize at this
rate. If you don't want to end up with no options, then
you will have to get your grades up and get into
physical shape. I'll help you if you want me to."

"I do want you to, Detective. Believe me. I'm
tired of living this way."

She turned to Benjamin's father and said, "As
for you, Mr. Laughlin, I have friends on the police
force that were Marines in the war. I asked them
about their training. They told me they weren't taught
hand-to-hand combat. The closest they came was
bayonet-type fighting with pugil sticks, which I
looked up and they are padded on both ends. Fist
fighting was not an official part of your training, or
even wrestling. Pugil sticks are not exactly a weapon
of the streets, which is where you live now. Your
main weapon in battle was a thirty-caliber M1 Garand
rifle, right? It weighs exactly nine and a half pounds,

but they told me it feels more like thirty pounds, and neither is it a practical sidearm on the streets. Let's face it. You are headed for a reckoning with Mr. Montes. I suppose I am also. You own a Colt .45 automatic, Model 1911, which you will now clean and oil and train yourself to become proficient with again. You are going to take Benjamin with you to the gun range and teach him to break down that gun, clean and oil it, and shoot straight too. He's the son of a Marine, the bravest of the brave, for heaven's sake. He's about to learn how to fight and shoot. Then maybe some of your Marine pride will rub off on him, Pops."

Thomas Laughlin smiled. "You're killing me, Detective James. I'll take him to the range in the next couple of days. I'll go with him to the fights at Madison Square Garden and I'll train with him in your martial arts. Thank you. I mean it."

Sandra said, "You're welcome, Mr. Laughlin. One more thing, sir. I may have been treating you disrespectfully about fighting techniques, and I'm sorry about that. I apologize. I want you to know that I have the utmost gratitude and respect for your courage, for your valor in the war. I am very sorry for the loss of your wife, Benjamin's mother. I hope that the memory of her and the care you have for your son are the excuse you need to come out of your sadness. You recovered from your physical wounds a long time ago. Now it's time to get the rest of you back in shape."

"Agreed," Laughlin said.

Alice White just stood by and listened.

Sandra James said, "I'm going to give you each a set of tools. You have to practice them day and night for a while to make them second nature."

She focused again on the teenager. "Benjamin, we will get your grades up. Your father has given you the freedom to lay around, eat candy bars, get fat, and let life pass you by. It's not all his fault. That's what families do, mine included. I was groomed by my parents to become a housewife, defenseless, protected by some imaginary Italian husband in my future. My brothers stood in for Mister Right when I was too young to marry off. I would have ended up being a victim the rest of my life if I hadn't taken matters into my own hands, like you are doing right now. I learned to defend myself and demand respect when I was about your age too."

Sandra continued, "We're going to begin with diet. You will start each day with this nasty concoction on the counter in front of you. It's called a prairie oyster. Two raw eggs in a glass with tomato juice, Tabasco sauce, and Worcestershire. It's got vitamins and minerals the three of you must be deficient of. Take my word for it. Down the hatch."

They swallowed the mess whole.

Sandra said, "I brought you a rope, Alice, and one for the Laughlins. Jump it fifteen minutes, twice a day. Then road work, two miles in the early morning, weekdays at least. Time off for snow in the winter. Then sit-ups and push-ups, twenty of each, three sets in a row."

She led them out of the kitchen into a large workout area. It was a classic boxing gymnasium, only cleaner and better smelling. There were the usual assortment of speed bags, heavy bags, and a couple of elevated boxing rings. There were also areas with mats on the floor for grappling. There was a section of weight benches, weights, and shelves with dumbbells. A number of men and women were already working out.

A man who looked ex-military, in a white T-shirt and navy shorts, stood at relaxed attention waiting for the small group. Detective James smiled at him.

Sandra kept her voice down and told her three pupils, "Because of my recent injury, Fred here is going to help me teach you punches, kicks, elbow and knee strikes, and how to break someone's foot with your heel. You'll be surprised how fast you pick this up. But, first, the speed bag."

She led them to a series of hanging speed bags.

"Watch Fred."

Fred stood at a speed bag.

Sandra said, "Put your fists in front of your face, like his, and roll them over each other, like he is doing. It's smooth and steady, like a windmill. Moving, missing, it's all good. Just keep rolling your fists up and over. It just takes practice. You'll get back to this, but now, to the mat."

Fred demonstrated the moves, starting with the heel strike and working upward to the knee, elbow, backfist, and headbutt.

"It's more mental than physical. This lesson has done more than you know. Don't forget: practice, practice, practice."

CHAPTER 25

GONE

     In a matter of days, lowering his blood sugar and seriously working out, Benjamin lost visible pounds of fat. He was sore all over. He lay on the couch only to sleep. He did homework and studied two hours a day at the kitchen table. He bounced out of bed when the alarm went off. Jumped rope, did push-ups and sit-ups every morning. Shadowboxing, hooks, kicks, jabs, elbows, and heel strikes filled his spare time. Swallowing those awful raw eggs with Worcestershire sauce became something he looked forward to. His diet was different. Steak, eggs, cheese, orange juice, bacon, salad, and whole wheat toast were his staples. In school he sat near the front of the classroom with the smart kids and gave the

teachers his undivided attention. They noticed the
dramatic change in the formerly listless, and visibly
bored, youngster. Gone were the after-school sugar
gorges. He ran distances down the city streets, a little
faster and a little farther each day. His posture
straightened.

Thomas Laughlin had new respect and
affection for the boy he had raised from infancy as
almost a stranger. When Thomas got home at night,
they wrestled and practiced punching each other
without breaking anything. Thomas agreed to take
Benjamin to the shooting range and to the fights at
Madison Square Garden on Saturday night. He so
looked forward to them spending time together in a
common cause.

On the steps of a Manhattan brownstone sat a
man smoking a cigarette. He seemed perfectly at
home, taking in the balmy spring afternoon. The
man's gaze wandered up and down the street, and
occasionally up at the few clouds floating by in an
otherwise clear blue sky. It was one of a run of
beautiful days with hardly anyone around at this hour

to enjoy it. The man saw the teenage boy drop into the butcher shop to say hello to his father.

"Son, you look like a different kid altogether. I don't know about you, but I am sore all over. That woman is killing us."

"I'm in pain too, Dad, but I like it, and I like her too."

"Would you do me a favor before you go upstairs to study?"

"I'd be glad to. What do you need?"

"This package needs to be delivered to the Stanislavskis."

"Sure, Dad. It'll give me an excuse to do some running."

Thomas hit a key and the cash register drawer popped open to give his son change for a twenty-dollar bill, in case that's all they had.

Benjamin pocketed the change, put his books in the back, and picked up the package wrapped in brown paper, tied with white string.

"Thanks, Benjamin. It's not far. It shouldn't take but half an hour round trip, less if you're going to run it."

The teenager started at an easy jog up the sidewalk.

The man on the stoop across the street stood up and flicked his cigarette into the gutter. Then he began walking at a brisk clip along the opposite side of the street, keeping pace with the boy.

Two hours later, the butcher called the Stanislavskis.

"No, Mr. Laughlin. Young Benjamin has not gotten here with our order," the missus told him.

"Okay, Mrs. S., would you please give me a call when he does arrive? He left two hours ago."

"Oh my."

"Yes. I'm concerned."

He hung up.

The butcher's CLOSED sign faced the street. Thomas Laughlin sat inside, in the dark, on a stool, hoping for a call from somebody, anybody to tell him where his son was and how much it would cost to get him back. It was now the middle of the night.

Finally, the wall phone rang.

"Hello," Laughlin said into the receiver.

"This the butcher?" grunted a man's voice Laughlin didn't recognize.

"Yes, it is. Who is this?"

"Never mind who it is. I want to talk to you about getting your kid back in one piece."

"If you touch a hair on his head, your life is over. Let him go now and I will let you live. What is it you think I'm gonna give you to get him back?"

"We don't want money. We just need a little time and we'll give him back to you. We need him as a hostage," the man said.

"Put him on the phone."

"Dad, I'm okay," was all Benjamin could say before he was cut off.

"You satisfied?"

"You're telling me I'm supposed to take your word that you won't kill him when you're done with whatever you're planning to do?" Laughlin said.

The voice replied, "Yes, that's right. It won't be long, mister. I promise. You don't have much choice but think about it. I'm not looking to have you hunting me for the rest of my life, so I'll keep him safe. Tell the cops we're taking good care of him. We got too much trouble already, if you haven't heard. We'll treat him good and give him back in no time, unharmed. You don't have to do anything, but it would help if you got that lady cop who got shot to slow down. We'll be out of her way quick enough. Don't tell me she won't do this favor for you. She's a fox and she stayed over with you."

"That's because you shot her, you moron. She hates me. She'll never let up on hunting you down."

"Not even for your boy?"

"She dislikes the boy even more than she does me."

"You are such a bad liar. A woman who looks like that stays over a man's house, you kidding me? Forget her. She'll never find us anyway. Let her knock herself out. Just tell her we have the kid and he's all right, and we'll bring him back real soon." *Click.*

It was the early hours of morning. Laughlin made the call anyway.

Forty minutes later the blond police detective was down from the Bronx, standing in his doorway wearing dungarees and a T-shirt with a kerchief tied around her forehead. Thomas hadn't closed his eyes since Benjamin disappeared.

The serious expression on the blonde's face made him wonder if he would ever see his son alive again. An oversized purse hung from her arm.

He said, "We can sit and talk. You want some coffee?"

She nodded yes and watched him carefully. She had seen the bullet holes in his back. From the moment she met him she was taken by the sadness in his eyes. Most women would have wanted to nurse him, that or turn away in pity. Her, it made her angry. Some of her anger was at him for letting himself fall apart like this. Some was at what life had done to him. His wife dying. The war almost killing him. This was a trained United States Marine and a veteran of a long, maybe the longest, most atrocious battle in the Pacific, maybe even in the history of war. He had been beaten up, honorably discharged, and dropped on the sidewalk in New York to make a living and raise a child by himself. She didn't regret agreeing to help train him and his son, and even goading him into getting into shape. But it was getting complicated. The bank robbers were using Benjamin as a hostage, probably for another job. She had done what she could for the father and son. She would help him get the kid back, but, after that, she was done with them. They were on their own. She had to cut them loose.

The father needed to find a woman who could shake him out of his fog and be a mother to the boy. She was a police officer, a barbarian, definitely not up to the task. This guy and his son were about to drive her around the bend as it was.

Laughlin handed her a cup of coffee. He said, "Thank you for coming all the way down here from the Bronx. You're busy, and you've been shot. I'm sorry I bothered you. We could've done this on the telephone."

Sandra said, "You sounded upset. Anyone would be. Besides that, I need my dressing changed and you couldn't have done that on the phone."

He said, "I told you, they have Benjamin. They want you and your partner to slow down the investigation and buy them time. I told them you hated me and you hated my son even more. Whoever it was on the phone said he didn't believe me. They're only using him as a hostage and, he said, they'd give him back very soon."

Sandra James said, "It sounds like they're planning something else. They're going to use Benjamin as a human shield."

She did a double take and smiled at him. It went to his stomach despite the fact that Benjamin was still out there, in danger.

"You told them I hated you? And I hated Benjamin more? That is so funny. A valiant effort he saw right through."

Laughlin said, "I couldn't think of anything else to say. His exact words were, 'You are such a bad liar.'"

"You make me laugh."

"I didn't want to dare them to kill him. I would never have lived with the guilt if they did it. What're we gonna do?"

"We're going to find them, kill them, and get Benjamin back."

"How can you be so sure?"

"Because I know who you are and what Benjamin is made of. And I know they aren't very bright. I'm a cop. You'll see."

"I'm glad you think so. What's in the enormous purse?"

"Bandages, what else? I'll be glad to be done with this hole in my stomach."

He took the bag from her.

"Lie down on the bed," he instructed her. "And lift up your blouse and lower your pants a little."

He flushed.

"I mean the outside pants, not your underwear, so I can get to the bandage."

She smiled at him again. He tried to ignore it. Benjamin's life was at stake. This was not the time.

"I know which pants you mean."

She lay down, unbuttoned her slacks, pushed them down a couple of inches, and raised her blouse so he could see the bandage.

"I'm gonna tear the tape off. It might hurt."

"I'm used to pain. Do it."

He ripped the bandage off and looked at the wound, which appeared to be knitting well. The bandage was damp, but there was no blood on it.

Thomas said, "The wound looks like it's healing well."

"Good."

"I want to do something to get my son back. You can't expect me to sit by the phone and wait."

"Please, Mr. Laughlin. Don't do anything stupid. At least let me know when you come up with a plan so I can advise you and even come along if you'll let me."

"I might end up breaking the law. I don't want to ruin your life, get you thrown off the police force."

"I can't speak for my partner, Louis, but I'll risk it. Yes, we'll work around the law, if we have to, to get your boy back."

Thomas looked down at the uncovered wound in her stomach. She could've died. He'd changed her bandage before when she was fresh out of surgery. This time he felt guilty. The redness was mostly gone, and her bare skin made him want to press his face into it, but Benjamin was somewhere in mortal danger, maybe afraid. He shook it off.

He said, "The wound looks clean. The bandage was a little damp is all."

"I showered before I headed over here. That's why I brought new bandages. You don't think I would have made this trip just for Benjamin, who, you told them, I hate, do you?"

Thomas smiled.

He said, "I'm sorry about hurting you yanking the tape off like that."

She said, "Think nothing of it. I'll take it out on you after we find Benjamin. I'm gonna make both of you run extra miles. What do you have in mind to get Benjamin back?"

Thomas said, "I have war buddies here in Manhattan. They would both willingly die to save my son, so I'll start with them."

"Please promise to call me so I can break the law with you?"

"Yes. I promise."

CHAPTER 26

CAPTIVITY

Half the space of the room Benjamin was locked in was taken by the cot he slept on. If it weren't for the window high on the wall, he wouldn't know if it was day or night. He had no clue where he was. An old lady who smelled like cigarettes and coffee was his only human contact. She brought him a crossword book, a couple of pencils, and the only Perry Mason paperback she could find, *The Case of the Howling Dog*.

"Did you feed the kid?" Christos Montes asked the woman. Her arms were crossed.

She removed the burning cigarette from her mouth and said, "Not yet."

He told her, "Make sure he goes to the bathroom. Get him whatever he wants, so he doesn't go crazy locked up with no place to go. We won't be here long."

She replied, "He's not like any kid I ever seen. He was in there doing his exercises on the floor all day yesterday. It's like he's doin' time in the penitentiary. Strange boy."

Christos Montes said, "He's like me. He doesn't need parents. His mother's dead. His father's a broken-down old soldier. He might as well be alone on this earth."

She asked him, "What're you still doin' here? Never mind. The longer you stay, the more I get paid. Forget I asked. I don't want to know nothin' about you or the kid. Nobody would use me if I started nosing into customers' business."

Christos Montes said, "Yes, I am paying you enough, that is for sure. You're a real jewel for taking care of the kid."

"It's my job. If you want a way to deal with being stuck here, I could get you some heroin."

"I'm not gonna stay here that long. There's one more thing I got to do, then I'm gonna blow this town forever. I'm not lookin' to become a junkie before I do."

"It's all good to me. I done this a long while, kiddo. I'll help you best I can. I'll even help you bury the boy if it comes to that."

"Are you married?"

"Why do you ask, honey? You in the mood?"

"Just making conversation."

"That's awright, sonny. I ain't a very nice woman to look at. I know. I's just havin' a little fun with ya. No offense. No, I ain't married."

"I gotta get some shuteye. God knows there's not gonna be much rest for me in a little while. Go on, take care of the kid. I got men I'm gonna want you to get in touch with later."

She said, "Okay, I'm goin'. I'll be back with food and stuff for the kid in an hour. I'll see if he has to use the bathroom before I leave. Anything you want? Sandwich, candy, magazines?"

"Can you cook me a steak?"

"No, I can't. No stove, but I can bring you a roast beef sandwich, soda, some French fries."

"Yeah, that'll do 'er. The kid's locked up tight, right? He's not gonna get away from you? I can't afford to lose him."

"He's locked up tight. I don't even let him use the bathroom, 'cause there's a window in there, and a fire escape. I give him a pail and some privacy. As far as him getting the best of me, he has no idea how strong I am."

In the 1800s the poet Edgar Allan Poe and his wife, Virginia, rented a white farmhouse in the Bronx, at Kingsbridge Road and Valentine Avenue. They lived there for three years. After he died, the house was moved to the Grand Concourse not far from its original location. It became known as Poe Cottage, in the middle of a little plot of land they named Poe Park. In the 1950s, young people hung out there in the afternoon after school. At night they sat on the benches munching White Castle hamburgers, a dime a dozen. Into the late evenings, the cigarette smoking and radio playing quieted down until the place was empty. At midnight it was usually deserted.

Harry Walker from Brooklyn, bodyguard, dockworker, muscle for hire, six feet tall, two hundred forty pounds, sat smoking a Lucky Strike cigarette down to its last few shreds of tobacco. Frank Watts, brother of the late Arty Watts, who was killed by the Wall Street bank executive, sat talking with Harry.

Harry said, "It's more than a week since we pulled that job on Wall Street. We lost your brother, poor Arty. I'm sorry. With all due respect for this Gypsy, Montes, I'm tired of hanging around here in the Bronx. My family's over in Brooklyn. I'm tempted to take the D train down there to visit them, but Earl said not to move. I don't know how a right guy like Earl Jones could hook up with a man like Montes. I'm getting tired of eating these black hamburgers. They're giving me gas."

"Phew, I'll say." Frank moved farther down the bench.

It was after midnight. They were sitting in the dim light from the Grand Concourse, a few blocks north of Fordham Road in Poe Park. Poe Cottage looked forlorn, tiny, and empty at their backs. It all just served to depress them more that they could not get out of New York City. Harry had his take from the bank. Frank got his brother's share on condition that he came along in his brother's place on this next job just a few days from now. At this hour, only an occasional car and an almost empty Concourse bus spewing black exhaust passed by.

Walker said, "We're sitting here just to get out of that crappy little apartment the Gypsy got us. We might as well be in lockup. I thought this was only gonna be one job and we'd be gone outta here. The Gypsy is a strange bird. He said he'd pay extra for the time, but I'm beginning to think it's not worth it. I feel like a sitting duck. We get caught here it's prison or the chair. I'll be glad when this is over."

Frank Watts said, "I'll be glad if we live through whatever he's got planned. He don't seem to know exactly what he's doin'. He got my brother killed. I'm thinking this next'll be another Friday morning job. Better get back to the apartment so we don't miss the call."

CHAPTER 27

EARRINGS

"Hello, Mr. Laughlin," Detective Sandra James said to her new martial arts protégé.

"Tell me you located Benjamin and he's all right," Laughlin said.

The detective responded, "It's not about Benjamin that I'm calling."

"So, what are you calling about?"

"Mr. Laughlin, I hate to be the bearer of bad news."

"What else could possibly go wrong?"

Detective James said, "An anonymous call was made to the department saying that you were the mastermind of the Wall Street bank robbery. The caller said we would find proof in your apartment. Men should be arriving at your door right about now."

Laughlin said, "I see them through the store window. What are they supposed to find in my apartment?"

"I don't know, they wouldn't say, but this is definitely not the time for you to go breaking any laws. You'd be playing right into their hands. Give them the key when they ask you for it and stay in your store. You just sit tight and let the officers do their job. Louis and I will be right along."

Baby Emily Applewood Bennett was propped up in a woven basket stuffed with blankets in the middle of the kitchen table. For the moment she was calm and contented, making verbal noises and reaching out her pudgy arms toward her mother, who was rolling out dough on the kitchen counter. Elaine pressed the rim of a glass into the dough to make biscuits for Andy Bennett's breakfast. Coffee was perking on the stovetop. The oven was at temperature, so she opened it, popped the biscuits in, shut the door, and set the timer.

"I'm home," Detective Andrew Bennett announced to his wife and baby.

Elaine raised her smiling face to her husband for a kiss. Flour was smudged on the tip of her nose. Emily reached out toward her daddy, her eyes shining, breaking his heart with her affection.

"How are my beautiful girls?"

Elaine said, "Fine. I just put biscuits in the oven for you. You'll smell them in a minute. They'll be ready to devour in a little bit. How was your meeting?"

Andy said, "Just fine. Same awful coffee. Someone brought a box of several-days-old donuts. I couldn't bring myself to have one. Now I'm glad I didn't. It's nice that you baked. As usual, the place was thick with cigarette smoke. Half the people there are replacing alcohol with cigarettes."

He walked over to the baby in her padded basket and kissed her on the forehead. She smiled and gurgled at him.

"She knows me. I think she almost said 'daddy.' She's the smartest baby I've ever seen. I'm gonna be outnumbered by the two of you."

"Pour yourself some coffee and I'll scramble you up some eggs to go with the biscuits. There's butter in the fridge. Alice dropped by to bring me a quart of milk from the store."

"Really? How nice of her. And how is Miss White doing? Is she recovering from her brush with death at the bank?"

"Andrew, I can tell when you're being sarcastic. You know how much I don't like sarcasm. She's my friend. She's a good girl. She's just a little high-strung."

"Oh, that is just begging for sarcasm, but I'm not gonna touch it," Andrew said and smiled broadly. "That's exactly what she is. She's 'high-strung.'"

"Honey, now, don't work yourself into a lather about her."

"Elaine, so what did you talk to her about? You remember, don't you, that I asked you never to discuss anything besides the weather with that woman without a lawyer and a psychiatrist present?"

"Andrew. What did I just say about sarcasm? You have no self-control."

"Okay. I'm sorry. It slipped out. You talked about the bank robbery, no doubt."

"Yes, we did."

"She wants something from me."

"Not really. She knows you're not officially on the case but was hoping you would keep an eye on it."

"I heard some news about it today," Andy said. "The gang that robbed the bank claims the butcher planned it. An anonymous caller tipped the department that there was hidden booty in his place. They searched it and, sure enough, found a ridiculously expensive pair of earrings some rich guy had made for his wife for their anniversary. She stored them in a safe-deposit box in the vault that was robbed. They found them hidden in his closet."

"That's exactly what Alice told me. The butcher identified the leader to the detectives. What do you think, Andy?"

He said, "I don't believe a word what this anonymous caller said. Alice and the butcher were there by pure chance. This sounds more like revenge. It's also kind of clever, sending the police on a wild-goose chase. This may even get the butcher charged with a crime."

Elaine said, "Alice wants to help the man. She can't represent him yet because she hasn't passed the Bar and she's not licensed, but she sweet-talked the lawyers in her firm into taking his case."

"You women are difficult to refuse when you're meddling in other people's business."

"Andrew, I have a soft spot for her meddling. She tried to save Emily's father, Harry. She was worried about me and kept at me until I admitted he was in trouble. She risked her life to save him."

He said, "I love to pretend she annoys me. I know she's a good person. The anonymous caller said the butcher forced the Gypsy to lead the robbery, that the Gypsy was the real victim."

"Andy, do you believe that?"

Bennett said, "No. I don't believe any of it. The caller said that the Gypsy kidnapped the kid as insurance against being killed by Laughlin. He says the butcher is a psycho and can't be trusted. You gotta admit it's almost convincing."

Elaine said, "I'm so glad that you and Alice are on the same side in this."

Andrew said, "My friend Sid Shapiro helped the detectives locate the gang leader's straw boss, but he escaped. He shot one of the detectives when they came looking for him."

Elaine said, "Alice says the butcher is a war hero. He fought in the Pacific, on Iwo Jima, of all the terrible places. He's just like Detective Shapiro with his medal. Alice told me she thought that Detective Shapiro was going out of his way to help the butcher because of that."

Andrew said, "Actually, this is getting interesting. You're a good influence on me, Elaine. I'll give my friend at Vice a call, see if I can help."

"Andy, that makes me very happy, only please be careful."

"Sidney, I hear you helped out the detectives on the Wall Street bank case," Bennett said.

"I suppose you could say I did, if you call getting one of them shot and almost killed helping them. I sort of did them a favor and got a lead on one of the gang members."

Bennett said, "My neighbor, the notorious Alice White, wants us to help the butcher get his son back and, while we're at it, maybe get him out of the frame he's in for the bank job."

"I'm willing to do anything. My undercovers have all the fun."

"Sid, you claim to be a coward who accidentally won a Congressional Medal of Honor, but I find that hard to believe. Alice doesn't always succeed at what she sets out to do. Elaine's late husband died when Alice was trying to help him. She thinks the butcher is about to reach his breaking point and take the law into his own hands, maybe go out guns blazing trying to free his kidnapped son."

Sidney Shapiro said, "Yeah, I heard his kid was taken. Guess who's got the scent on the robbery? Angelo "the Angel of Darkness" Mancuso. He's gonna want to nail the butcher, even with such pathetic circumstantial evidence. Yes, Andy, I want to stop this foolishness and get the kid back. But I'm single. You have a wife and a kid."

"My wife knows the risks. In fact, she encouraged me to stick my nose in this."

Shapiro said, "The butcher and me were both whatever, heroes I guess, in the war, Andy. I was the big celebrity, but all I did was shoot one Nazi officer. Laughlin was on Iwo Jima. He went through the torments of hell every day for over a month. I don't even know the guy, but I can tell you this about him. He's depressed, he's afraid, and he's angry. This may be more than he can take without breaking. He's gotta still have his .45 auto. Heck, I'm practically a pacifist and I do. I clean and oil mine too. I could be him, Andy. Tell the detectives on the robbery, and Alice White, to keep me in the loop."

CHAPTER 28

LOUIS MARAGLIA

Detective Sandra James was back on the job just days after she'd been shot. The man who shot her, Earl Jones, was still at large. Young Benjamin, her new student, the butcher's son, was still being held hostage, God knew where. Time was not on their side. These guys were either gonna get off scot-free or pull another job and, maybe, kill more people. It seemed that she and her partner, Louis Maraglia, could not catch a break.

Louis told his partner, "They're here, in New York City. We need to get a bead on what they're still doing here. It would help if we knew where exactly they were."

Sandra said, "The obvious reason is another job. These are killers, Louis. They almost killed me. I need them. I want them. Let's be careful. There are some neighborhoods I'd like to check, residential, but close to the bank."

The "wifebeater" became the popular nickname for a man's athletic undershirt in 1947. A picture appeared on the front page of a Detroit newspaper showing a man in an A-undershirt who had just beaten his wife to death.

A disheveled gentleman stood in the doorway of his un-luxurious Manhattan apartment wearing such a shirt. It was a sixth story walk-up, and this was the top, referred to laughingly by residents as "the penthouse." Sandra just about burst a gut making the climb. The man stood in the wreckage of what had once been a high-rent building. The paint was now peeling off the hallway walls. He looked at the two detectives with brazen contempt. Slovenly, unshaven, the man looked every inch a wifebeater. He stood there with his hands on his hips just begging for a broken jaw, Sandra thought.

The attractive blond police detective was gripped by the urge to inflict bodily harm on the man but thought better of it. She brushed it off as back-to-work jitters every cop experiences from time to time. Instead, she bent forward and put her hands on her knees to calm down and catch her breath.

"What can I do for you?" the man asked.

Detective James smelled beer on his breath and wondered what he did for a living. Hopefully he did not split diamonds. She raised her head and looked at him.

Finally able to speak, she said, "My partner here and I are canvassing the neighborhood, looking for anyone who saw anything the morning of the bank robbery on Wall Street."

"How's that going for ya?" he asked sarcastically.

She envisioned a hard left elbow to his nose and the satisfying crunch of bone and cartilage versus a kick to the groin. With the utmost restraint, she responded, "Not at all well, sir. You could help a great deal if you would just answer my questions. Did you see anyone the Friday morning of the robbery? Maybe notice masked men with guns driving by, one of them tall and skinny?"

Even a thoughtless twit such as this man could sense an explosion, rumbling in the distance, headed his way. He did not want any such trouble. He was taller than her, but she was in fifty times better condition to tear him apart. He was already in the doghouse with his wife for not taking out the garbage. He imagined his bloodied corpse on the hallway floor, so he did a 180, stood up straighter, and spoke more politely. "No, ma'am. Sorry to say, I did not."

"Okay," she said, pleased with his attitude adjustment.

He said, "Nothing like that. I wish I had."

Detective James said, "What is it you do for a living, Mr. uh . . . ?"

"Bus driver. Name's Haggerty. James Haggerty, but they call me Jim. And I didn't mean no disrespect."

Detective Louis Maraglia spoke for the first time. "I'm curious, Jim. How did you know you were in trouble with the detective? I have to guess the nearness of death has a way of waking a person up."

The man did not answer. He just gave Louis the hint of a grin, in acknowledgement that he had just dodged a bullet he didn't see coming.

Sandra said, "I forgive you, Mr. Haggerty. You think of anything or hear anything, please give us a call. Here's our card."

The man looked at the card and said, "Sure thing."

He smiled pleasantly. She turned and walked the few feet to the next apartment.

Out on the street again, Sandra said to Louis, "That was a complete waste of time."

Louis said, "Let's get some coffee. How's your stomach?"

"The wound is healing good. The pain isn't so bad. I keep thinking, if the bullet had gone a few inches in any direction, it could've been a lot worse. Thanks for saving my life, partner."

"Think nothing of it. I gotta lose some weight. If it had been reversed and I was the one who got shot, I would'a bled to death 'cause you could never have carried me to the car. I think we've had enough for your first day back. What do you want to do?"

"I want to go visit the old bag who claims to have given birth to Earl Jones. Looking at her, it's hard for me to believe that some man lent himself to that process. You never know. She might have been a fabulous beauty for a few minutes in her youth, before the ravages of smoking, drinking, and not giving a crap about her fellow human beings set in. Anyway, who am I to pass judgment on anyone?"

They went to a luncheonette. While Sandra was changing her bandage in the bathroom, Louis ordered two cups of coffee with cream and sugar.

"You again," the old lady groaned over the speaker. "Earl ain't talkin' to his mom anymore thanks to the two of you. You should be ashamed of yourself, coming between a mother and her child like that."

"Mrs. Jones," Sandra said. "Given that your son shot and almost killed me I think we can safely say that your family dynamic is the last thing you want to be talking to me about. You called ahead to warn him we were coming, didn't you? Right after we told you not to. You did it anyway. You know, Earl could've gotten himself killed because of you just as easily as he shot me. Do you have any idea where he is now? Chances are, sooner or later, your precious baby boy, Earl, is gonna die in a hail of bullets or fry in the electric chair. I'm sure he's not that bad a man from a mother's point of view, but I'm too busy trying to stay alive in my job to give a damn. Why don't you do Earl and yourself a favor and tell us where he is. This time, try not warning him in advance so you give him at least a chance of surviving, because I will kill him if I have to."

The old woman gave them a neighborhood. She swore that was all she had. Thanks to them, she said, Earl couldn't trust his own mother with the address.

Detectives Sandra James and Louis Maraglia climbed the stairs to the front porch of a wood-sided house. Sandra rang the doorbell and they both stepped aside, out of the line of fire, in case somebody fired a shot through the door. Neither of them was going to catch a bullet that way again.

Chimes sounded inside, a stately, substantial sound. No gunshots rang out. A white-haired woman, maybe in her sixties, in a kitchen apron, answered the door.

"Yes. Can I help you?" she asked.

Sandra slid over to the center of the doorway, showed her badge, and said, "I am Detective Sandra James of the New York City Police Department. This is my partner, Detective Louis Maraglia. We are going door to door to see if anyone saw or heard anything related to the bank robbery on Wall Street.

In particular, have you noticed any suspicious characters or new arrivals in your neighborhood?"

"Please come in. You both look exhausted. You caught me baking bread. I see you both have coffee, but there's a fresh pot on the stove. Why don't you let me dump yours out and pour you some refills?"

Louis spoke up, "That's very nice of you. I don't mind if I do." They followed the woman in and handed her their cardboard cups.

They sat at the dining room table. The woman detoured with their coffees and replaced them with ceramic cups filled with a strong brew.

"My name is Helen Forrester, Detectives. I'll try to be as helpful as I can."

Sandra said, "Thank you for that, Helen. Do you live alone?"

"No. I'm a widow, but I have a boarder. She's not home right now. Her name is Mary Beth Perkins, a nice girl going to school at NYU, undergraduate. I put the room up on a bulletin board at the college.

"I heard about the bank robbery, and, in answer to your question, yes, there has been a new resident in the house right next door, a man."

"What does he look like, Mrs. Forrester?" Louis asked.

"He's medium height, big around the middle. He seems nice enough. Looks like he can do some heavy lifting, like a longshoreman. He only just showed up in the last week. Does he sound like someone you're looking for?"

"Maybe," Sandra said, her pulse quickening.

The woman said, "My husband was a police officer, Joe Forrester. Does that ring a bell?"

"Yes, it does. I knew him," Sandra said. "Your husband was at a number of crime scenes I was called to. I heard he was shot in that big jewelry store robbery last year. What a nice guy he was. I'm sorry for your loss."

"Me too, and I'm sorry I can't help you more with your investigation. I heard a bank executive was killed."

"Detective James," Louis said with some urgency in his tone. "We have to be on our way. Thank you again, Mrs. Forrester, for your hospitality."

Louis and Sandra swallowed down some of their coffees then set them on the table. "Here's our card." He handed the woman one from his pocket.

"I'll keep my ears and eyes open," Mrs. Forrester said.

Louis said to their host, "I'd like to ask you to stay indoors for a few hours. As a policeman's widow, I think you will know when it's okay to come out. Am I making myself clear?"

"Yes, you are. I will stay put until this is over."

"And stay away from your windows," Louis added.

On their way down the front steps, they agreed to call for backup before going anywhere near the house next door.

Six uniformed police officers gathered out of sight of the suspected residence of Earl Jones, the house next door to Helen Forrester. The owner of the house was contacted and gave the name of the current renter as Arthur Price, in his thirties, hefty of build, gave his occupation as a sign painter, very polite. There were no photographs, but the best guess was that Arthur Price was Earl Jones and they weren't taking any chances of another police officer being shot by him.

Louis Maraglia said to the assembled officers, "Watch yourself. You know the drill. On my count."

Thud, crash, pop, the sound of boots on the floor. Inside, Sandra had gone left, Louis right.

Louis yelled, "Police officers. Put your hands where we can see them."

Then the single exploding sound of a bullet leaving a weapon and all hell broke loose. What seemed like hundreds of shots were fired.

The man, Earl Jones, was literally shot to pieces and lay dying in a puddle of his own blood on the kitchen floor.

Earl whispered, "Tell Ma I said goodbye. I had this coming and I'm not afraid of dying. She raised me the best she could. And you coppers ain't worth a damn, with all due respect."

He stopped talking. His breathing stopped. He lay still.

"Officer down!" the shout came from the living room in a straight line with the kitchen door. "Oh God," the voice yelled. "It's Louis. It's Maraglia. Louis, stay with me. Somebody call an ambulance."

Sandra James plunged into the living room toward her partner. "You hang in there, Louis, dammit. Don't you go anywhere. They're coming to get you. An ambulance is on its way."

She could hear an officer talking to the hospital on the telephone.

"I think I bought the farm, San," Louis told his partner in a whisper. "I knocked on one door too many. Do me a favor and nail them bastards. Make me proud. Tell Annie I love her."

"Don't you die, you son of a bitch. Please, Lou. Don't leave me. I need you. You saved my life, made me into a cop. Please. I'd be lost without you. You can't go."

Louis gurgled, "San, San. It's not like we'll never see each other again. We'll meet up, I promise. You have what it takes. You're going places. Exactly where I could never figure out, but you're gonna find what you're looking for. You don't need me anymore, sweetheart. I love you too."

He lay still. Eyes open, but empty. Tears streamed down Sandra's face. She kissed him on the cheek.

One of the other officers gave her a handkerchief, put his hand on her shoulder, and felt her sobs and her pain.

CHAPTER 29

SANDRA

Laughlin heard it on the radio, closed his shop, and hightailed it to the neighborhood the anchorman said the police were at. It wasn't hard to spot the crowd of cop cars parked at angles, blue uniforms, and ambulances with flashing lights.

He approached slowly, feeling the terrible tension in the air and not wanting to impose on the personal tragedy that had just occurred to every man and woman on the site. He walked gingerly to a spot close enough to see Detective Sandra James without distracting her from her grief and the camaraderie he too had felt when one of his fellows had died in combat. Sandra looked up, saw him, and managed a slight, sad smile, but immediately turned back to her colleagues on the force. They needed comforting also and reassurance that she was all right. Thomas looked around on the ground and saw what must have been the covered bodies of her partner and the outlaw, Earl Jones, who they had identified on the radio. A bare-headed, bookish man with a square name badge on his jacket that Thomas couldn't read must have been the medical examiner. The official moved slowly and patiently so as not to disturb the site or the solemnity of loss and bitterness surrounding the job most of these people did, all day, every day, for a living.

After they carted the bodies away, Sandra came over to Laughlin and said, "Take me to a telephone, Thomas, please."

They walked the blocks to his shop in silence. It was a hike. He could've gotten a cab, but he knew she needed time to gather her thoughts, so he didn't speak. When they arrived at his business he took her around back, left the CLOSED sign in the window, then pointed at the wall phone.

"Are you going to be all right?" he asked her.

"I'm not sure if I'm ever going to be all right, Thomas. Louis was my second father, my second family. He looked after me on behalf of my parents and my brothers. You know, he just saved my life."

"The front door is locked. Here's a stool to sit on. There's a crate I sit on in the alley behind the store. That's where I'll be. Do you want a cigarette?"

"Yes."

"Something told me to get a pack on my way to see how you were. In the war these were the times I found myself smoking the most. I picked up a pack of Pall Malls, long, unfiltered, harsh."

He tapped the pack until a cigarette protruded, and when she took it and put it in her mouth, he fished some paper matches out of his pocket, scraped one against the striker, and lit her up. As an afterthought he tapped one out for himself and lit it too.

"Come get me when you're done with the phone."

"That'd be good," she said. "Thank you."

Laughlin walked out the back of the store to the alley and closed the door behind him. He sat down on the crate and leaned up against the side of the building. He took a deep drag on the cigarette and tried not to think of what Sandra James must be feeling, but he couldn't help himself. Tears came to his eyes. He cried over all the life he had seen lost and felt pity for Sandra James, and for himself.

When Sandra was done with the long, tearful phone calls, she came and found Laughlin.

"I called Louis's wife, Annie. How will she ever live without Louis? How will I ever live without Louis?" Sandra's shoulder erupted in spasms of grief, then she stopped.

Thomas said nothing. Words were inadequate.

"Then, I called my mother."

Sandra stopped talking and, once again, began crying like a baby.

"My mother's the only one in my family who doesn't expect me to be tough. She knew me when all I needed from her was for her to feed me and change my diaper."

Thomas Laughlin said, "You don't know me very well, but you know I was in the Pacific during the war. I know talk is cheap at a time like this, so I'll give you space, but I won't leave unless you send me away. If you ever want to talk about this, call me. There were times since the war I wondered if I would've been better off dying. Nobody understands that, except, now, I know you do. It's going to eat you up from time to time. My advice, what I do, is to let it eat me up. I do not drink at a moment like that because I've seen what that's done to my friend, Hal, and I have a son to take care of. If I have to, I curl myself in a ball and shut myself in a closet. After a while the grief loses its appetite and goes away for a bit."

One single, solitary tear fell from his eye. He didn't wipe it away. He just let it drop to the floor.

Sandra James said, "It's not over for you either, is it? Now your son's been taken. And they want to pin the robbery on you. My God, Thomas, life is so unfair."

"Sandra, I want to tell you everything is gonna be okay, but it's not. It's never gonna be okay. It's been fifteen years since Patsy died bringing Benjamin into the world, and now I've gone and lost him. I'm gonna let Alice White worry about me supposedly being the mastermind of the bank robbery. From the little I've seen of her, she is fully qualified to have been a Marine on Iwo Jima herself. With a little training from you on top of her inbred bravery, she'll be a killer with her hands, her feet, and her gun. She is a woman in love with danger. And she's headed to a courtroom to wreak havoc on the criminal justice system. That guy she lives with has got to have nerves of steel."

Sandra said, "I saw your back without a shirt. All those bullet holes. You're not short on nerve yourself."

Sandra looked at the butcher. She couldn't conceive what he'd been through.

She said, "Thank you for consoling me on the death of my partner. In the war, you weren't given a moment to recover from the loss of your comrades, were you? So, you understand more than anyone that I don't mean any disrespect to Lou, or to his widow, but I am going to tear this town apart to find these guys and bury them."

A thirty-second spurt of tears followed.

He smelled the cigarettes on her, but he also smelled her. He wanted to wrap his arms around her, but he thought she might misunderstand and physically hurt him if he did.

He said, "I do understand, and I'm here to help you. My God, they have Benjamin. I do not want you to lose your anger. I heard you say you were willing to break the law. I haven't talked to my friends yet about getting Benjamin back, but I am about to, and I can assure you that we will at least come close to breaking laws. If you want, you can keep an eye on us by working with us."

Sandra said, "No matter what it takes, we will get your son back, Mr. Laughlin. I promise. Louis and me just shredded one of the major players in the gang, and I'm not gonna stop until I get Benjamin back in my hands to torture him with schoolwork and physical training. For a short period of time, he was a terrific student. He is young and open-minded. If I were to guess, wherever he is, he's doing push-ups and sit-ups. I am not gonna lie around and grieve because Louis is dead. I am frustrated about how

slowly the wheels of justice are turning, and I intend
to kick them into high gear.

"There are five boroughs for them to hide out
in, and they're not invisible, especially the Gypsy,
Montes. Benjamin's got to be with him. They still
have a getaway driver. He's still around somewhere.
And, if they're gonna do another bank, they'd keep
the guy who blew the vault too. He knows what he's
doing. They got away with over a million dollars,
more like two million. Too much dynamite and the
bank would have come down on their heads."

"Meanwhile," Thomas said, "I'm gonna rouse
the two guys I survived Iwo Jima with and do some
snooping on my own. I'll leave you and Alice White
to get me out of the trouble these people think they
put me in."

Sandra said, "Thomas, two other detectives
have offered their services, with or without backup. If
we find out where and when they're going to hit, I
want them with us and I want us inside the place
when it starts. We'll get Benjamin back and square
things for Louis. I'll call it in after we have it under
control. Hopefully, by then, half of them will be dead.
Montes has to be thinking his chances of being caught
and killed have increased a hundred times because of
Louis dying. He's got to be thinking that the next job
will be fifty times more dangerous. I hope he's scared
to death. If he gets caught, maybe having Benjamin to

trade was the smartest thing he ever did. He'd still be facing life in prison, but he might be able to avoid the electric chair by turning Benjamin loose."

Thomas said, "Sandra, this kid is all I have left in the world. I want him back."

Sandra said, "I'm willing to murder the whole bunch of them, if that's what it takes."

CHAPTER 30

THE HUNT

Thomas Laughlin sat on the ground in an alley somewhere near Canal Street in Manhattan. He was leaning against a brick wall, his service .45 wedged into the small of his back. It was loaded. Two magazines were taped to his left calf. There were army surplus stores in the neighborhood, wholesale electronics places, a Salvation Army, and a soup kitchen. It was a favorite haunt of less-solvent New Yorkers wishing to drink themselves to death, out of brown paper bags, with no cover charge and no minimum.

Hal Ferragamo, late of the United States Marine Corps in the Pacific, and one of Thomas

Laughlin's few surviving buddies, lay sprawled on the broken pavement, passed out, arms and legs akimbo. It was obvious that, at some time during the night, Hal had vomited his stomach contents all over himself and loosed his bowels inside his dungarees.

Hal roused himself from slumber, like some hideous monster in a Japanese horror movie about to terrorize a city. But this monster wasn't going to terrorize anyone because he had awakened with an even more hideous hangover.

Thomas Laughlin said, "At last. It moves. It's about time. It is me, Hal, your old pal, Thomas. I need your help. They've taken Benjamin."

Thomas put his hand on his friend's shoulder. He said, "What happened, man? We both should've died a thousand times on that island. I lost count. You were doin' so good after we got home. You were the strongest of us. Then all of a sudden you disappeared into the bottle. I understand, man. Believe me, I do. You needed a break from the nightmares. We all did. But, please, for God's sake, don't leave me now. I need you. I got no one but you and Reggie left from the war to help me get your nephew, Benjamin, back."

Hal suddenly stood up to complete attention in a frightening transition very few drunks could ever have pulled off.

"Where we go, kemosabe? Your son is my son. Coffee. I need coffee. And pills, bennies, and aspirin. My God, my head hurts. What're we doing standing here? Let's go."

Thomas said, "You are amazing, Hal, truly amazing. I knew I could count on you. Let's get you under a shower. Then we go hunting. When this is over, I'm taking you to a meeting. Don't give me any trouble about that. This here is slow torture. You got things to do, women to make miserable, a nephew to help me finish raising, if we get him back."

Hal said, "I'll beat the booze, Thomas. I got to."

Thomas said, "No more promises. You better do it. I'll take you at gunpoint if I have to. Get used to bad coffee and stale donuts. You may have to visit me in prison 'cause these guys that took Benjamin are telling the story that I planned this bank robbery I walked in on to make a deposit. They actually took Benjamin and sicced the police on me at the same time. I'm gonna find them and beat them to death with my bare hands."

Hal said, "Don't worry, man. We've been here before. They throw everything they got at us and expect we'll just lie down and die."

Thomas said, "Let's get you into the shower. Then we'll go find Reggie."

Thomas got Hal home.

"First aspirin," Thomas said. He found the bottle and gave Hal six.

He helped his friend out of his clothes, which he stuffed into a pillowcase and put out on the fire escape because of the smell.

"In the shower, old timer."

He held his friend's elbow, so the big guy didn't crack his skull on the edge of the tub. Thomas turned the cold-water valve in the shower all the way open. He made sure Hal was wedged into the corner, stable enough to let go of, before he went to find coffee.

By the time Hal was sparkling clean, clothed in fresh underwear, pants, and boots, the coffee was ready. Thomas had dumped a generous helping of grounds into the aluminum basket of the percolator to make it strong.

Hal put a Lucky Strike in his mouth, offered one to his friend, and Thomas lit them both up. Then Hal took a pill bottle out of a kitchen cabinet. He dumped a palmful of little white pills into his hand and did likewise to Thomas. They swallowed the pills with coffee. Hal said, "Bennies and java, breakfast of champions."

"Hal, where's your piece?"

"Pressing into my back. I put it there after my shower. I'll never be too drunk to forget my .45. There's spare mags in my boots."

"Good," Thomas said. "Sun's coming up. Butter some bread and stuff it in your mouth. It'll coat your stomach. I'll have some too. Then we'll go find our bud Reggie."

It was a good-sized garage. High-end cars were scattered across the floor in various states of disassembly. Towels were draped over car fenders to protect the finishes from grease monkeys working on their engines. A sky-blue, brand-new Cadillac Eldorado convertible was up on a lift. The shine off the paint job was blinding. There was a dark red Triumph Roadster with its hood propped open standing alone in mid-repair.

Thomas and Hal found their friend bending over the engine of a green Chevrolet four-door sedan.

"Reggie," Thomas said.

Six feet tall and chunky, Reggie looked up, saw his friend's troubled face, and gripped Thomas in a bear hug. "What're you doin' here? Not that I'm not glad to see you, but it's not even light outside and you don't look like this is a social call. Aren't you supposed to be opening your butcher store?"

"Reggie, something came up."

"What can I do? Spill it."

"I need you to help me find Benjamin, my son. They took him."

Reggie lowered the hood of the car he was working on.

"I'm with you, buddy. Tell me where we're going."

"A Gypsy and his gang robbed a bank. I walked in on it when I went to make a deposit. He and me have a history. He sells protection. He's a window breaker, throws paint all over the inside of stores. As far as I can tell, he's not a bank robber, but there he was, plain as day, wearing a mask. But still I could tell it was him. He's gangly, has long black hair. What did he expect? I told the police who he was."

"So, what happened?"

"I still can't believe it. He took Benjamin, kidnapped him off the street. Planted jewelry from the robbery in my place. Now there's a big-time prosecutor thinking I'm good as the gang leader, the mastermind. I'm gonna kill the Gypsy when I find him, but I need help tracking him down, and I need you to cover my back because now, he's not alone. He has a gang. After the robbery the cops hit his place and it was empty. Big surprise. He kidnapped Benjamin, so he hasn't left the city. He must be planning another job and he's going to use my son as a hostage. Can you get away?"

Reggie said, "I won't even dignify that with an answer." He yelled, "Hey, Alfie," to a distant corner of the garage. "They took my buddy's son. I got to go help get him back."

A voice shouted back, "Go on. Get out of here. Call me if you need anything, including me. And you better have good news when you get back here. You're still on the clock, so I want something to show for my money. Get the hell out of here."

"Right," Reggie yelled back.

They walked as they talked.

Reggie asked, "What do the cops say?"

Thomas answered, "It's out of their hands. The prosecutor is not gonna let me walk. The cops are a whole tragedy in themselves. There's a very nice, blond police detective who was assigned to the robbery with her partner. One of the gang members and a bank executive died in the robbery, you may have heard. Right when they began the investigation the ramrod of the gang shot the blonde in the stomach. She would've bled out if her partner hadn't gotten her to Bellevue where they operated on her and stopped the bleeding. When she was back on the job they tracked the shooter to a house, broke down the doors. The guy went down in the gunfire, but a stray bullet killed the blond detective's partner. She's nice, a martial arts prodigy, but she is now insane with thoughts of revenge on the remaining members of the gang, especially the leader. She is willing to break the law, risk jail or death, to get these guys, and to get my son back too. There's two other detectives also willing to risk jail to take these guys down and get my son back. The blonde was just starting to teach Benjamin to fight and help him with his schoolwork, so he doesn't end up on the street. She wants him back. She's a good person, but she's still recovering from being shot and now, from losing her partner."

Reggie said, "Sheeit. I thought about being a cop when I got back from the war. Thought it would be a piece of cake compared to Iwo. Guess I was wrong. So, where we goin', Thomas?"

He grabbed Thomas and Hal by their arms. "I'm carrying. It's my old service automatic. In the small of my back. You work in a garage on expensive cars in New York City, you gotta be prepared."

Reggie snagged a brown leather vest off a hook on the wall and pushed Laughlin and Ferragamo toward the street. While he walked, he took out a pack of Chesterfields and lit one up. He saw his friend Thomas was upset and he wasn't going to leave his side.

As they walked Thomas said, "There's a guy my new lawyer told me to call for help with the search. My new lawyer is a woman, very nice looking, but don't get any ideas. She's taken. She just graduated law school, so she's not licensed yet, but she got her law firm to agree to defend me. You're probably gonna meet her, so get it out of your system now because she's practically married to a carpenter, another vet, army, who builds sets for Broadway shows. He makes up for not being a Marine by having the guts to deal with her. She has a reputation for causing mayhem and aggravation wherever she goes. So, we need her on our side, and you don't want to hit on her, if you know what I mean."

Reggie said, "I am always a gentleman, I'll have you know, but thanks for the warning, Thomas."

Laughlin went on, "The guy she told me to get hold of is named Antonio Vargas. He's a whole other level of badass. He's in the security business, ex-con, covers high-end clubs and restaurants downtown and around New York. We're gonna need all the help we can get to smoke this Gypsy out and get my son back."

Reggie said, "Yeah, I know who he is. Boss is considering hiring him for security."

Thomas said, "An army is what it's gonna take to beat these people. So, we have the outlaw Antonio Vargas, and the would-be lawyer Alice White, about to be licensed to lay waste to the law. We have one raging blond police detective who's willing to do time in jail to get revenge for the murder of her partner and for being shot in the stomach herself by one of the gang members, who is now dead. Oh, and two police detectives who are already involved want in. As for me, they have my son. You are my friends. Let's kick these guys' butts so bad that they never see the inside of a bank again for the rest of their lives. They will either be dead or sitting on death row waiting to take a seat on Old Sparky."

They came to a pay phone.

Thomas dropped a dime into the slot and got hold of Alice White at the number she gave him and told her he needed her, Antonio Vargas, and their new mutual martial arts instructor, Detective James, to all meet up as soon as possible, meaning today. Alice told him Antonio had already picked the time and place.

Thomas Laughlin did not believe in God, but he'd prayed on Iwo Jima, and he prayed now. He asked whatever power ruled the universe to save his son even if it meant he had to die in Benjamin's place. He had been a rotten father anyway. He also asked the power to help Sandra James find peace over her partner's death. Maybe destroying these guys would help with that.

The meeting was set to start at ten thirty in the morning, to last an hour so the employees of the establishment would have time to prepare for their opening at noon.

The original Delmonico's restaurant opened in the year 1827 at 23 William Street. It was one of America's most famous fine-dining establishments. It was also, of course, the birthplace of the Delmonico steak.

In the late 1940s, Antonio Vargas served a prison term as a favor to the head of a criminal family for a crime he, Antonio, had not committed. In exchange, on release from prison, Antonio Vargas was handed the reins of, perhaps, the most powerful security company in New York City. It served elite nightclubs and restaurants, as well as private gatherings in and around the city. It provided bodyguards for select individuals. It came as no surprise to anyone who suspected the truth of Antonio's rise to prominence that he immediately landed Delmonico's as his flagship client.

Antonio arrived first, alone, with no entourage, to greet his guests. The interior was in its usual state at this hour. Most of the chairs rested upside down on the tables. The floors had just been mopped. The excited sound of multilingual cooks, their helpers, a gang of Hispanic busboys, and an assortment of auxiliary staff echoed from the kitchen.

Recent law school graduate Alice White and her new sensei, Detective Sandra James, were Antonio's first guests to arrive. Antonio Vargas stood, bowed slightly at his waist, and gave Alice a hug and the detective a handshake.

Antonio said, "Detective James. I am very sorry for the loss of your teacher and partner, Louis Maraglia. May our endeavor here bring you a degree of peace."

Sandra said, "Mr. Vargas. You have no idea how much I appreciate hearing a human voice speak Louis's name. And with all due respect, from the look of you, I think you will understand that I would like to live to see the men responsible for his death catch fire in the electric chair at Sing Sing Prison if at all possible."

Antonio smiled slightly and said, "I understand your feelings in this matter, and I will do all that I can to help you realize that vision."

He gave Sandra a brief hug, stepped back, and said, "Please tell our real host whatever you would like to drink, from water to Scotch."

Antonio nodded at a handsome man in a collared, white dress shirt, no tie, sleeves rolled up, black slacks, and expensive black, laced oxfords. He came to the table.

The man said, "Ladies. My name is Mario. I am the manager of Delmonico's and I welcome you warmly. Please ask me for your heart's desire and I will attempt to fulfill it. Something to drink perhaps?"

Sandra James spoke, "Mario, I am pleased to meet you. My partner in the police department was just shot and killed. Regardless of the hour, would you please bring four shot glasses of something expensive for us to toast him a safe journey?"

Tears filled her eyes and nobody looked away. They were all of a cloth. Tears came to Mario's eyes also. He said, "It would be an honor, signora. I have just the thing. I will return in a moment."

Not long after the shot glasses were emptied and taken away, Thomas Laughlin, Hal Ferragamo, and Reggie Johnson came in off the street, and Antonio rose again to shake their hands.

"Please sit down," Vargas said. "We must eat as we talk to allow the staff to prepare the restaurant for the public. The menu for us is simple. Steak sandwiches are the specialty of the house at this hour. Beer, soda, water, or perhaps something stronger is at your disposal."

Conversation went on through the ordering, service, and consumption of the early lunch.

Antonio informed the assembled parties that every one of his employees was working around the clock, except for shifts at their assigned nightclubs and restaurants, searching for a whiff of Christos Montes and his fifteen-year-old captive, Benjamin Laughlin. It was only a matter of time before something broke, but time, they all agreed, was not on their side. If these men were planning another robbery, it would be very soon.

Sandra said she had every available officer in the New York City Police Department, especially personal friends of the late Louis Maraglia, looking for suspicious activity around the banking industry, armored car companies, Western Unions, diamond merchants, and the like.

CHAPTER 31

JIM PETERS

Jim Peters stopped at a downtown watering hole, on his way home, to collect his thoughts. He had worked late on the stage set of *West Side Story,* scheduled to open in four months. He no longer enjoyed the convenience and luxury of the vast home he had occupied until recently, spread out over an entire floor of a commercial building near Broadway. He gave up that luxurious space to live with Alice White in an apartment in the Bronx.

"Bartender, I'll have a shot and a beer."

"Okay, buddy, coming up."

The heavyset barman with his sleeves rolled up, an anchor tattoo on his forearm, glanced back at his customer to see if he was okay, then went on to fill his order.

Jim bummed a cigarette from a man and woman down the bar. They gladly interrupted their conversation to light him up. He returned to his stool, cigarette in hand. The couple reminded him of the wonderful times he had spent with Alice, drinking beer in places like this, and playing pool. The smoke helped him relax and think.

Three shots and three beers later, the bartender stood on his side of the mahogany looking at his customer.

"What's up, man?" the navy vet asked Jim.

"Not much," Jim said.

The bartender said, "Girlfriend trouble?"

Jim smiled. "First guess."

"I am a bartender. I might as well hang up a shingle, 'The doctor is in!' You live together or just dating?"

"We just moved in together. I gave up my huge place down here, near the Broadway shows, the only residential tenant in a commercial building. A magnificent spread. I gave it up to live with her in an apartment in the North Bronx."

"She must be a fine woman."

"Excellent deduction. She's a heartbreaker. She's beautiful. She's smart. She's funny. It makes my teeth ache to look at her. She's independent, stubborn, crazy, and she's a magnet for danger. If that doesn't make a man want a drink, nothing ever will."

"I have no advice for you, I am not even jealous. Part of me feels sorry for you. One thing I will say is that almost no one in this world ever once meets a person that they feel the way you do about her. What do you do for a living?"

"I'm a carpenter, a stage set designer on Broadway. It's a good job. Now I commute to the Bronx, an hour each way, just to be with her."

"I can see you are in deep trouble, my friend. You're sitting here wondering if you should get a hotel room and not go home. Am I right? Don't answer that. Of course, I'm right. I haven't got a thing to tell you. There's a Jamaican song, I think it goes, 'If you want to be happy for the rest of your life, never make a pretty woman your wife.' If you ask me, we all think we're not good enough for a good woman. But think how lonely pretty women would be if men like you weren't willing to take one for the team."

"Lucky me. I should be more grateful."

"Well, man, this takes no thinking at all. First, a cup of black coffee. Next door is a flower shop. Get her some roses. Not too many or she'll think you cheated on her. If that happens, you're gonna wish you were back in the war, army."

"That's an interesting skill you have. Yes, I was army in the war. So, then what, Doc?"

"Get on the train and go back to the Bronx. You're nuts about her. She sounds like one in a million. You fought and almost died in the war so this kinda thing could happen to you."

"I know you're right. What's wrong with me?"

"We're all a little crazy in the head, us who traveled over the ocean to get shot at and came home to put a life together. Don't think yourself out of a good thing. It'll get better. Just hang in there."

"Thanks, man."

"One more piece of advice. You're not really a drinker. I hate to turn away good business, but stay away from the booze, d'ya hear me? There's a big hole in your heart, same as in mine. Too many guys fill it with hooch. Don't tell anyone, but I don't drink hardly a drop. Otherwise, I would'a poured myself one and bumped glasses with you to hoping I ever have your problem. I should be so lucky. Go home to her and hug her like your life depends on it, 'cause it does. Don't put any money on this bar. You're an investment in my future. Use the money next door at the flower place. Drop in again sometime for a cup of coffee and let me know how it's going."

CHAPTER 32

THE ANGEL OF DARKNESS

Some say Hell's Kitchen is the toughest neighborhood there ever was in the history of America. It ran from west of Eighth Avenue to the Hudson River and north and south from 59th Street to 34th Street on the West Side of Manhattan, New York City, the Atlantic coast of the United States. By the mid-1850s the area was predominantly occupied by Irish immigrants escaping the great potato famine in their home country. A hundred years later, in the mid-1950s, a wave of Italian and Puerto Rican immigration was underway. Street gangs coalesced. There was trouble.

Into the waterfront cauldron of the West Side was born Angelo Mancuso of modest circumstances. He was brought up in a hardworking Italian family. Early on, Angelo determined to go to law school. Fordham University showed financial favor to children of immigrant parents who wished to study law.

"You want to do this?" Angelo's mother questioned him. "Then you have to stop fighting the Irish. You gonna end up in jail. How you be a lawyer then?"

"But, Ma, they attack me. I don't start anything. I can't just let them push me around, take my money, disrespect my family. But I'll do better, Mom. I promise. Only please, tell me it's all right with you if I go to study law."

"It's okay with me if it's okay with your father, but, also, I forget, you have to stop pulling your little sister's hair. What is it with you two? You play rough. What did I tell you about doing that, eh? How's she gonna get a husband if she's bald? You think about that? Do you want to have to support her her whole life?"

"Okay, Mom, I'll stop. I don't want Anna living with me when I'm married and a big famous lawyer."

"And sonny, how much they gonna charge you for that fancy law school? How you gonna pay? And lawyers wear expensive suits. What you gonna do? Deliver groceries?"

Angelo said, "No, Ma. I asked around and I'm gonna work the night shift in the morgue at Bellevue. That way I get time to study. They give me a meal. I can even take a nap if it's not busy."

And that's exactly what Angelo did. He got a little studio apartment and rode a bicycle to Fordham University School of Law, on Broadway. He worked the aptly named graveyard shift at the morgue. He became the lawyer he dreamed of becoming by the sweat of his brow and the help of a partial scholarship, and then made his way up the ranks of the New York City District Attorney's office, under David M. Falcone.

In March of 1952 a man named Arnold Schuster, a twenty-four-year-old clothing salesman, helped the police locate and capture the famous bank robber Willie Sutton. Schuster was shot and killed outside his home in Brooklyn. The execution prompted Angelo Mancuso to start a fight for a witness protection program. The law enforcement community loved the idea, and he continued the inevitable climb toward his goal of becoming governor of the State of New York. As he stacked up convictions, Angelo became known among defense attorneys as "the Angel of Darkness," and sometimes, with his growing success prosecuting capital cases, "the Angel of Death."

In the spring of 1957, Angelo Mancuso spoke with the police commissioner about the brutal robbery and murders at the First National Bank on Wall Street. He saw an opportunity to put another notch on his belt by convicting the Marine veteran, Thomas Laughlin, of the planning and execution of the robbery and the brutal murder of the bank executive. All Angelo had to do was ask his boss, David Falcone, to assign him the case.

CHAPTER 33

LAUGHLIN AT LAW FIRM

"Mr. Laughlin, first off, on behalf of our law firm, I would like to thank you for your service during the last world war." Clarence Eaton, storied defense attorney at law, spoke for the three partners present and the assembled staff.

Thomas Laughlin said, "It is me who should be thanking you for taking my case. My business is doing well. I can pay whatever you ask."

"That's very good of you. Before we begin, let me introduce you to my partners, who started this law firm and who were kind enough to bring me on board. Jack Bryce and Rich Adams."

The partners stood and shook hands and they all sat down.

Eaton said, "I just wanted you to meet my partners and to know that we will do all we can to defend you in this matter and, of course, Alice White will keep us appraised of the situation with your son, Benjamin. For now, you can pay my secretary, Miss McDonald, five hundred dollars as a retainer. She will keep track of our expenses as we proceed. We intend to earn every cent of our fee."

Thomas Laughlin took a check from his wallet, wrote it out, and handed it to Laura McDonald, who handed him back the receipt she had already written out.

Eaton continued, "We are very sorry about the kidnapping of your son, Benjamin, which must take priority over everything else.

"As for the rest, we will do our best to defend you against this ridiculous assertion that you had anything to do with the commission of the robbery of the First National Bank last Friday."

Laughlin said, "The charge may be ridiculous, but it is backed up by the so-called 'discovery' in my apartment of a pair of expensive, one-of-a-kind earrings, reported taken from a safe-deposit box during the robbery. That and my coincidental appearance at the bank while the robbery was in progress. I heard they have assigned the case to a prosecutor out of my worst nightmare by the name of Angelo Mancuso. Is that correct? Should I be concerned?"

Eaton said, "Yes, Mr. Laughlin, we are aware of the district attorney's appointment to your case, and we are prepared to fight tooth and nail for your speedy vindication. Mr. Mancuso does indeed have a reputation for aggressive prosecution, but what he doesn't like people to know is his passion for the truth winning out over all other considerations, including his own political ambition. This flimsy story about the kidnapping of Benjamin being insurance against a double cross simply does not pass muster. I understand this blatant lie has become known to the district attorney. It is obvious that they want a hostage for their next action, possibly another bank robbery, to prevent one of their number being killed again, as happened to Arthur Watts, a longshoreman and, before his death, resident of the Bronx. Frankly, I think there is a chance that Mr. Mancuso will dismiss this charge as being unworthy of his office and we will be free to focus all our attention on insuring your son's safe release."

"Mr. Mancuso from the DA's office is here to see you, boss. Shall I show him in?" Laura McDonald asked her longtime employer, Clarence Eaton, Esquire, over the intercom.

"Yes, please, Laura. And when you get a chance, please bring me a fresh bottle of gin, as the current bottle is almost empty, and another carton of cigarettes."

"I'm on it, boss," Laura said, then in a whisper, "if you ask me, the Angel of Darkness does not seem all too friendly. Watch yourself, boss, with all due respect."

"Warning noted and appreciated, Laura. I am afraid that my fervent prayer that he would back off the butcher was merely wishful thinking. Be prepared to earn your keep, Laura. Bring him in."

"Good day, Clarence," District Attorney Angelo Mancuso said pleasantly enough, with a smile on his face. They shook hands.

Clarence motioned his guest to a comfortable, upholstered armchair and Laura McDonald left the room. Clarence took his seat behind the desk.

"It was good of you to come all this way to see me, Angelo. Dare I hope that you are dismissing the insane charge that the butcher, Mr. Thomas Laughlin, late of the United States Marine Corps on Iwo Jima, masterminded the robbery of the First National Bank on Wall Street this last Friday?"

"Hope all you want, Clarence. I intend to do no such thing. That's the bad news. The good news is that I am willing to deal."

Clarence Eaton said, "What kind of a deal can any defense attorney possibly make against a charge of bank robbery and murder in the first degree? Make that double murder. What part of 'totally absurd' do you not understand? Planting possibly the most expensive set of real gold and extravagantly priced pearl copies of costume-earrings in the squalid apartment of a butcher and his, now kidnapped, son? Even if they were worn by Grace Kelly in a movie, it doesn't make the charge any less ridiculous. Insanity! Pure insanity. The offer I was hoping to come from you was dropping the entire preposterous charge and focusing all our attention on getting his kidnapped son back, intact, before he gets used as a hostage in yet another bank robbery, with no guarantee the boy will survive."

Angelo Mancuso squinted and said, "The charge has not been officially made yet, Clarence, so your client is free to confer with you here, in this office, and construct a defense. I realize the evidence is circumstantial, and I'm not looking to hang an innocent man. Please do not let him leave this city. I'm in the business of putting criminals behind bars. This robbery was a tragicomedy of errors masterminded by an amateur, which, unfortunately, perfectly describes Mr. Laughlin. Give me something to work with here, Clarence, besides just dropping the case. I don't want to be right about a war hero. But this is just too much evidence to turn my back on."

Clarence Eaton, Esquire, said, "I'm going to ask you to go now, Angelo, because my doctor has serious concerns that one more outburst of indignation from me and I will have the stroke he's been trying to prevent. Not to mention the rise in blood pressure will worsen the effect of my chain-smoking and exorbitant ingestion of gin with or without vermouth and olives. You, Angelo Mancuso, are a bully of the first order. Laughlin is a child of immigrants, same as you, same as me. You are familiar with my practices enough to know that, if I thought he was guilty, I would insist that he plead guilty or find another lawyer. You just don't care. Shame on you, Angel of Darkness."

They both rose from their seats.

Eaton said to the prosecutor, "See you in court."

There was no handshake.

CHAPTER 34

AT THE POST

"You have time for a visit?" Alice asked her reporter friend, Franklin Jones, on the telephone.

"Alice, my dear, you know you are always a most welcome respite from the harrowing trials of this New York City newspaper reporter. Please, come ahead," Franklin responded.

"Franklin, hold that thought. It'll take me an hour to get downtown. I have to switch trains on the way. Can I bring you coffee?"

"Yes, Alice, how very nice of you to offer. Black is good. And, if it's not too much trouble, a buttered hard roll, also."

The *New York Post* was founded by
Alexander Hamilton in 1801. It was housed in a
fourteen-story Parisian-style building, located in the
Financial District of Manhattan, between Church
Street and Broadway. It carried daily columns by
Drew Pearson, Earl Wilson, and Eric Sevareid.
Eleanor Roosevelt, wife of the late President Franklin
D. Roosevelt, contributed a column, six days a week,
on women's issues.

Franklin Jones was forty-six years old,
divorced, the father of a twelve-year-old girl who
lived with his ex-wife. He was also the veteran of
multiple dead-end relationships with women much
younger than himself. He was five feet ten inches tall
and weighed two hundred eighty pounds. He was a
heavy smoker, a heavy drinker, and flushed from the
addition of those predilections to his uncontrolled
high blood pressure, for which he refused treatment.
Alice had been on him to slow down his drinking, but
he could not.

Alice found her favorite reporter sitting at his
desk on the red velvet cushion he insisted on telling
everybody he stole from the house of ill repute in
New Orleans where he lost his virginity. No one

believed him. The cushion was supported by an oversized swivel chair. He was typing furiously on his Underwood, oblivious of the lit cigarette hanging from his mouth about to drop its ash in his lap.

Franklin Jones existed during working hours on the tenth floor of the *New York Post*.

Alice emerged from an ocean of scarred oak desks, through a fog of cigarette smoke produced by dozens of reporters and secretaries. Franklin lifted his flushed, perspiring face and smiled broadly in welcome.

"Ah, my dear, you are a sight for sore eyes. Please have a seat."

He kissed her on the cheek.

She slid an unattended chair to the side of his desk, close enough to hear herself think.

"How may I assist you?" he asked, relieving Alice of two coffees and a bag of buttered rolls that were precariously balanced in her grip.

Alice had taken the D train from the Bronx to 59th Street, Columbus Circle, where she switched to the C train, and got off at Fulton. On her way to the paper, she stopped at a luncheonette to collect the coffee and rolls.

"In a nutshell, it's about me, minding my own business, walking into a bank on Wall Street last

Friday morning to deposit my paycheck. This local butcher beat me to the door and gallantly opened it for me, like a knight of the round table. Unfortunately, we walked right into the middle of a bank robbery, realizing what was happening too late to make an exit. I want you to know, Franklin, this man is a widower, a Marine survivor of Iwo Jima. You get the picture?"

"Alice, Alice, I am familiar with the bank robbery in question. How is it that you find these cataclysmic events so irresistible? These things are not all that common. This is just like the garage robbery you walked in on and nearly killed the armed robber by smashing him in the head with a wrench, which, come to think of it, was also on a Friday. By the way, congratulations on your graduation. If memory serves me, you are facing an even worse trial with the Bar in, eh, July? Good luck. I'm sorry for your trouble, but you provide me with more entertainment than any single human being in this city. What can I do for you?"

"July it is, Franklin. Good memory. So, the butcher, the war hero, who walked into the middle of the robbery with me, recognized the masked gang leader and told the police who he was. As I'm sure you know, there were two fatal shootings during the robbery. They kidnapped the butcher's fifteen-year-old son and planted jewelry from the bank's vault in his apartment. The earrings were originally costume jewelry made for Grace Kelly to wear in *High Society,* but this woman's husband had a copy made with real gold and real pearls as a twenty-fifth anniversary present for his wife, who stored them in their safe-deposit box in the Wall Street bank we are talking about. The gang is claiming that the butcher is the real mastermind of the robbery. In my brief, uncredentialed psychological assessment, this widowed, war-ravaged single father was already profoundly depressed. I cannot imagine the pain of having bank robbers kidnap his child and blame the robbery on him. He must be on the brink of suicide. I would be. They want the son as a hostage, for what they haven't said, but it doesn't take much imagination to guess it's probably another job of some sort."

"Alice, you want me to write a hit piece on Mr. Mancuso."

"Exactly, my friend. District Attorney Angelo Mancuso, the so-called Angel of Darkness, or Death, has expressed sympathy with the plight of the butcher, but he has absolutely no intention of delaying a high-profile prosecution so tailor-made for his rise to the occupancy of the governor's mansion in Albany. I mean over a million dollars taken, two deaths. A war hero gone bad. It almost doesn't matter if the Marine vet had anything to do with it. Mancuso has thought it over and decided to make an example of our butcher, Mr. Thomas Laughlin. I want you to use your talent with that typewriter of yours to crush the honorable Mr. Mancuso like a bug."

"Delightful. Let us adjourn to my office on Church Street for further discussion."

Alice said, "If we're going to Cleary's Pub, I would be honored if you would at least let me buy you lunch to go with your whiskey."

HEROIC MARINE SURVIVOR OF IWO JIMA TO BE CHARGED WITH MASTERMINDING BANK ROBBERY ON WALL STREET

by Franklin Jones

The New York Post

A popular Manhattan purveyor of fine meats, Thomas Laughlin, is to be charged by District Attorney Angelo Mancuso for masterminding the Friday morning robbery of the First National Bank on Wall Street in which two men were killed.

Laughlin is a Marine survivor of the more than one-month-long Battle of Iwo Jima, a hero, a widowed single parent, who arrived at the bank to make his business deposit only to find the institution in the midst of an armed robbery.

Mr. Laughlin was able to identify the masked gang leader as the man who had previously visited his butcher shop to extort him for protection money. Subsequently his fifteen-year-old son, Benjamin, was kidnapped and is being held as a hostage by the gang. An anonymous tip led to the search of Laughlin's residence, which turned up a unique pair of custom-made earrings, removed from a safe-deposit box during the robbery.

District Attorney Angelo Mancuso, famous for supporting the witness protection program, is considering prosecution of Mr. Laughlin to the fullest extent of the law, an action in blatant opposition to the values of the witness protection program he was instrumental in establishing.

A cooperative eyewitness, incriminated by the very bank robbers he has helped identify, is now charged with the crime itself. Good luck, Mr. Mancuso, in your bid for the governorship of the State of New York. A successful prosecution, in such a heinous crime, would certainly lend a much-needed boost to your success.

The penalty for armed robbery and murder is electrocution. Which begs the question, "What price political ambition?" Lady Justice must be rolling over in her grave.

Respectfully submitted, Franklin Jones

Antonio Vargas parked his Pontiac Star Chief in front of Alice and Jim's apartment building in the Bronx. The trunk of the four-door sedan was loaded with ammunition and gun-cleaning equipment.

Riding shotgun, next to Antonio, was Thomas Laughlin.

In the back seat sat Detective Sandra James, whom they had picked up on the way north through the South Bronx.

Alice White got in the back seat next to Sandra.

"Hello, everybody," Alice said. "I brought coffee and a stack of paper cups. Please take some and pass it around."

Sandra said, "Thanks, Alice. I'd like a cup. And, Antonio, thank you for helping us get ready. There's not much time. The next robbery could be as soon as tomorrow."

Antonio nodded.

Sandra said, "The two Marine friends of Mr. Laughlin are going to meet us at the gun range."

Laughlin said, "We could all use some time on a range to get the kinks out before we take these guys on. I never thought I'd have to use my gun again. But I cleaned and oiled it once in a while for old time's sake. It did save my life, a time or two, in the war."

Thomas turned around in his seat and said, "Alice, I appreciate what your firm is doing for me. I am certainly grateful to all of you for helping me get my son back. And that piece in the *Post* was not lost on me, Alice. I suspect you're a close friend of Franklin Jones."

She said, "Shucks. Who, me? Yes, we are acquainted."

They got there, rolled up on the gravel parking lot, and emptied the trunk of equipment and sandwiches, as if they had done this together a million times.

Hal Ferragamo and Reggie Johnson pulled into the lot right behind them.

When he saw Laughlin, Hal walked up to him and said, "We're gonna do it again, aren't we, Thomas? Those bank-robbing fools do not know who they have messed with."

Reggie approached them and said, "Amen, brother."

CHAPTER 35

EMPIRE STATE BUILDING

Benjamin was locked in a small room a few inches longer and maybe two feet wider than the cot he was given to sleep on. It was a huge utility closet emptied of mops and brooms. He had nothing to complain about. He hadn't taken up much more space than this for the past few years, lying on the couch, a bag of chips on his chest, and a *Mad* magazine in his hands. That was his whole world until the blond police detective entered his and his father's lives. Now he had purpose. He had a pencil and paper to write and do crosswords. There was room for sit-ups and push-ups. He could shadowbox, kick, and run in-place. If he kept his eyes and ears open, there might even be a way out of here.

He heard talking in the next room. The smell of cigarettes came in under his door. The old woman stuck her head in and asked him what he wanted for lunch. He asked her for a tuna fish sandwich, carrots, and apples.

The door latch locked automatically when she closed it on her way out. When she emptied the bucket, she made him use as a toilet, her hands were full. When she was down the hall rinsing the bucket in the sink, he jumped up and jammed the tip of one of the pencils into the latch, hard as he could, broke it off, then jumped back on the cot before she returned. She came in with the empty pail and a fresh towel and put the pail in the corner. She looked at him. His heart froze, thinking she knew something was wrong. She said, "I'll get your lunch while I'm out." With that, she went into the hall and jammed the door closed tight from the outside.

Benjamin heard the faint sound of a man's voice talking to her: "Bring me back a pastrami on rye. I gotta go out to run some errands later. But I'll be back in time to catch a few hours of sleep. We're leaving early tomorrow morning, before sunup. Thank you for taking such good care of us."

"Think nothin' of it," she said. "You sure paid me enough."

The man said, "The kid and me are going digging for treasure tomorrow."

The woman said, "You takin' a boat to some island?"

"We're not going that far. The treasure we're looking for is between Broadway and Amsterdam. Ha."

The man cringed inside, sorry he had said so much. The sheer amount of money they'd be hauling away from this next job must be getting to him.

Broadway and Amsterdam? Benjamin thought. *I'm gonna be with him. I guess I'll find out soon enough.*

Benjamin shook it off. It didn't matter what the man was talking about. He was a prisoner. This might be the end of his life. Strangely, he was not afraid.

"Okay," Benjamin heard her say to the man. "I'll be back in an hour. I called the number you gave me. Told 'em where you'd pick them up. They said they'd be there."

Benjamin listened to her footsteps recede down the hallway.

After a time, he quietly pushed open his door and carefully pushed it closed behind him. He tiptoed his way down the hall to a public bathroom, closed the bathroom door, and bolted it from the inside. He spotted a wall phone, but it was a pay phone so he couldn't use it. He pushed the bathroom window open in its tracks, slowly, and quietly, and began to climb out onto the fire escape. Suddenly he remembered the change for Mrs. Stanislavski in his pocket. He checked and, sure enough, it was still there. He reversed his direction and fished out a dime from the change and deposited it into the coin slot on the phone. He held his breath when it made its ding, but there were no hurried footsteps toward him in the hallway, so he dialed his father's number.

He whispered, "Dad, I'm in a hurry. I got out of the room they had me locked in, but I'm still in the building where they've been keeping me. I'm sure they're gonna come after me once they know I escaped. I have no idea where I am. I have to keep moving. I heard the man who has me say they're gonna do something tomorrow morning, early, and something about digging for treasure between Broadway and Amsterdam, if that means anything to you. I thought maybe it was a sewer or a subway tunnel. Then they're gonna leave New York. Dad, I gotta go. I just wanted to tell you I'm free and on my way home. I wish I could tell you more about where I am. I love you."

His father said, "That's plenty, Benjamin. Hang up the phone and get out of there."

Benjamin took a deep breath and climbed out the window.

Down the metal fire escape stairs he went, stepping as quietly as he could. The part at the bottom was tricky, but he was able to slide the retracted length of ladder down to the ground and make his way into the alley. When he was out on the street his eyes darted from side to side, squinting in the sunlight. He hunched his shoulders and headed in the direction of the only landmark he could recognize, the Empire State Building.

At the next corner he turned left to keep the Empire State Building in sight. He kept looking up at it. A couple of blocks away from where he had been held, he walked straight into the arms of the man who had kidnapped him in the first place. A handkerchief covered his nose and mouth. As soon as he took a breath, he smelled something like cleaning fluid and felt the blood rush to his face. As he was passing out, he noticed a car pull to a stop at the curb.

CHAPTER 36

CONFESSION

"Thank you for seeing me at this late hour, Father. I am thirty-five years old. I have never been married. I'm a Romanian Gypsy, born in America somewhere, I think. I am probably Catholic, but I am not certain. I do not know how this goes."

"Start with, 'Bless me, Father, for I have sinned.'"

"I am not sure what sin is, but, if it is bad, I have done it. I hear you are not allowed to tell anybody what I say to you. Is that true?"

"That is correct, my son."

"So, here goes. 'Bless me, Father, for I have sinned.' I am not making excuses, Father, but I am telling you, I was abandoned on the street by my parents, who I cannot exactly remember, to fend for myself. Were they wrong to do that, Father? I have hated them for that my whole life. I don't know why I am telling you this about my parents. Maybe it is because I think I might die soon. I have never confessed before."

"You are doing fine, my son. It is not necessary to ask why you are here. I don't judge people's behavior, and you might consider doing the same with your parents' behavior, and with your own. It is a far lighter burden to bear. Take as long as you need."

"I will then, Father. Gypsy families are supposed to be close. Who were these people, my parents, to just leave me like a mangy dog to die? Maybe from starvation, maybe from exposure? It has left me feeling worthless my whole life. It makes me angry."

"I don't know what circumstances your parents were facing, and neither do you. How can we? We are not God. They may have been trying to protect you from some danger, maybe an immediate threat to your life. We are all so quick to judge and quick to blame, ourselves and others. And we are slow to forgive. All of us. You are not alone. Go on."

"I suppose I was angry at them for forcing me into a life of violence. I always thought that if I ever found my parents, I would kill them."

"I understand, but you never know the capacity of your heart to forgive. Continue."

"I became a thief, a pickpocket, a prostitute, and, it goes without saying, a liar, a cheat, unkind, and unworthy of forgiveness. I'm sorry I bothered you, Father."

"Don't apologize to me, my son. No one is unworthy of forgiveness. This is what I am here for. This is your pain you are dealing with. Confess your sin, if you can. Then we will talk about repentance and forgiveness. There are things to be done."

"I've killed people, Father. One recently."

"Listen to me. I will not tell you what to do. I don't do that. Some priests, maybe, but not me. I can tell you what I understand from my limited experience. You will have to find a way home to yourself and to whatever idea of God you have, and that will not be easy. But you are up to it. Your soul is not beyond saving."

"But this is the only life I have ever known, Father. I'm in too deep. How can I give it up?"

"It's not going to be easy. You will have to make better decisions. That is difficult. Your attitude is going to have to change. What you call anger is really fear. You will have to admit your fear and walk through it. I would normally tell you to say a certain number of Our Fathers and Hail Marys, but you're not sure you are a Catholic, and besides, you need something more concrete you can relate to. A man like you speaks with action, and you clearly are braver than many men. Your penance is not going to be to repeat a prayer. You have to find peace, which means you have to look for it inside yourself. There is kindness in you. You have to guard it, feed it with as much love and forgiveness of your fellow man as you can muster. You are going to have to forgive yourself for what you have done in the past before you can forgive anyone else. Can you do that? Can you try?"

"Father, I am in a situation that I cannot discuss. It may make repentance impossible."

"Another thing I have learned being a priest and seeing sinners come and go."

"What is that, Father?"

"This may sound empty to you, but I have seen with my own eyes that with God in your heart, all things are possible. Not the darkest secret or the most desperate circumstance can overcome the power of God. Believe that, or at least pretend you believe that. It doesn't matter what religion you are or who and what is threatening you. You can and will find a way to redeem yourself. Hold that thought in your heart."

"I will try, Father."

"And son."

"Yes, Father?"

"The thought may have occurred to you to kill me where I sit; right here, right now. You feel vulnerable. I know that. But I am not a threat to you, so don't do it. Don't kill me. It won't help you find what you are looking for, and it will only have you dig yourself a deeper hole. Don't get me wrong, I am not afraid to die. You came to me for help, for advice, and here it is. Save yourself. You can do it."

"Okay, Father. I'll give it my best try."

CHAPTER 37

CHANGE OF PLANS

"You're taking my little brother, Freddy, with you tomorrow," the woman said. "He's gonna take Earl's place. Poor Earl went and got himself killed."

Christos Montes said, "I am not taking your brother with us; not at the last minute like this. I don't even know your brother. I don't need anybody coming in now and messing everything up. I put together my own crew for this job. I'm gonna use the same explosives and tool guy I used on the last job, and the same driver. We did perfectly good with the crew we had. We got away with over a million dollars. I got Frank Watts to take his brother's place.

When we scoped the new bank out, your brother wasn't with us."

She said, "I took Freddy down to see it. A bank's a bank. He said it would be like takin' candy from a baby."

Montes said, "Did he see the whole layout?"

She said, "More or less."

"We already got masks."

"I bought him a Halloween mask. He's gonna be Bing Crosby."

"Him and you are gonna get us all killed. I swear. I didn't sign up for this."

She didn't say anything.

"I guess he's coming along, no matter what I say?"

She said, "My mother would never forgive me if I left my baby brother, Freddy, behind on this heist."

Montes said, "Your mother must be a piece of work. No offense. I never met the lady, but she should be keeping Freddy safe at home for this. Does she know that two of the guys in my first crew are dead now? Is she willin' to visit Freddy on death row, sit in the gallery, and watch him die when some other mother's son straps him in and pulls the switch on the electric chair? She should be tellin' Freddy to stay as far away from this job as possible. But who am I to talk? I'll probably be in the cell next to Freddy's, waiting my turn."

She said, "C'mon. Cheer up. This'll go like clockwork. We already pulled one bank heist off without a hitch, and we made a ton of money."

Montes said, "You don't call Arty and the banker getting killed hitches? And what about Earl Jones getting blown away? This needs to go as smooth as silk. Smoother. We need to get in there, blow the vault, clean the teller windows out, and get away from there as fast as possible, hopefully without any more people dying."

She said, "It can be done. I have faith."

"I'm glad somebody has faith. This time we got a hostage, the kid, which should improve our odds of living through this. That was a great idea you had, taking the butcher's son in case the cops show up. And planting the jewelry, that was beautiful. Now he's got the DA, Mancuso, all over him. Afterwards, when this is over and we kill the kid, daddy's gonna put a bullet in his own head."

She said emphatically, "Do not touch a hair on that child's head. We need to send him back to his father without a scratch. Killing him would be as idiotic as killing the banker on Wall Street was. You kill that boy and his father, and every veteran in the country, will follow us to the ends of the earth. And our deaths will not be quick."

"That broken-down old soldier? Are you serious?"

"You so underestimate that man. I asked around. He has been through the kind of hell almost nobody ever goes through and survives. There's a statue to that one battle he was in, in Washington. Almost everybody died who was in that place. When he's a hundred years old he will be just as frightening as he ever was on that island. There's a reason they mention the name of the battle he was in when they talk about him. The battle of Iwo Jima lasted a month and change. Practically everyone was killed around him, Japanese and American. Before he was even on the island, his wife died birthing that kid you're talking about killing. That boy is all he has left to show for any of it. The father has got to be deranged. Anything happens to that kid, he's gonna find you and me both. He will not give either of us an easy death. The electric chair has more mercy in it than he does."

"Okay, all right, you made your point. I'll let the kid be."

"Now you're talking."

"To this unlucky crew, you are asking me to add a guy whose own sister, you, and his mother, are willing to see him blown away in a hail of bullets or watch him fry in the electric chair."

She said, "That's the deal. Either that or we call the job off altogether."

Montes said, "I'm not backing out now. Hopefully nobody gets cute and pulls a gun or trips an alarm. After it's over, you and me are gonna get out of the country, maybe forever. We'll leave the butcher's son on some street corner for his father to pick up."

She said, "So it's settled. Good. Freddy is a great guy. You'll see."

Christos Montes said, "I don't want to be looking over my shoulder to make sure he's okay when this is going down."

"Trust me, Christos, baby. Freddy's a good'ne. He'll do what you tell him. You know, he already did a bank job once? In Chicago."

"No kidding? I'm impressed. How'd that go?" Montes asked her.

She said, "Not so good. Three of them got killed by the guard and a teller. Freddy made it to the street, but the getaway driver took off as soon as the shooting started. So Freddy had to hoof it outta there with just the cash from the tellers' windows. We went to the Bahamas together. Got a terrific suite in a dynamite hotel just like you and me are gonna do right after we get out of that bank tomorrow."

"I hope so."

"At least if Freddy gets caught, he won't rat the rest of us out."

Montes said, "That's easy for you to say. It'll be a different story when they sweat him with a bunch of murders hanging over his head. He'll squeal like a pig. Probably tell 'em all about me, the gang leader of both bank robberies. I'll go down in history as the dumbest crook that ever lived. Oh, Freddy'll protect you all right, but he'll crucify me. He'll probably die in the exercise yard of a prison somewhere, probably Sing Sing. They hate snitches in there. Don't you worry though. You'll probably end up on an island, sunning yourself with some other man."

"Oh, honey, I would never."

"Yes, you would, and I don't blame you. You're the first real woman I ever knew, and for that I thank you from the bottom of my Gypsy heart. Stay alive, you hear me? If I die it'll be worth everything to know you're well fixed and safe somewhere."

She said, "So it's settled. You're taking Freddy?"

"You are one hard-hearted woman. Freddy will take Earl Jones's place," he said. "And may the Lord have mercy on our souls."

CHAPTER 38

RESURRECTION

Hal Ferragamo's shirt was doused in cheap wine, but there was no alcohol in his bloodstream. Maybe when this was over, he would try to stop drinking for real. Maybe he would swallow his pride, what there was left of it, and get help from the old drunks in the meetings. Who knew? All he knew for certain at this moment was that his .45 was cleaned, oiled, locked, and loaded, in his belt, ready to flip the safety off and start killing bad guys.

The years since the war ended were lost. He could never get them back. But he was still alive, and there was still time to do some living. There were people to meet and places to see. There were women to ruin, and he wasn't too old to be a father. All he had to do was live through this day. There was some nasty work to be done here, in this bank, and maybe worse afterward, getting sober.

Hal was sitting on the ground just inside the mouth of an alley at the intersection of Broadway and Amsterdam Avenue. They had solved the mystery of what Benjamin overheard about buried treasure at Broadway and Amsterdam. There it sat. The Treasury Bank of New York. Christos Montes planned to rob it, using Thomas Laughlin's son, Benjamin, as a shield.

Hal wore tattered rags and a bent-up gray brimmed hat with a stained band that looked like it had been retrieved from a garbage dump. He caressed a paper bag with a bottle sticking out of its mouth.

Thomas Laughlin was dressed the same, there to share the drink.

Hal kept his voice low. "I can't wait, Thomas. After so long, I finally get to do something right. I'm gonna help you get your son back and, maybe, kill the son of a bitch that took him."

Thomas said, "This is the place. There's only one treasure anywhere near Broadway and Amsterdam and it's in the vault of this bank. We've done this before, Hal. I know it's been a few years, but you never lose the skill set. It's Friday morning.

The bank's about to open. Benjamin will be with them, so let's try not to shoot him. Where's Reggie?"

Before Hal could answer, an unkempt Reggie Johnson shuffled across the sidewalk into the alley and sat down on the ground to share their bottle.

Hal asked him, "What's a matter, Reginald? Couldn't sleep."

"Sorry I'm late. I wasn't about to miss out on the action," said Reggie. He slid an impressive knife out of its sheath on his hip. "And here we have every Marine's pride and joy, a genuine USMC KA-BAR, for those sticky situations where only the best will do and guns are too noisy, or you're out of ammo."

Hal said, "My God, man. You sure kept it in mint condition. Now that this gang of hoodlums have had some practice robbing a bank, they're gonna hit hard and hit fast. When it's over they won't care if there's blood everywhere so long as they have the cash. They got nothing to lose. They're already up for murder, all of them. We gotta watch out for Benjamin."

Laughlin said, "I have a feeling he's gonna wish he was still a hostage when that blonde police detective gets her hands on him and forces him to swallow those raw eggs and Tabasco at three in the morning. His break is over. We're gonna start running together. She's gonna drill him on his schoolwork.

She's brutal. I wonder where she is right now. She's gonna have a lot of explaining to do for not calling for backup, maybe even face jail time if anything goes wrong. She doesn't care. She owes it to her late partner, Louis Maraglia."

Hal told his friends, "We checked our weapons. We checked our ammo. No sense getting killed unless it's absolutely necessary."

Antonio Vargas arrived looking nothing like a wino. He was dressed in his usual black pants, black T-shirt. black motorcycle boots, and black diver's watch. A shotgun was in his hands like some rancher in a Dime Western looking for a varmint to shoot. That wasn't far from the truth. An automatic stuck out of his belt. A sheathed knife was tied to his thigh.

He said, "I'm here."

Laughlin grinned and said, "You think you're well enough armed? Two guns and a knife seems about right for a man like you."

"Be prepared, I always say," Antonio commented.

Laughlin said, "You'll recognize my son. Please kill whoever has him."

"I will do that. It is my top priority," Vargas said.

Thomas said, "Good, Antonio. Thank you for being here. I will never forget it. We want them all dead or in custody. No one gets out of here alive, unless they're in handcuffs."

Hal said, "Roger that, Thomas."

The front door of the bank was unlocked by a teller. Sandra James was nowhere in sight. Alice White must have slept late.

On cue, a macabre, choreographed ballet unfolded. A rumbling, souped-up black Ford sedan pulled sharply to a halt in front of the bank. Almost simultaneously, out of the shadows, there appeared two women headed for the front door. At a glance, one was clearly the blond police detective, Sandra James, looking every bit like the bubble-headed housewife she was not. The other was strangely familiar, but more like a boozer wearing a ratty scarf, a secondhand raincoat, and a bad wig. They walked toward the entrance, not exactly together. The dainty purse hanging from Sandra's forearm carried her Colt Detective Special. Alice White had no purse. Her Browning .380 automatic was securely fastened to the small of her back in a holster. Spare magazines were taped to her leg. They proceeded into the bank like two spiders drawing flies into their web.

Laughlin, hardly containing himself, said, "There they go, beating us to the punch. What women. We better get in there before they steal the show. They're gonna need our help, I guess."

Out of the Ford emerged five masked men, one of them leading an unmasked teenager, Benjamin Laughlin, handcuffed to him. All wore Halloween masks with pirate faces, except one that looked like Bing Crosby. They were circus clowns from a nightmare.

Thomas said nothing when he spotted Benjamin. His heart broke at the sight of the son he had neglected for most of the kid's life but burst with pride at the way Benjamin carried himself: defiance in his step. Gone was his belly flab. His face was gaunt. He was a handsome young man. That was all Sandra James's doing.

The driver, Richy Anderson, remained behind the wheel, planning to hop out and watch for trouble as he had done on the Wall Street job.

The gang moved quickly. Jimmy Cage, the explosives expert, and Freddy Hill, the one wearing the Bing Crosby mask, now the ramrod of the gang, went to the trunk of the car and emptied it of tools, explosives, and canvas sacks to carry the loot. They joined the others.

Just before they entered the bank, Frank Watts said to Benjamin, whose right wrist was handcuffed to Frank's left wrist, "Listen, sonny. You move when

I move, and as fast as I move, you hear me? Don't make me have to hurt you, 'cause I will."

Benjamin, his tone neutral, but compliant, said, "I hear you."

There they stood, about to go down in history as either the most successful modern-day gang of bank robbers since the Brink's job, or the unluckiest, most pathetic excuse for a gang that ever lived, who would all probably die, in the bank or in the death house at Sing Sing. They paused, waiting for the signal from the boss, Christos Montes. It looked for a moment like they were posing for an oil painting . . . a strange gathering for the Last Supper.

Christos Montes stood out for his height and build. Freddy Hill was the new foreman of the team, replacing the late Earl Jones. The now-dead Arty Watts, Bronx muscle, was represented by his brother, Frank Watts. Being the junior member of the gang, Frank got the honor of being handcuffed to the hostage, Benjamin Laughlin. Harry Walker, the Brooklyn muscle man, had survived and was there because he was offered a bigger cut than last time. Jimmy Cage was smiling at the prospect of blowing open another vault.

Montes signaled the gang to proceed through the door of the bank. They slithered in like a poisonous snake. When they got inside, they spread out in front of the tellers' windows, Benjamin keeping up with Frank Watts, step for step.

Harry Walker disarmed the uniformed guard. Neither of them said a word. The guard raised his hands.

Walker then turned and took charge of the two female customers, the housewife and the pathetic woman with the bad hairpiece. He motioned them, with his gun, to step away from the tellers' windows and move to the side.

He told them, "You just stand here, out of the way where you won't get hurt. Keep your mouths shut and you'll live. Understand?"

They nodded.

Sandra turned her head and gave Benjamin Laughlin a quick look. Benjamin blinked back at her and turned away.

Richy Anderson, the wheelman, was outside standing fully alert beside the Ford.

Hal Ferragamo, Thomas Laughlin, Reggie Johnson, and Antonio Vargas surveyed the scene, from the mouth of their alley.

Reggie waited for the last gang member to enter the bank and was about to jack-rabbit to where Richy Anderson stood but was beat to the punch by Police Detective Sidney Shapiro, who hit the hapless driver in the head with the butt of his gun. Detective Andy Bennett taped the unconscious driver's mouth and restrained his arms and wrists behind his back. He removed the keys from the ignition. Together the detectives lifted Anderson into the trunk and shut it.

Reggie Johnson said, "Who invited you guys? Don't get me wrong. I appreciate the help. You look like policemen. I'll bet you're not on the clock."

Shapiro said, "You're right. We're not on any clock. You can visit us in jail when this is over, but we had to be here to lend a hand. Let's go."

Inside, Montes announced, "This is a stickup. No alarms, no guns. Keep your hands where we can see them. Anything goes wrong, we kill the boy. Then we kill you."

The gang was too busy watching the tellers for false moves to notice they had company. Six armed men had slid in the front door and were preparing to attack.

Amazingly, that same teller from the bank on Wall Street who had gone into shock was practically having a stroke behind her window, groaning loud enough to be heard all over the bank, "No. Not again. Not you. This cannot be happening. Please don't hurt me. I'll do whatever you say."

Sandra and Alice were standing perfectly still, listening and waiting for the moment to act.

Montes looked at the teller and said, "It is you. I remember you, Margaret. Do not worry. Do what we say, and everything will be okay, just like before. What are you doing here anyway?"

Margaret's hands were shaking. She said, "I asked for a transfer. I told them I couldn't work at that bank anymore. It was too frightening. Now it's happening all over again. I should've found another way to make a living."

Montes said, "It was destiny. Never mind. You know what I want. Empty your cash drawer into the bag and pass it along."

Jimmy Cage was about his business with the vault. He lost sight of the front of the bank altogether. He was placing the charges to blow the vault.

The guard found himself ignored, so he moved ever so slowly to get another gun from a panel in the wall. He knew it was dangerous, but he was supposed to try. That's what bank guards did.

Everything was going smoothly. None of the gang even noticed the seeming crowd of armed strangers, hunched and drifting in from the front, guns in hand.

Sandra scanned the bank and saw her armed friends moving in. She decided this was her last chance to defuse the situation, before a full-scale gun battle took place with unnecessary casualties. She caught Benjamin Laughlin's eyes with a hard stare and a grimace. He knew what she wanted him to do, and he smiled back to let her know he understood. Sandra slowly removed the Colt revolver from her purse, grasped it with both hands, pointed it at Christos Montes's head, and shouted, "Police! Freeze. Everybody stay right where you are! You, Mr. Montes, don't make a move or I will blow your head off."

The hysterical teller, Margaret Hopkins, started yelling and applauding, "Thank heavens, the police are here. We're saved."

At the sound of Detective Sandra James's harsh announcement, Benjamin Laughlin lifted his right knee in front of him, pointed his heel toward the floor, and stomped down hard and fast on the back of Frank Watts's booted left foot, hard enough to break the bones, which, he knew instantly, he had done. He could hear the sound of bone snapping. Frank let out a yell and bent forward in pain.

"Why you little . . ."

He was interrupted by Benjamin smashing him in the nose with a hard left uppercut. The nose gave way. Then, again with his less restricted side, the boy slammed his left knee into Frank Watts's crotch, and the monster hit the floor. Benjamin followed with a hard kick to the head and the man lost consciousness.

Sandra James observed the series of moves and her heart swelled with pride.

"You are a great student, Benjamin," she yelled at him. "Now get the key from his pocket and unlock the cuffs, and cuff him quick, before he comes to." She stared into Christos Montes's eyes and saw that he was getting ready to make a move.

"Don't even blink, Mr. Montes. I'm dying to kill you for your boy killing my partner, Louis Maraglia. He is why I did this without police backup. So, I could kill you with as few witnesses as possible. I don't care what happens to me."

She kept her eyes on his and said, "Alice. Call it in."

Alice White told the nervous teller to let her in. The teller fumbled and tried to get the door to the tellers' positions open but was shaking too badly.

Benjamin bent quickly to retrieve the handcuff key from Frank Watts's pocket while Watts was still out cold. The pocket was empty. He tried the other pocket, found the key, unlocked himself, and cuffed Watts's wrists behind his back as instructed. He looked around on the floor, found Frank's gun, and grabbed it.

Alice looked at the teller in disbelief. "You have got to be kidding. You can't get the door to open?"

She yelled, "Any other teller, get over here and open this door."

The next teller down buzzed Alice in to make her call.

A shot rang out, and Freddy Hill, in his Bing Crosby mask, was dead before he hit the floor. The intrepid uniformed bank guard, Samuel Brown, had finally earned his pay.

Another shot rang out and Samuel Brown was alive no more.

Detective Sandra James and Christos Montes both turned to see who had fired. There stood the bank teller, Margaret Hopkins, no longer the trembling victim in near hysterics. She was standing rock steady, arms stretched straight out in front of her, with a two-handed grip on a large automatic handgun. There she was, a cold-blooded killer. She shouted at Sandra and Christos in her defense, "Freddy was my brother, dammit. I couldn't just let the guard get away with killing him. Mother would strangle me with her bare hands. Now I'm done for."

Detective James pivoted toward Margaret Hopkins and, with a bead on the center of her forehead, said, "You. You're the brains behind these robberies, aren't you? Answer me."

Margaret said, "Yes, it's true, I am."

Sandra said, "Louder."

"Yes, I am," Margaret yelled. "This jerk, Montes, fell in love with me. Now he's done for too."

The other tellers were witnesses to the confession.

Margaret said to Montes, "I was just using you, baby. I'm sorry. They're gonna fry us both, Christos honey."

Sandra told her, "Put your gun down or not. Your gang is responsible for the death of my partner, and I'm just looking for an excuse to blow you away. Put the gun down. Heck, I want so bad to shoot you now and save you the trial."

Sandra kept her gun pointed at the bank teller and told the other bank employees, "The police are on their way. Someone call and tell them we need ambulances, four or five. This one"—indicating the real gang leader—"is not going down without a bullet."

Harry Walker, the muscle from Brooklyn, felt invisible. With the shooting, no one seemed to notice him standing down at the far end of the row of tellers' windows. He pointed his gun at the teller who had finished emptying her drawer into the canvas bag.

"Gimme," he said.

She slid him the bag.

"Use the side door and come out here."

She did what she was told.

He put his gun to her head.

He yelled, "Anyone tries to stop me I shoot her dead."

He started walking her straight toward the door of the bank into what appeared to be a convention of armed men who had appeared out of nowhere.

Bang!

Hal Ferragamo shot Harry Walker in the head. The teller held her face in her hands and began to sob. Hal grabbed her, hugged her to him, and let her cry.

Detective James focused on the teller who still had not laid down her gun.

"Last call for the bus to heaven for the two of you. Drop your weapons or die. Give me an excuse. On the other hand, a fast-talking lawyer might find a way to save you both from the electric chair. C'mon, lady, make up your mind. You too, Mr. Montes."

Montes looked around and saw the butcher and his friends. Instead of dropping his gun, Montes pivoted and shot Thomas Laughlin in the chest. The butcher dropped to the floor.

Sandra James knocked the Gypsy's gun out of his hand. Instead of trying to retrieve his gun, Christos Montes raised his empty hands in the air, flipped off his mask, and proceeded toward the fallen soldier.

"Stop," Sandra yelled at him.

"I'm going to help the butcher," Montes yelled back at her. She believed him. With all the guns in the front of the bank there was no escape for the Gypsy.

Alice White pressed the muzzle of her Browning directly into the side of the teller's head, placed her finger on the trigger, and began to squeeze.

Margaret quickly responded, "After careful consideration, I have decided to take my chances with a lawyer rather than commit suicide in this damn bank."

She put her gun down on the counter, raised her hands, and backed away.

"Dad, dad. Please don't die. Please don't, please." Benjamin was hugging his father's fallen body, crying and sobbing.

Christos Montes reached Laughlin, removed his own jacket, and used it to staunch the blood flow from the wound, which was already sucking air into the butcher's chest.

Frank Watts came to consciousness from being mauled by the teenager, his supposed captive. He wriggled his feet through his cuffed wrists and made his way over to the dead bank guard. They had left the guard's gun on the floor next to his body. He grabbed it and took aim at Detective James and began to pull the trigger.

Before Watts could pull the trigger, a shot rang out and his head exploded.

Sandra absorbed what had happened. She half turned to look right next to her. There stood Alice White. Her feet were shoulder width apart, her arms outstretched, holding in a two-handed grip the .380 auto she had just fired.

Sandra said, "Well I'll be damned, woman. You saved my life. Is this the first time you ever killed anyone?"

"Yes, it is."

"Let's talk about it, real soon. Just not right now. Okay?"

"Sure, yeah. I'd like that."

"Thank you, Alice. I mean it. You know I do. I owe you."

"Sandra, for heaven's sake. You've been more than generous to me."

"We'll talk."

Hal Ferragamo and Reggie Johnson crouched next to their dying buddy. The Gypsy continued to hold his jacket against the chest wound, but he could tell it was no use.

Sandra walked her prisoner, the real power behind these bank robberies, over to where Thomas Laughlin lay.

"Reggie," she said, handing him her handcuffs. "Cuff this woman, would you. I want to pay my respects to your friend, Thomas Laughlin."

Reggie took the handcuffs.

Sandra kneeled down next to the butcher, who was barely conscious and breathing with difficulty.

The detective whispered, "Thomas. I hope you can hear me. The ambulance is almost here. Don't you dare go anywhere or I swear I'll come after you, find you, and hurt you." Tears were in her eyes.

"Hey, man," Montes told the still body of Laughlin. "I didn't mean to kill you. Please forgive me. You are twice the man I ever was. You are a war hero. I thought it would be me who died today."

Reggie was cuffing the prisoner, Margaret Hopkins, and she actually reached around his back and grabbed his gun. Reggie, in disbelief at her gall, quickly slid his hand to his hip, came up with his KA-BAR fighting knife, and stabbed her in the thigh, hitting bone but not killing her. The gun dropped out of her hand. He finished handcuffing her wrists behind her back.

Laughlin looked up and whispered to Montes, "I'm not dead yet, you kidnapping, evidence-planting son of a bitch. Don't rush me."

Then he turned to Sandra. "I heard what you said. It sounded like you really care what happens to me."

She said, "I was under stress. Don't believe a word I said."

Jimmy Cage peeked out from the vault area. He hadn't blown the vault door because he knew the jig was up. The electric chair or life without parole were not options he was willing to face. He pulled the gun out of his belt. The place was teeming with police, and ambulance people were starting to show up. The fire exit would be covered. He might as well leave the way he came in. He pointed the gun ahead of him and began walking briskly toward the front door. He swung his aim side to side, acquiring targets. Before Cage could pull the trigger, Antonio Vargas lifted his Ithaca 37 shotgun, loaded with 00 buckshot, aimed, quickly checked to see that no one was in front of or behind him, squeezed the trigger, held it back, and slam-fired the weapon, repeatedly pumping it, until Cage lay lifeless on the floor.

Uniformed officers and ambulance attendants streamed into the bank.

The first attendant wheeling a gurney ahead of him spotted Laughlin on the floor and pulled Montes away from him. Sandra backed off. The medic kneeled to assess the pulseless, breathless man. There was no need to listen for breath sounds with a stethoscope because there would be none on either side. The man had been shot in the left chest, so the left lung was collapsed against the heart, preventing it from beating, and pressing on the right lung, preventing it from inhaling.

Laughlin lay totally still on the marble floor. He was beginning to lose color.

"Help me lift him," the medic said to the men standing around. "His lung is collapsed."

Hal Ferragamo and Benjamin Laughlin lifted Thomas onto the stretcher. The medic sealed the bullet hole with tape and plunged a large bore needle into Thomas's left chest, between the ribs, straight into his empty chest cavity. Air tinged with blood filled the large syringe as the plunger was withdrawn. The medic unscrewed the barrel, emptied it onto the floor, and screwed it back into the needle he had left hanging out of Laughlin's chest. He repeated the procedure several times as Laughlin came around and his color began to improve. The weathered veteran looked at his friends and Montes. Sandra moved in close, and he could feel her breath on his face.

He said to her, "Thought I was a goner, didn't you?"

She gave him a sour look and a smile.

"Dad, you're gonna make it. Please don't do that again."

"Son, something tells me you are gonna be all right too."

Laughlin looked up at his war buddies and Antonio.

"Some reunion, fellas. And you, Antonio, are one hell of a man. Mr. Vargas, thank you for your help. Next time we have lunch at Delmonico's, I'm buying."

Benjamin Laughlin almost suffocated his father with hugs and tears. Then he backed off and told the medic, "Take him away. He did what he came here to do."

Freddy Hill, Frank Watts, Harry Walker, Jimmy Cage, and the bank guard, Samuel Brown, lay dead. Margaret Hopkins, Christos Montes, and Richy

Anderson, who was restrained in the trunk of the getaway car, were taken into custody. An ambulance attendant taped a pressure dressing to Margaret's bleeding leg.

CHAPTER 39

THE ANGEL AT EATON

"Show Mr. Mancuso in please, Laura," Clarence Eaton told his secretary.

District Attorney Angelo Mancuso, aka the Angel of Darkness, sat in the client chair across the desk from his host. He said, "It's good of you to see me, Clarence. I came here to eat crow face-to-face, and to beg your pardon for being so close-minded and pigheaded, blinded by dreams of moving into 138 Eagle Street, in Albany."

Laura McDonald had not left the room and was gratified to be witnessing this act of humility on the part of the feared prosecutor.

Clarence Eaton, Esquire, responded, "Angelo, I'm amused that you know the actual address of the governor's residence. I can't blame you for your political ambition. Somebody has to step up and take that kind of responsibility. It's not all about prestige, and I sincerely wish you well in that endeavor. I must say, however, that I was disappointed in you in this matter of the veteran. I've always thought of you as someone who put justice before personal considerations. Nevertheless, your apology is heartily accepted. Would you like a drink?"

"Yes, please. I know you incline toward martinis, so I'm sure they will be excellent. Dry. An olive would be nice."

Clarence nodded at his secretary, who smiled and closed the door on her way out.

"While we're waiting for our drinks, Angelo, I'd like to ask you a favor."

"Name it. I nearly sent an innocent man to the electric chair. A war hero for crying out loud. I owe you."

"There's a woman who's worked here since before I arrived. She lost her position as a clerk at the department store, Strawbridge and Clothier, in New Jersey, to a returning soldier at the end of the war. She began here at the bottom of the ladder, on this seedy end of Nassau Street, as a secretary in what was then a two-man law firm. They specialized in wills, contracts, real estate, taxes, patents, and general law, but not criminal defense. They asked me to join them and fill that spot. By the time I got here she was already serving as their investigator and also attending NYU Law School at night. Alice White is her name."

Angelo said, "I've read about her in the papers. She must be quite an employee. It sounds like she is poised to become a force to reckon with, in and out of the courtroom."

Clarence went on, "Precisely. She only just graduated law school and is hard at work, preparing to take the Bar exam in July. She's divorced from a uniformed New York City police officer. She currently lives in the Bronx with the set builder for *My Fair Lady, Mame,* and now for the upcoming production of Leonard Bernstein's *West Side Story,* opening in September. She's lost her father to emphysema, and the worst tragedy of her life was the death of her older brother, Phillip, in action, in Korea."

"I've also heard her name in the last few days," Mancuso said, "in connection with the attempted second bank robbery by the Gypsy gang on Broadway. It was reviewed by the police commissioner. Before the call for backup was even made to the precinct, there were already three undercover police detectives in attendance, which begs the questions, what were they doing there without backup in the first place, and how did they know the robbery was going down in that bank at that time? Quite a coincidence, to say the least. The two witnesses from the first robbery were there. One of them was the father of the teenage hostage, and the father's two war buddies were there. The other was the lady we were just discussing, Miss Alice White. God knows what she told the responding detectives she was doing there, because she has no account in that bank, either. She shot and killed one of the gang members. I cannot imagine why. I think she said it was because he cut in front of her at the teller's window.

"Then there was the legendary Antonio Vargas, who just happened to drop by with a shotgun, a pistol, and a knife. He doesn't have an account at that bank either, so that rules out a coincidence too. This all happened within thirty minutes of the bank's opening. Five people were left dead. Four were members of the gang. One was the bank's guard. It would make more sense to ask who in New York City was not in that bank. There was a closed-door hearing in the commissioner's office. I was invited since I already had a vested interest and he knew I would approve his decision not to press charges against the detectives or the civilians, but to privately beg them all never to do this kind of thing again. I doubt they'll comply."

Clarence Eaton laughed out loud.

Mancuso asked, "Geez, Clarence. What can I possibly do for her? She just shot and killed a bank robber. She seems quite capable of taking care of herself."

"Watch over her. Whether she becomes a DA or a defense attorney, I want you to get over your prejudices and do what you can to protect her no matter what else she does. She's just like you and I were when we got started. Impulsive, hotheaded, not even afraid to break the law in the interest of justice."

"I get it, but where will you be when her illustrious career is unfolding, Clarence?"

"Do I have to spell it out for you, Angelo?"

Angelo dropped his head, so he was looking down at his lap.

Laura entered the room with a tray of martinis and an open pack of Chesterfield Kings. She sensed that her timing was inauspicious, so she put the tray down on Clarence's desk and did not look up. On her way out, however, she caught sight of a tear on the district attorney's cheek and withdrew without speaking.

When she had closed the door, Angelo asked, "How long?"

Clarence said, "Not very long. In fact, not counting my doctor, and me, you're the only other person that knows. I'm working up the courage to go home and tell my family."

"Anything you need, Clarence. Miss White, of course, I won't forget. I'll keep an eye on her, protect her in the extreme, which means I may end up as a gardener at the governor's mansion, instead of as its occupant, maybe even wearing a prison outfit and shackles."

Eaton smiled slightly. "Yes, thank you. I love her like a daughter. There's one thing you may not know, but as an Italian, you may or may not like it."

"You're talking about the old mustachios, yes?"

"Yes."

"They and I already have an understanding. If the old Italian gentlemen have a vested interest in her well-being, that will be a big help to keeping her out of danger. Please tell Alice to contact me anytime and for whatever reason and ask her to tell her Italian gentlemen to contact me on her behalf also, although, frankly, they already have contacted my office about a gun permit for her, that they wanted dated a few years ago. It may be the first of its kind in the history of New York City. I guess I've already been on the job."

Angelo stayed quiet for a while. Lifted his martini and took more than a sip of it.

Then he said, "Clarence, I am very sad about your news. I have never relished the thought of going up against you in court, but I never walked away from an encounter with you without learning something about the law, or, even better, about human nature. I will miss you, but I will think of you whenever I'm extracting Miss White from her difficulties, which, if what I've read in the newspapers and what I just heard in the commissioner's office is any indication, will be often and dramatic."

Angelo Mancuso put the remains of his martini down and stood up. He extended his hand. "Thank you for forgiving me about my mismanagement of the innocent veteran affair and for entrusting me with your protégé. Now go home and kiss your wife and children."

CHAPTER 40

CANNOLIS

Detective Sandra James inhaled the smell of fresh bread, pastries, and the fumes from the pot of coffee brewing behind the counter.

"I'd like a dozen cannolis, Mrs. Giacomo," she told the proprietress of the bakery.

"Hm, you got company?" Mrs. G. asked her.

"No, not company. I'm taking some friends to visit my parents."

"A man?"

James said, "A man and his son."

"I heard something about you and a downtown butcher with a boy. You know you can't keep secrets in this part of the Bronx. People would have nothing to talk about if it wasn't for talking about each other. If you are with this man, I'm happy for you. It wasn't easy for you growing up the only girl with all those brothers. They scared the other boys away. I heard this guy you're talking about was a soldier, and a widower. I heard he got shot in the bank robbery."

"That's right."

"Is he Italian?"

"That's so funny, Mrs. G. You'd be great questioning a suspect. You should consider a career in law enforcement. Here's a little tidbit for you to feed back into the rumor mill. I just started teaching the boy and his father to fight the way I do. They're on their way here from Manhattan. That boy had one lesson before he was kidnapped. He kicked the butt of the man he was handcuffed to, a grown man, a freight-hauler, longshoreman, tough as nails. The kid was handcuffed with his right wrist, so he did it left-handed. I was in the bank. I was there to stop the robbery. I nearly cried when I saw the kid drop the man to the floor and then kick him in the head to knock him out. I was so proud of him."

"How old is he?"

"Fifteen years old."

"You know, I have a cousin with a beautiful daughter. The daughter's thirteen, perfect for a young man his age with prospects. Maybe the boy wants a little company on a Saturday night?"

"It's no wonder you have so much business. The bakery is just a front. People come in here for news and to get fixed up on dates. I got a feeling he's gonna be a big draw to the ladies when the bank story gets out. I'll let him know about your cousin's daughter when I see him."

"It is worth a try, Miss Sandra, my beautiful blonde Italian maiden, with a badge and a gun no less. That's not a big sales advantage when you're looking for a man."

"No, Mrs. G., in answer to your question I ignored, they are not Italian. The father and son helped me out when I was shot, is all. They took me in for a couple of nights and helped me change my bandage when I got out of the hospital. They wanted to meet my family, my brothers, and my parents, see where the crazy police lady was hatched. So here I am, gossip central. I should charge you for this chat. They're from Lower Manhattan and they're coming to sightsee up here in the South Bronx. Saves them the expense of a European vacation. They're Irish. Are you happy? Totally incompatible with a wop like me."

Mrs. Giacomo said, "Oh my God. You dear girl. You are never going to find an Italian man. Still, I am happy for you finding someone to spend time with."

"Mrs. G., he's a crusty old bachelor. I am never going to go out with him, let alone marry him. He is not my type. We did each other a favor is all. He hasn't gotten out much since his wife died and he came back from the war. This'll be a great visit. My brothers are gonna love him, a genuine survivor of Iwo Jima. Are you kidding? My parents will love him too. He asked to meet my family, and his fifteen-year-old son wanted to come along. The kid is more likely to ask me to marry him than his father is. So I called my mother and she said fine, bring them over. It'll be like visiting the Vatican for him. She wanted to know does he have a job? Can you believe it? Yes, I told her. He owns a butcher shop. She doesn't care if he's Italian, as long as he has a job. So that's all that's happening here. That's why I need cannolis. They're like a peace offering for the man to give to my mother. She loves manners."

"That's very romantic."

"You know I am the one with a badge. I'm the one supposed to be asking you the questions. So can I have my cannolis, please?"

"You're so funny, Miss Sandra. I love you. Sure thing. Coming right up."

CHAPTER 41

RECKONING

Benjamin's stomach was flat. His baby fat was gone, even from his face. He had a Hollywood look under all that padding. His arms and chest were sculpted. Following his release from captivity and his heroic actions at the bank robbery, he spent endless hours lifting weights, punching and kicking the heavy bag at the local gym, rolling his fists like a windmill at the speed bag, jumping rope, and running miles of New York City streets.

He ate mostly a carnivorous diet now, meat, supplied by his father from the shop below their apartment. There was force in his stride.

He spotted the bully, Fred, from outside the schoolyard. The bully had heard the boy was kidnapped so he gave him a pass for a while. But now, the vacation was over. It was time to remind the kid how low he still was on the food chain.

A lit cigarette dangled from Fred's mouth. He was strutting around, combing his hair with the black plastic comb he carried in his back pocket. Susan looked on with disgust. Susan was the prettiest girl Benjamin had ever seen. Fred was the peacock courting the hen, but not getting anywhere. Benjamin took the strut out of his walk and slouched into the yard.

"Hey, Benjamin," Fred called when he saw him. "How're you doing? I ain't seen you around lately. You're looking good. Come over here. I need a couple of dollars to buy this pretty lady a hamburger and a soda. Don't make me have to chase you down."

Benjamin made eye contact with the girl named Susan, who he had pined for through most of his time in high school but never had the nerve to speak to. In classes, when they were in the same room, he tried not to let her catch him staring at her. She had those droopy eyes that made him want to wrap his arms around her and kiss her, but he had never exchanged a single word with her. He figured she wouldn't give him the time of day.

She was standing in the crowd that was slowly gathering to watch Benjamin take a beating.

Susan saw Benjamin looking her straight in the eye for the first time and thought it was about time.

No one really wanted to see Fred tear the youngster apart, but no one had the nerve to stop him, and no one could bring themselves to look away. It was like getting to see a car crash in slow motion, close up.

Susan held Benjamin's gaze. She had known who he was for a long time, caught him staring at her like she was a cupcake, and he was starving for something sweet. Boys were always staring at her like that, and looking away when she looked back, but not this time. His boldness excited her. He really liked her; she could tell.

Benjamin looked different. This was not going to go the way everyone thought it would. Susan just knew it. She imagined Benjamin was sending her a message like a knight of England, dedicating the merit of what he was about to do to the fair maiden, her. Tears of emotion came to her eyes. Just like that she fell in love with the butcher's son. She nodded her head at him and silently wished him well. Fred disgusted her. She had always dreamed of someone knocking his block off.

"Awe, come on, Fred," Benjamin whined. "Don't you ever get tired of taking money from kids smaller than you? I can't give you my money anymore. It's too embarrassing. Why don't you pick on someone your own size? Someone the size of, like, say, an elephant."

Susan smiled at Benjamin with admiration. Benjamin saw the look and blushed.

Fred was blinded by his own arrogance. Something was different about the boy that he had pushed around and taken money from so many times. He recognized the face, but the rest of this kid was different. That was it. The kid was on some kind of diet. In preparation for the violence he was about to do, he pulled the comb back out and ran it through his hair. He hummed the Brylcreem commercial: "Use more only if you dare. But watch out, the girls'll all pursue ya. They love to get their fingers in your hair. Boom. Boom." After all there were ladies present.

"You must be crazy, calling me names. I'm gonna have to make an example of you. 'To those who are about to die, I salute you.'"

Benjamin stared back. "I think the time has come for someone to teach YOU a lesson, big bully-butt."

"You're making me very mad, little man. Saying things like that. Have you completely lost your mind? It looks like you're in for a good old-fashioned thumping."

"Maybe so, but it'll take more than your sorry self to give it to me. 'To those who are about to die, I salute YOU.'"

The crowd became hushed. Benjamin Laughlin was about to be slaughtered, annihilated in front of their very eyes. They were about to witness a human sacrifice. A few of the Catholic kids crossed themselves. Others wondered if they should call for an ambulance, or maybe the principal, or the police.

Fred wasted no time throwing the sucker punch all seasoned bullies use as an opener, to end the fight before it began. A left hook! Benjamin watched it in slow motion. Hard. Hard enough to turn his lights out and break his face. Only it didn't connect. He ducked. The swing left Fred off-balance. Benjamin threw a right into the side of Fred's head. Hard enough to ring Fred's bell and put him face-down on the ground. The crowd went wild.

"Stand up, Freddy baby," Benjamin said, bouncing up and down like a prizefighter. "You've had this coming for a long time. Try taking it like a man."

"Lucky punch, kid," Fred said, getting up and brushing himself off. "This is your last chance to avoid cremation. Either hand over your money or start running. Otherwise, you are definitely going to the hospital. Somebody, call his mommy."

Nobody moved.

Benjamin had settled down and was standing still, his hands hanging at his sides. Susan was aroused, to say the least.

Fred suddenly started toward Benjamin at a sprint, head down. Benjamin moved to the side. Fred caught the butcher's son with a shoulder to his stomach. Benjamin buckled forward, but stayed on his feet, pivoted, and delivered an upward strike with his elbow to Fred's face, breaking Fred's nose and splitting his lip. Fred dropped to his knees. Blood ran from his mouth. He looked like he wanted to puke, but he held it together. The crowd went crazy again.

Fred started to get up, but Ben walked around him and kicked him in the backside, sending him sprawling.

Benjamin was bouncing again, off the balls of his feet, waiting for the next round to start. Fred got to his feet and said, "Why you . . ." and punched at Benjamin, who bobbed out of the way. He slapped the bully in the face with an open hand, exactly what Fred had done to him so many times. It was the most humiliating thing one man could do to another man. Then Benjamin punched his opponent in the stomach. While the heavier, taller boy was leaning forward, catching his breath, Benjamin reached into Fred's pockets and emptied them of sticks of gum, dollar bills, change, and a lunch pass probably taken from some other innocent victim.

Fred was on his feet but did not look like he was up for much more of this punishment. He stayed out of range, seething at Benjamin from a distance.

Benjamin stood straight, unthreatening, but spoke so everyone could hear him, "Mend your ways, Fred. Don't make me have to find you and publicly humiliate you again. Your sad life is about to get sadder. Every shrimp in school is gonna disrespect you to your face, knowing that if I hear you laid a hand on them, I'm gonna find you and beat you to a pulp. Do you hear me? Get a job, Fred. I'm gonna keep doing this until you start treating people with respect. Comprende?"

Fred stood at a crouch and said, "What happened to you, Benjamin? You used to be easy pickings."

"You did me a big favor, sending me home with black eyes and no money. I got up off the couch and learned to fight. My father was a war hero, and his son couldn't defend himself. Oh, and since we're conversing all friendly like this, for your information, my mother is dead. You telling me to go home and cry to my 'mommy' was the last straw."

Fred said, "I'm sorry about that. I gotta hand it to you. You did good fighting me. I'm gonna graduate soon and then I'll be just like my father, taking crappy jobs nobody else wants, and drinking himself to death."

"That's exactly where I was headed, Fred. There's still time for both of us to turn our lives around. If a wimp like me can do it, you can do it. Get someone to help you in school. If you want, go to the gym and learn to fight. You already paid the price of admission. You could be one heck of a fighter. You got nerve. Now you just need to learn how to use it to protect the weaker kids instead of terrorizing them."

Benjamin held out his hand and they shook.

"I deserved what you did to me just now, Benjamin. I hated you because you were gonna graduate this place and make something of yourself and I was gonna end up a bum, on the streets or in jail. Maybe I'll give it a try. Heck, if you can turn into the man you are from the disgraceful loser you were, no offense, there might be hope for someone like me."

Benjamin headed home after the fight. He felt a tug on his sleeve and turned to see it was Susan. His face went into full flush.

"Oh, hi," he said.

"Benjamin, I'm Susan."

"Yeah, I know who you are."

"Benjamin, it was very nice of you to treat that boy with such respect. I've never seen anybody our age have that kind of dignity and courage. You may have changed his life."

Benjamin's face turned even redder.

"Benjamin, I'm not saying this to embarrass you, but I've been aware of you for the longest time, watching you staring at me, but never saying a word to me. It's painful to see someone as shy as I am. Well, you just showed me who you really are, whether you like it or not, so that makes it my turn to tell you how I feel. Benjamin, ask me out on a date already. I promise, I won't bite, unless you ask me to."

Benjamin just stood there speechless; his mouth slightly open. Susan smiled at him and turned to walk away. Then she turned back, took a ballpoint pen out of her purse, and wrote her number on the palm of his hand.

CHAPTER 42

SOLDIERS

Hal Ferragamo announced to the waiter, "I'm buying. Give me the tab when we're done."

"Yes, sir."

Reggie Johnson asked for Scotch straight up.

Hal said, "Bring me a glass of ice water and a cup of coffee, please."

Antonio Vargas said, "Just coffee for me."

Thomas Laughlin asked for Scotch, a double.

Detective Sidney Shapiro ordered a triple Scotch.

Andy Bennett stuck with water.

Thomas said, "Hal, thank you for the drinks. You're not drinking. What's up?"

"I stopped, man. I got sober. I got a job."

"Doing what?"

"I'm working for Antonio, bodyguarding, working the clubs, depending on the night. He's making me go to those meetings, says else I can't work for him. They're not as bad as I thought they would be. And I got me a sweetheart."

"Hal, everybody knows they say not to date for at least a year after you get sober. Otherwise, you could end up in serious trouble."

"We didn't date. We went directly to bed."

Laughlin laughed and said, "If it's possible, Hal. You're gonna give being sober a bad name."

Then to the assembled men, Laughlin spoke seriously. "I want to thank you all for taking care of me when I was shot. I should be buying you the drinks, but Hal beat me to it. I wasn't scared, lying there on the floor of that bank, trying to breathe, thinking I was dying. I was disappointed because my life was just beginning to get better, and I wouldn't be alive to see my son become a lawyer and maybe even to have a social life myself. I was gonna check out and miss it all. Wouldn't you know it, in the end the Gypsy tried to save me. So, now I promised myself, when the time comes, I'm gonna drive upstate to Sing

Sing and thank him for helping me and watch his execution."

Hal said, "We should all go."

Antonio said, "I feel like an outsider to you Marines. I missed the war and went to prison. Thank you for allowing me to be part of your inner circle, to assist you at the bank. You must know by now that Alice White saved my life a few years ago. That's how we met. I take that very seriously. If it comes to it, and her or me has to die, I would rather it be me. If she was going to be in that bank, in danger, I had to be there too. Thank you for accepting me."

Reggie asked, "Antonio, since it's only us men here, and Alice's boyfriend couldn't make it, did you ever have a thing for her?"

"You have seen her. Even in the bank dressed like a homeless woman, she was beautiful. How could I be in close contact with her without, as you say, 'having a thing for her'? She did not have a boyfriend then, and I was not yet married. The tension was so great that if she hadn't run away, I would have taken her somewhere private. She is crazy brave, and I will always be there for her, but I am married now, and my wife doesn't mind me looking at Alice, as long as I bring my appetite home to her."

Hal said, "So, Thomas, we all saw that blond policewoman in action. How's that working out for you?"

Laughlin said, "She's nice. Just knowing her this little time has helped me get over a lot of the past. I helped her when she got shot and when her partner died, and she helped me. I don't think she likes me all that much. I suppose I repel her because of how I let myself go after the war and failed to be a righteous father to Benjamin. I don't think there's any future for her and me, if that's what you're asking. We helped each other out, is all. Maybe we'll stay friends."

Hal finally said, "Thomas, that story is so thin. I'll be sure to never ask you about your love life again. Just remember, in the unlikely event that anything does happen with her, do not hurt yourself or the lady catching up on a fifteen-year dry spell. She looks like she can take care of herself. It's you I'm worried about. Drink plenty of water. I gotta say, with all due respect for the lady, that when she held her gun up and said, 'Police. Freeze. Everybody stay right where you are,' I got more than a little aroused."

Thomas said, "Hal, you finally just now got sober. A lamppost would excite you. You took a woman you knew for fifteen seconds to bed with you. I am so happy you got help. I owe you so much, my brother. Treat that woman like a goddess. As for the lady cop, get that thought out of your mind. She would kill you before you even got unbuckled. That said, if you ever need advice about sex or marriage, don't call any of us."

Reggie said, "When I told the owner of the garage that your kid was home and okay, he actually cried, Thomas. He gave me a raise. In that bank, when the time came, that kid of yours stood up like a man. He kicked the butt of that guy he was handcuffed to, a longshoreman, had to have over a hundred pounds on Benjamin. Geez, man. You must be so frigging proud of that boy. He's another Marine in the making."

"The Marines didn't turn out to be as uplifting as we thought it would be, did it?" Thomas said. "He wants to be a lawyer. When he does, if he wants, I suppose, he could practice law in the military. That's his business."

CHAPTER 43

SANDRA JAMES AND THOMAS

"Could you bring some sort of Italian vegetable dish to go with the steak?" Thomas Laughlin asked.

His chest was healing. The coughing had stopped, but he still had a bandage that needed changing every day.

"I can do that," Sandra James said. "My mother taught me a few tricks in the kitchen. I'm not just all about fighting. I'll see you in about an hour, make that an hour and a half, so I can do a casserole."

Laughlin trotted down the steps to the sidewalk in front of his shop. He went around back and unlocked the door in the alley to retrieve steaks for dinner. Benjamin was out on an actual date with an actual girl named Susan. The boy had gone a little heavy on the Aqua Velva, but hopefully it would wear off by the time he got to her house to pick her up. Back upstairs the butcher poured wine, turned on the gas broiler, and splashed a little Aqua Velva on himself.

After dinner Laughlin said, "I'll wash. You dry."

"Deal."

Laughlin scrubbed the dishes and the silverware and put them in the drying rack. Sandra dried and found the cabinet for dishes and the drawer for silverware. Laughlin finished rinsing a dinner plate and placed it in the rack just as the detective was reaching for the next plate to dry. Their faces came within an inch of each other, and Laughlin impulsively mashed his lips into hers for a brief moment, then regretted it and pulled himself away like it had never happened. He was surprised, shocked, that he had done it. Sandra, mortified, slapped the butcher hard in the face. He reached up with his hand to see if she had broken the skin or dislocated his jaw. Finding that he could open and close his mouth, he looked into her eyes and said, "I think I love you."

To his surprise, she responded, "I think I love you too."

"Well then, what did you do that for?" Thomas asked her, still holding his face.

"I don't know. I'm sorry. It was a reflex. I didn't mean to hurt you. This is all new to me. I never felt like this before." She reached up and touched his cheek, gently, where she had slapped him. Then she leaned in and kissed it. He moved his mouth to her neck and kissed her there, behind her ear, then he put his nose into her hair and smelled it and hugged her to him and she hugged him back.

The sound of a key in the door roused them both from their rest on the living room floor.

Thomas spoke loud enough to be heard through the door, "Benjamin, don't come in. Give me a minute."

He squatted over the floor and picked up Sandra's scattered underwear and clothing, handed it to her, and whispered that she should get dressed in the bedroom. When the bedroom door was closed, Thomas slipped on his slacks and called to his son, "You can come in now, son."

The butcher asked Benjamin, "How was your date with the fair princess?"

Benjamin smiled. "I think I love her."

"What happened?"

"We saw some movie, I don't remember the name of it, I was so nervous. Then we went for chocolate malteds. I was trying to think of what to say. Then she kissed me. Uh, on the cheek."

"My gosh, Benjamin. It's like we both came out of the deep freeze at the same time."

"Dad, where is our instructor?"

"She's in the bedroom freshening up. Dinner was fine. Steak and vegetable casserole. Then we washed and dried the dishes together."

"Dad, you look different. Something happened."

"Yes, son. In your whole life I haven't been close to a woman. Part of it was loyalty to your mother. Some was sadness because of the war and that she died. But it took an Italian, blonde police detective to break me down. That and being shot. Do you mind?"

"Dad, if I was older, I would ask her out on a date myself. Does she like you?"

"Yes, I think she does. She's been alone for a long time herself. When she finishes what she's doing in the bedroom, I'm gonna take the subway back with her to the Bronx, if she'll let me. It's certainly not to protect her. More, just to be a gentleman and to spend more time with her. Don't wait up."

"You know you didn't have to escort me all the way up here to my house. I could've taken the subway myself," Sandra said.

They were walking down the street, approaching Sandra James's small wood-framed dwelling.

"I certainly didn't escort you for your protection," Laughlin said. "It's just I haven't had a date with a woman in a very long time, and I wanted to do all the things I was taught as a kid that a man should do for a woman when they go out together. I can't believe you let me get this close to you. I will try not to smother you."

"That's very thoughtful of you."

"I would have spent all night lying awake thinking about you, wondering what you were doing, who you might have had to beat up on your way here, wishing I was with you to hold your badge and gun while you destroyed whoever it was. I'm disappointed we haven't been attacked."

Sandra said, "In all fairness, Thomas, this is the first time I've enjoyed being a girl. I missed that part growing up. I like to blame my family, but they loved me the best they could."

"I'm happy, Sandra."

"You can come in if you want. I promise I won't strike you again. I'm really sorry about that."

Later Sandra said, "I wish I smoked."

"Nah, it's only in the movies that people smoke afterwards. Bogart and Bacall."

Sandra said, "Are you ever going to get dressed and go home?"

"No. I plan on staying here for the rest of my life."

"How will we live? We'll run out of food. I'll lose my job on the police, your shop will fall apart, the meat will all spoil, they'll shut off your electricity. Come winter, Benjamin will freeze to death."

"If I leave, can we do this again sometime?" he asked.

"I don't see how we could avoid it."

"I wonder how it's going to be having a girlfriend who can take me in a fight?"

"Gives you incentive to train harder. Want some raw eggs and Tabasco before you take the subway back downtown?"

"It's practically daylight. Almost time for my workout. I'd like that."

CHAPTER 44

ON THE ROOF

The stars sparkled on a black velvet sky as the warmth of the day subsided.

Alice White carried two beach chairs up to the roof of their building. Jim brought a cardboard box with whiskey, glasses, a couple of American cheese sandwiches, a couple of filter-tipped cigarettes, and two paper napkins. He also brought an ashtray and a book of matches from Luigi's. She was doing well staying away from cigarettes, but he knew she was dying for one now.

They unfolded the chairs and Jim poured them each a generous drink. Alice took a drag on a cigarette, blew the match out, then swallowed half the glass of whiskey. She took a deep breath, exhaled, and lowered her shoulders from her ears.

Jim said, "I know you feel unnerved by the thought of taking a human life. You carry a gun, and you practice with it, but nothing prepares you for the reality of ending someone's life. Alice, I know firsthand how you feel. As much as I love you, I know this is personal, private, so have this moment alone. I'll take care of you. I brought lots of whiskey, but I went easy on the cigarettes."

"You are so good to me, Jim. Thank you."

After a while Jim said, "Alice, not to change the subject, but this neighborhood is so peaceful. It's like a night in the Caribbean. My exotic digs near Broadway, with horns blowing, engines ripping around the streets at all hours, bright lights, doesn't hold a candle to this."

Alice asked him, "Do you smell the garlic and tomatoes? It's not completely quiet. You can still hear the kids and the little dogs. It's all the things I liked about growing up in Queens with my brother, Phillip. There's a feeling of love and support I haven't felt since he died in Korea."

"That was only a couple of years ago, Alice."

"It was, and in case you're worried about how I feel, killing that man in the bank, I'm fine, Jim. It does, however, make my graduation from law school seem somewhat anticlimactic."

"I'm glad you feel that way. You did a good thing. You saved a life. It's why you carry a gun. I'm so proud of you I could scream. Have another drink."

He topped off her glass.

He said, "I'll try not to crowd you, Alice."

"I love you being here with me," she said.

Jim said, "I'll never be good for any other woman, Alice. I don't much care if you marry me, as long as we can be together."

"So," Alice said. "How am I gonna steady my nerves to meet Mr. Leonard Bernstein?"

"Get drunk beforehand. Ha. I'm kidding. Last week a bartender downtown told me I shouldn't drink, that I should stick with coffee. That's the night I brought you flowers. He told me not to buy too many or you would think I had a mistress. I was afraid to come home."

"Why, Jim?"

"Because you're different, Alice. You're a cyclone. I never felt this kind of affection for anyone. He said he understood. The bartender wasn't even jealous of me, but he wouldn't serve me anymore, except coffee, because I would give alcohol a bad name."

370 | Marc Hirsch

"What a sweet story, Jim. I'll do my best to overcome my fear of the people you work with."

"Alice, have you ever considered that when you're around them, they don't even know I exist? Have you checked the mirror lately? I'm the one that can't speak. I'm too busy watching them look at you. You're not exactly hard on the eyes. Half of them know you carry a gun. They read the newspapers. When you go into practice, they will all want you as their lawyer."

"I never thought about that."

"As far as you killing someone, Alice, I think it adds to your credibility. I think every lawyer should have to be in a gunfight to be licensed."

"You're kidding, right?"

"Yes, Alice. I am."

Later, he sat in his pajama bottoms, with a pillow between his back and the uprights of their fire escape. His ankles were crossed on the lowest step up to the roof. His arm was around Alice's shoulders.

She said, "I feel like the hard work will be over as soon as I take the Bar in July. All I'll have to do is wait three months for the results, but I have a good feeling about it. I think I'm going to pass. What am I going to do with all that time? You'll still be getting ready for the opening of your show."

"I have this idea, Alice. It's the expensive graduation present you haven't stopped torturing me to find out about for the past month. As a reward for your patience, I thought I'd give you time to prepare."

"Out with it. What is this big surprise?"

"It's a trip to British Columbia, off the west coast of Canada, to a little island in the Strait of Georgia, protected from the open Pacific by two-hundred-mile-long Vancouver Island. I read about it in a magazine. It's called Vasquez Island."

"When on earth will you have time to leave your project on Broadway?"

"*West Side Story* goes out of town before it opens on Broadway. First to Washington, D.C., then to Philadelphia. It opens on Broadway at the end of September. That's just before your Bar results come back and you are licensed. I'm taking you to opening night and to the party afterwards to celebrate what I know without a doubt, that you have passed the Bar and will be licensed to practice law. You will get over your stage fright and shake hands with Leonard Bernstein. I assure you; he will be more impressed by you than you are by him.

"We leave in late July after you take the Bar. That'll give us time to pack at our leisure. We'll come back in September. That way we get to see the beautiful colors of autumn in Canada. I'll have just enough time to inspect the stage sets before opening night. You'll be able to assemble a wardrobe for court. It may be your last real vacation for a while. What do you say?"

Alice batted her lashes at him and said, "I haven't got a thing to wear."

CHAPTER 45

RETRIBUTION

Christos Montes and Margaret Hopkins were sentenced to death by electrocution, which, by New York State law, required a two-year waiting period before being carried out. Richard, Richy, Anderson, the driver, received a life sentence without the possibility of parole to be served at Attica Prison, in northern New York State.

The newspapers had a field day, drawing parallels between Christos Montes and Margaret Hopkins, and Julius and Ethel Rosenberg. The Rosenbergs were electrocuted on June 19, 1953. Ethel was older than Julius. Margaret Hopkins was older than Christos Montes. Margaret and Christos were scheduled to die in the electric chair, at Sing Sing, sometime in 1959.

May 15, 1959

At Christos Montes's request, the prison tracked down the priest who had heard his confession two years earlier and convinced the man to administer last rites to both inmates on the day of their execution.

"Cigarette, my son?"

"I haven't been a smoker, Father, but yes, I'll take one now."

The middle-aged priest lit two cigarettes and passed one to the condemned man.

"Did you enjoy your dinner?" he asked the Gypsy, Montes.

"It was okay. Under the circumstances, my appetite wasn't very good. Talk to me, Father. Tell me if what they say is true about the streets of Glory being paved with gold."

"It's not mine to speculate, but, yes, I would guess that's true. Dealing with more immediate issues, my boy, it only takes one act of kindness to wipe the slate clean. I asked around the police department. Many police officers find me when their souls are troubled, the same as you did. I found out what you did to save that dying man in the bank, the man you shot. That's repentance. He's here today as a token of his gratitude for your help. He tried to get in to see you, but they wouldn't let him. He asked me to thank you for coming to his assistance in the bank and to tell you he forgives you for kidnapping his son."

"Incredible, Father. It's just what you said. It wasn't too late."

"Exactly. You took my advice and, when you got the chance, you saved yourself by administering to him. You performed an act of contrition. It means you are forgiven. You can meet your Maker with a clear conscience."

"That's good, Father. I'll remember that when they're strapping me into the chair."

"You do that, young man."

"How's Margaret doing?"

"She's doing well. She's made her peace, and in fact, she sent you her love and asked you to forgive her."

"Sure, Father. This was bound to happen. It wasn't her fault. I'm a Gypsy. I would have gone insane on a beach somewhere, drinking cocktails with little umbrellas in them. I'm glad they found you, Father, to listen to my confession. You did good by me. Would you say a prayer?"

"Certainly, my son. It's the prayer Jesus used to teach his disciples how to pray. It goes like this: 'Our Father, who art in Heaven, hallowed be Thy name. Thy Kingdom come, Thy will be done . . .'"

THE END

ABOUT THE AUTHOR

 Marc Hirsch was born in Washington Heights, New York City, in 1945. He grew up in the Bronx on the Grand Concourse at 205th Street, in Alice White's dirty white brick building. He walked down the hill, through the southern Italian enclave, to attend the Bronx High School of Science. He entered Boston University's School of Medicine in Boston's South End, adjacent to Boston City Hospital, and graduated in 1969. He was a medic at the Boston Garden and got to watch the Boston Bruins play hockey, the Celtics play basketball, Killer Kowalski and Haystack Calhoun wrestle on Monday nights, and Country Joe and the Fish sing about Vietnam.

After graduation, he moved to San Francisco for postgraduate training. In November 1969, he was asked to render medical assistance to the Native American Indians of All Tribes who had illegally occupied Alcatraz Island in protest of the historical removal of their lands and the establishment of the policy of assimilation of tribal culture into mainstream American culture. This policy had been instituted by the federal government in 1948, and effectively wiped out Native American traditions. These were armed people, illegally seizing federal land, and Dr. Hirsch was informed he might be arrested, imprisoned, and lose his medical license. A medicine woman accompanied him on his rounds to approve his treatments. In the end, the cold drove many families off Alcatraz. Thousands of acres were subsequently restored to Native Americans, and the policy of assimilation was officially ended.

After training, Dr. Hirsch lived for several years in a small cabin on a cliff on an island off the coast of British Columbia. He bought cartons of used detective fiction from a bookstore on a neighboring island. He discovered the works of Raymond Chandler, Dashiell Hammett, and Earl Derr Biggers (the last was the creator of Charlie Chan), which he consumed voraciously at night by kerosene lamp. It was the first nonmedical literature he had read in many years and helped develop his lifelong passion for detective fiction.

While living on the island, he rendered prenatal care to a woman on another island and delivered her beautiful baby girl. The "baby" is grown now and has children of her own. Marc and his wife, Millie, visited them in 2011. The baby's mother has offered suggestions for the writing of the next book in this series, which is titled *The Case of the Little Island in the Pacific*.

Eventually Marc returned to mainstream medical practice in California, New York, and finally Kentucky, where he retired in 2011 and now lives with his wife, Millie, and writes his own detective fiction, the Alice White Investigator Series.

Visit www.marchirsch.com.

DISCLAIMER

This book is a work of historical fiction. Names, characters, places, and incidents that correspond to real people, places, and events are used as entirely fictional products of the author's imagination. References to the *New York Post,* Delmonico's restaurant, the several banks mentioned, and all streets and landmarks are used in a fictional context.

The author has been a fan of Jack Kerouac and Pablo Picasso, and he does know a curator at the Museum of Modern Art.

The only Broadway show of the three mentioned in this book that the Hirsch family ever actually attended together in Dr. Hirsch's childhood was *My Fair Lady,* with Julie Andrews and Rex Harrison.

The Bronx drugstore, Luigi's restaurant, and Cavuto's Funeral Home were real places with different names, but the activities described within them were, again, purely fictional, products of the author's imagination, with no disrespect intended for actual people, including the author's father, and events that occurred during the 1950s. The pharmacist, Manny Harrison, was a respectful representation of Marc's father. His references to Marc's fiscal irresponsibility were based on several talks Manny had with both his children. Mr. Hirsch, the pharmacist, was indeed held up at gunpoint. That was true. A zip gun, made with a car antenna, very unstable and known to discharge by accident, was actually used in the robbery. In lieu of intravenous sedation, Mr. Hirsch had several stiff drinks when he got home from work that night. The fate of the robber is unknown to this day.

ABOUT THE SERIES

The Alice White series started as an exercise in fiction writing. The author set out to compose his memoirs and was sadly disappointed by his inability to write an entertaining story, so he registered for a writer's workshop. He was asked to write a chapter of fiction for admission. He placed his older sister, Nancy, on a fire escape in the Bronx, New York City, in the 1950s, where and when they grew up. She was drinking whiskey and smoking cigarettes in the dark of a hot summer night, taking in the sights of other buildings, a couple stringing laundry to dry on a nearby rooftop, the sounds of children playing, dogs barking, and the smells of Italian cooking from the

Italian neighborhood below. That became the
beginning of Chapter 5 in his first book, *The Case.*

From there he took up the plight of postwar
women in the workplace and in society in general,
under the cover of historic detective fiction with a
female protagonist he named Alice White.

Alice had been married and divorced from a
New York City uniformed police officer and vowed
never to engage in another romantic relationship for
the rest of her life. The coup de grâce to that vow
came when she seduced the client on her first outing
as an investigator. Jim Peters was the builder of a
home in which an explosion had killed a doctor.
Peters was charged with homicide. Lynch mobs were
forming. Alice proved it to be murder by a third party,
and she walked away from upstate New York with
Jim Peters in tow.

Alice White's adventures play out against the
backdrop of her studies at NYU Law School's night
session and her interactions with her southern Italian
neighbors in the Bronx, who more or less adopt her.
As mentioned in the disclaimer of this book, the
people portrayed are purely fictional for the purposes
of entertainment, with no disrespect intended toward
the author's wonderful Italian neighbors.

ACKNOWLEDGEMENTS

First and foremost, I want to thank my wife, Millie, for her encouragement and support in my medical career and now, in my career as a writer. During more than half my life as a doctor she fed me, kept a beautiful home for us, and reminded me that there was life outside the hospital and the office. Now that I have become an author, she has again encouraged me and given me room to work, but not so much that I miss the rest of what life has to offer.

Half the fun of writing these books has been the people who I consulted for technical advice in their professional specialties and persons living and dead who served as models for characters in my stories and/or directly helped me with technical detail.

Early in the writing of this book I consulted Rian Barefoot, owner of the best butcher shop I was ever a customer of, in the creation of the butcher and veteran, Thomas Laughlin. Rian lent me books and encouragement for which I remain grateful and hopeful that he thoroughly enjoys this book.

My meditation teacher, Sokuzan, was a United States Marine in his youth and gave me factual advice regarding the training he received, which I have used in this book.

Master Tom Pardue has been invaluable, not only as a martial arts consultant, but as a fan of Alice White. He has read and critiqued my martial arts scenes in both this book and others in the series.

John Firmin is a law enforcement officer in Louisiana who has been a fan of my work and has reviewed selected scenes in this manuscript.

Attorney Matt Baker has been an enthusiastic supporter in the writing of this book, and he especially helped me craft the evil prosecutor, the fictional Angelo Mancuso.

Gunsmith Gary Smith of Precision Guncrafters has been fun to work with in arming my characters and advising me on best practices and terminology.

My late dear friend Joseph Trusgnich allowed me to use his nationality, his last name, and some of his physical attributes—his frozen face, rigid spine, raspy voice—in the mobster Enzo Trusgnich. His wonderful children have been terrific fans of my writing, and they are looking forward to the publication of this work.

Gene Lazaroff, carpenter, my good, good friend, has allowed me to use his career as a stage set creator, a home builder, and a Renaissance man in the character of Jim Peters, Alice White's boyfriend. In these books I've had him reading works of Allen Ginsberg, Jack Kerouac, and Anthony Bourdain.

My first cousin Robin Wachtel's daughter, Amy Kesner Kean, a New York City event planner, kindly advised me about accurately presenting subway routes and switching trains to get around underground in New York City.

As is our custom, my wife, Millie, has read the manuscript before it was sent to my wonderful editor, Laura Dragonette, in New York City.

Made in the USA
Columbia, SC
01 August 2024

39457166R00215